Tipping Point

Michelle Cook

www.darkstroke.com

Discover us online:
www.darkstroke.com

Find us on instagram:
www.instagram.com/darkstrokebooks

Include **#darkstroke** in a photo of yourself
holding this book on Instagram and
something nice will happen.

For Reuben and Martha

Acknowledgements

I always love reading the acknowledgements. All those strangers' names whizzing past. Til now, I've always thought how kind it was of the author to thank these people, who probably just smiled politely as they blathered on about plot holes and structure.

Now I know what they do. And it's a heck of a lot more than that, though that's a lot.

There's nowhere else to start but by thanking Laurence, Stephanie and all at Darkstroke Books for giving me this opportunity, and working so hard with me on editing and cover design. I love this story, and it was the best feeling in the world when someone agreed it was worth publishing. And thank you, too, to the lovely family of writers at Darkstroke, especially Charlie Tyler for her generous words, and making me feel like a proper author from day one.

I'm indebted to the fabulous writers and editors I've met along the way: Rufus Purdy for his support and excellent Write Here course; the immensely talented Thumb and Finger Pool, whose care, tender and otherwise, helped shape an awkward, gangly early draft into a book. And all my fellow Scribophiles, too—every single one who stopped by gave priceless advice and made some heroic catches.

For working her organisational magic, thank you to Rachel Gilbey, and to all her fabulous bloggers who agreed to take part in the Tipping Point blog tour. And who could ever forget Johnny Hill, uber-lawyer, his disclaimers and priceless advice?

To Mum and Dad, thank you for keeping up with my lifelong habit of switching course to follow my passion. Guess what? I finally caught up with it. And a special thanks to my kids for basically not caring if I'm a proper writer or not, as long as they can have chicken and chips for tea and no electronic device ever runs out of charge.

For inspiring me, though she may never know it, I thank Greta Thunberg, and all the young people who fight every day to turn a seemingly unstoppable tide. We owe you more than most of us will ever be honest enough to admit.

Huge and eternal thanks to you, dear reader. Without you, none of this stuff is ever possible. I hope to repay your faith with a good yarn.

Finally, thank you to my husband, Daniel, whose support and forbearance is exceeded only by his bizarre compulsion towards coasters.

About the Author

Michelle lives in Worcestershire, UK, with her husband Daniel, their two young children, and a cat called Lyra Belacqua. By day, she works for the NHS, a job which she has almost as much passion for as fiction.

Her first joyful steps into creative writing were at the age of ten, when the teacher read out her short story in class. A slapstick tale of two talking kangaroos breaking out of a zoo, the work was sadly lost to history. Still, Michelle never forgot the buzz of others enjoying her words.

More recently, she has had several flash pieces published, was long-listed for the Cambridge 2020 prize for flash fiction, and placed first in the February 2020 Writers' Forum competition with her short story The Truth About Cherry House. Tipping Point is her debut novel.

Tipping Point

Chapter One

24th April 2035

Splashes of bluebells line the way to the crematorium. They were Mum's favourite, so I pick a handful for the plaque, though their petals are browning. If I had my way, there'd always be bluebells for Mum. Everything flowers earlier each year and there can't be many anniversaries left until they've been and gone when the day comes around.

Hard to believe it's been two years since the attack. The press like to call it *Twenty-four/ Four*. An ugly name, but it's a tradition from way back when people started naming these events for the day they happened. God knows how many more there've been since then. They must have run out of dates to use by now. I try not to pay attention.

At the iron gates, I swipe a hand over my clammy face and enter the merciful shade of the crematorium. It's so much greener here than everywhere else, they must irrigate the grounds in the dry spells, though they're not supposed to. Perhaps the ashes keep the soil fertile.

I approach the black marble of the plaque—donated by the survivors' fund—with shaky legs and dry mouth. Like it's a wild animal I'm forced to sit and pet.

Their names and dates glitter in embossed gold:

George Glass	(1985—2033)
Alice Glass	(1985—2033)
Willow Glass	(2010—2033)
Darya Glass	(2019—2033)

That's all of them. My whole family.

Beautiful as it is, the alignment of the four *2033*s is stark and goading. I close my eyes, imagining my name among them.

Essie Glass   *(2016–2033)*

To distract myself from the barb in my throat, I pull at the crispy weeds that criss-cross the plaque. They come out of the earth with a dry snap.

I lay the wilting bluebells on the marble, and wipe my eyes with gritty fingers. There must be something more I can do to mark the day, but no ideas come to mind. There are no words.

What did I do last year?

The first anniversary is an angry blur. I was drunk through most of it, trying to unwind my twisted guts. It didn't work. I've dim memories of my flat, dark and stale, Maya hugging me for hours, whispering. Later, long, sweet messages from FractalEyes. But I recall nothing from the crematorium. Why can't I remember?

Taking a last look at the plaque, I turn away and begin the sweaty walk home. It seems wrong to leave so soon, but the tightness in my chest lifts a little all the same.

A breeze eddies towards me along the lane. My phone buzzes with a text. It's Maya.

Maya: *Hey lovely. How crappy is this year's Crappy Day?*
Essie: *Crappy. How was the audition?*
Maya: *Crappy. Though obviously not in the same magnitude. Sorry I couldn't come to the crem.*
Essie: *I understand. You're busy. Post-audition shag with [insert current boyfriend]?*
Maya: *His name's Lawrence. And* we*'re at it right now.*
Essie: *You disgust me. Impressive multitasking, though.*
Maya: *Thank you. Just wanted to say, don't be a masochistic moron today. Stay off those ranty forums, OK?*

She means PolitiWorld. And she's right. I was headed straight there when I got home. Maya gets me like no one else. Or not, but she's an actress, and she does a fair job of pretending.

She's texted again.

Maya: *Anyway, you in work tomorrow? I wanna talk to you about an idea Lawrence and his mate have. You are gonna LOVE it.*

Essie*: Huh???*

Maya*: Wait and see my lovely but deranged bestie.*

Essie*: Okayyy. Is it a bank job or a killing spree? Both?*

Maya*: Let's just say, it's right up your street, my crazy but righteous revolutionary.*

Essie*: Come to the Braai at 12. Leave your sense of humour at home X*

Maya*: See ya tomoz, freak. Don't wreck your head X*

***

Face-to-face, I'm not a confrontational person. It's just sometimes a good argument is better than silence. I need to fill the void the crematorium left in me today.

On the PolitiWorld forum, this evening's top thread is on fire. They're blaming immigrants for the bombings. Again. Today of all days, I can't resist. Taking a generous swig of cider, I bash at the keys.

Stop spouting pointless slogans from the headlines. You know nothing. Most of the attacks are by English people.

Everyone knows PolitiWorld isn't the underground movement it used to be. When the government discovered it, instead of banning the forum, they twisted it to their own advantage. Typical subvert and control.

I grab my faithful, rickety old laptop from the twenties, and type again.

It's all about the Good Citizen points with you lot, isn't it?

5

That stirs the hornets' nest, but it's true. They all chase the credit because higher GC points mean a better life. Who wouldn't want that?

As I field the worst of the online abuse, a private message pops up.

FractalEyes*: Hope you're not winding up crazies again. Don't poke the bear.*

Corny as ever. I roll my eyes, spark up my last cigarette, and reply as my persona.

Vixie44: *What are you, my grandad?*

Another forum post—a suggestion that if *[MaskedSession1343]* likes immigrants so much, they should screw them all. I can't help it.

Vixie44: *Yeah, why not? Wanna join us?*
FractalEyes: *Seriously. Do yourself a favour. Go out clubbing or something. Celebrate life.*

I wince.

Vixie44: *Your timing could be better, Fracster.*

He doesn't deserve that, but off it goes into cyberspace. There's an awkward, over-long pause.

FractalEyes: *Shit. Sorry. It's today. In my defence, I am a complete idiot.*
Vixie44*: Don't stress. I'm just a bit edgy.*

I should say something more meaningful, make him feel better.

FractalEyes*: You okay?*

I can sense the mortification in his typing fingers.

Vixie44: *I'm fine.*

FractalEyes: *Must have been a rough day. I'm sorry. Do you need anything? Need to talk? Or just swear at me? I'm here for that.*

I can't help a smile. Maybe the swearing would help… but the black knot inside me has to stay tied for now. Vile_Forum_Man is back with more poison. Tired of anger, I slam the laptop closed. It emits its disappointed shutdown whine as I grimace at my improvised vegetable curry. The sight of congealed lentils makes my stomach clench.

I switch on the TV, which goes exactly as expected. The reasons I've been avoiding it all day beam back at me. Head shots of the victims indecently juxtaposed with mug shots of the perpetrators; it's like the pictures of the wreckages are piercing my chest. I don't know why I'm shocked to see a clip of myself included.

The editors have chosen to show footage of sixteen-year-old me scurrying away from a horde of ravenous reporters, exposing themselves as the predators they are. Inside the TV, I mutely repeat the phrase, *No comment*, as the present-day newsreader recites from the autocue. My solicitor, a square-shouldered, ex-Navy guy in a blue suit, swats the microphones away to clear my path to a black cab.

That was the day of the inquest. I know that for sure because it's the first and last time I wore that dress. It was blood red and too far above my knees, which didn't go unnoticed in the gutter press the next day. Like my dress was the most important thing about that circus. Makes you sick.

The newsreader drones on from her heavily glossed mouth. "… took place on this day in 2033. It was the largest and most coordinated terrorist attack on English soil. The attacks, at seven locations across–"

I turn it off.

Pacing round my flat doesn't take long. It's a shabby, ground floor one-bedroom box, all frayed threads and vintage

Swedish flatpack. Brown lounge, beige kitchen, magnolia bedroom, white bathroom. That's it. The letting agent reckons it's 40 square metres. I think that's a lie, but when the social worker found it for me, I was in no state to argue.

Our family home had to go when they all died. The insurance companies wouldn't pay out for an incident on that scale. The government felt bad for us—just not bad enough to help. We had their thoughts and prayers and deep admiration for our dignity, all 11,000 of the bereaved and injured. But deep admiration didn't pay the mortgage.

Text from Maya.

Maya: *Essie you're Masking, but I can tell it's you ranting on there. Get off the forums!!!*
Essie: *I'm off now, okay, Mother Hen?*
Maya: *Good. Now stay off!!*

I send her a thumbs up and a heart, then pull back the purple curtains my social worker bought me as a moving-in present. I'm not sure what she was thinking, buying velvet in this unrelenting year-round heat. Did she think it was all going to stop? But I suppose she has to clutch a nugget of optimism to her soul in that line of work.

I've kept the curtains up, though, because they're about the only thing in this whole place that isn't broken or worn out, or both. They remind me that life isn't universally crap, and that my social worker—with a caseload of maybe a hundred screwed up teenagers—thought to remember my favourite colour.

The window is open but there's no breeze, just a heat so intense it feels like a fever on my damp skin. All that reaches through the opening is the hot oil stench from the chippy over the road, and that makes me queasy.

I shouldn't have cut FractalEyes off like that. He meant well. And his messages have seen me through some dark days in the last two years. There are times I wonder if someone up there sent him to me. He came just when I needed him, like a guardian angel.

We don't use real names, just handles. What I think of as the Second Level of security clearance. There's Level One: MaskedSession, which I use for the forum nuts; Level Two is Vixie44, for him. You have to know me personally for Level Three—just plain Essie. I'd recommend this approach to anyone. It works for me.

Should have stayed online and chatted, though. Eased his guilt for overlooking the day. Sometimes even I forget it happened. Not today, though. Not a chance.

***

The next morning, the sun is already blistering through the taupe haze on River Street. There's no hint of the freshness of a new day as I walk to work at Bri's Braai. Instead, it feels like yesterday is still breathing its sweaty fog over me.

Two lads of about fifteen are sitting on the pavement, backs against a charity shop window, one smoking. A pocket of air wafts from their vicinity and the sweet, emetic smell tells me it's not a cigarette. I'm guessing their parents have high GC ratings if they can afford weed. These kids must have set a pile of empty boxes alight two shopfronts away: no one else is here. The cardboard crackles, expelling acidic smoke.

There's a lazy hostility in the boys' eyes. *Wanna make something of it, babe*? they seem to say.

I move on without comment, side-stepping the bonfire. The drones will pick them out if they hang about long enough. I'd give them half an hour tops until the next one. Though they're likely too stoned to notice.

I have to be at the Braai for seven to open up. We start trading at seven-thirty, but I need to get the fresh stuff prepped and make the sandwiches. Brian tackles the more exciting dishes. I'm a decent cook, but his bobotie is better than mine.

The early start doesn't bother me. I've never been a late sleeper, and it's the coolest part of the day, which I like. The gangs of listless adolescents and short-tempered men are mostly off the streets by early morning, and the walk helps get my head together. I can get some work done before Bri's kitchen gets too steamy.

On my right, Bank Lane descends towards the river. A gentle breeze picks up from the water, cutting through the haze. People complain about the smell of rotten eggs, but to me it's wild, unsuppressed life. Down there, away from the fierce heat and trade, all the sleeping bags lie huddled with the discarded humans inside. When I was younger, I used to hate coming here. Too embarrassed to make eye contact with the people and ashamed when I didn't. Now I'm so close to being among them that some are my friends.

There's no movement in the sleeping bags, so everyone must be asleep. The heat will wake them soon enough. Or some soulless idiot will flick a cigarette at one of them.

A soft, sniffling sound draws my eye back there. A man with dark hair and a coarse ginger beard huddles in the sleeping bag nearest to the junction, sobbing. When a filmy brown eye pokes through the red hair, I realise it's not a beard, it's a dog. The man cries out and squeezes the dog into a hug. From the stiffness of its posture, the dog's dead.

Oh, god. Poor things.

He lifts his head from the tarmac. I know him a little: his name's Merrie. Maybe that's not his real name. There's an upended, empty vodka bottle on the floor by his arm. My face grows hot as his eyes shoot a spark of recognition at me. All I have is a wonky smile. On the way home, when everyone's awake, I'll come back to see if he's okay.

Fifty yards past the junction with Bank Lane sits Bri's Braai. The customary scowl at the Unity sign must be observed. Why did I get a job right opposite one of these things, with its deceitful *Hands of Kinship* logo? They're meant to represent two hands clasped in support, but to me they look more like they're holding some poor sop below the waterline. This morning, for Merrie's dead dog, I add an extra one-fingered greeting to my sneer at the sign. I'm brave

10

enough when the drones aren't about.

Right on cue, I hear a blue-bottle whine, and squint up to see one of the hateful things hovering twenty feet above, its triangular beams casting a spindly shadow against the pavement. They've painted the underside with a smiley face. With a poorly stifled grimace, I unlock the door and slip inside the café.

How you experience the Braai depends on when you come in. Early in the day, it's a generic coffee shop on the approach to the station. Two mornings a week, after nine, it's more like a soup kitchen. Tuesdays and Thursdays, Bri does a free breakfast for the rough sleepers.

Come in at night and you'll find it a hedonistic carnival, with abundant wine, dancing and experimental music. Sound bounces off the rough plaster walls, dancers bounce off the dark-stained wooden floorboards. Angled lights pick out the many framed photos on the wall: landscapes and street scenes of the South Africa of Bri's youth.

Brian arrives about nine, with a pale grey face behind his craggy beard. I give him a few minutes, then follow him into the kitchen.

My eyes slip past his bulk to my drawings. About six months ago, he 'borrowed' two of my sketches—a sample of the happy ones. There's one of Maya reading a script on my sofa, and one of the river. He framed and hung them on the kitchen wall, by the door where the steam doesn't reach. There was no persuading him to take them down.

"Bri... can I have the early break? Maya's coming in."

"Don't see why not. It's worth it to gaze upon the Asian goddess again. Anyway, I'm not doing hot lunches today—got no bookings, and this headache is a mother. Can't face the oven."

I can't believe he's still in business.

"Asian goddess?" I say with a squint. "Bit racist, or not? Also, creepy. She's half your age."

"Not racist." He winks at me. "You're jealous. How sweet. Don't worry, you're still my crazy, flame-haired princess."

The fact is if either of us ever came on to him he'd freak

11

out. He only says these things to bother me. Like the flame-haired thing. He knows I've only ever wanted dark hair. But short of dyeing myself head-to-toe it's never going to work. Maya says I'm all pale and English freckles on the outside and dark-hearted emo on the inside. I always reply she's the opposite.

There's a mid-morning trickle of coffee drinkers, but it's otherwise quiet. Brian makes more sandwiches for the lunch trade. Maya's late, which is annoying because I only get half an hour's break. She bounces in, with sleek black hair and lip gloss. No sheen of sweat on her face, unlike me when I walk through the same door. Which is incredible because she comes in on a waft of steamy heat from the street.

"Hi Bri," she calls through to the back, and he blows her a kiss.

"You're late," I say as we hug, and she follows me to a window table.

"Sorry. Lawrence's fault."

I don't pursue that. Brian brings us coffees so fast they must have been meant for customers, and flashes a smile at Maya.

"Also, the trains from Worcester are all cancelled." Maya beams her thanks at Brian. "Something about melted lines or some other garbage."

"No excuse. You could have got a DEV car."

"Don't trust them," she says. "My sister got stuck in the Birkenhead tunnel in one of those. It ran out of charge and the helpline was out of service. She nearly pooed her pants. They thought she was setting a bomb in there. I mean, they shouldn't operate driverless when the helpline's down and the power's out half the time. I heard they're gonna ban them in Worcester–"

"So anyway, since we're short on time…" I say. You have to cut off her stream before it overflows.

"Oh yeah," she says. "Get this: Lawrence wants us to join his gang. Well, me really, but I persuaded him to include you."

I blink in the pause. "His gang. Maya… is he five?"

She laughs. "Not like that. It's not the Secret Seven. He's into..." she looks around, ducks low and drops her voice. She's enjoying the performance, and I tap my fingers on the table. "... a*ctivism.*"

Not what I was expecting. "Okay. What kind of..." I mimic her spy moves, "...a*ctivism?*"

"The good kind." When I frown, she says, "The kind you're always muttering about. Climate change and such. He kept on about me joining up. Said it would be great to have a famous actress involved. Give them an air of legitimacy. When we can come out in the open, obviously."

Where to start? "Maya, you're not famous."

She shrugs and stirs her coffee. "Yes, well, I might be. One day. And then we can bring the argument to the mainstream, he said. It's the long game."

"Well, he is a genius. If only someone had thought to bring the argument to the mainstream before. It's not like it's illegal or anything. 'Out in the open'? Are you mental?"

Maya presses her lips together and pulls her head to the side. "Come on, Ess."

I try to soften my expression into a grin. "Sorry. Been a tough couple of days. But it's still illegal."

She nods slowly, twisting her hair, but then it seems she can't help buzzing again. "So, will you come?"

Brian hovers in my peripheral vision. My break is over. To Maya, I must look blank at her words.

She rolls her eyes. "To the meeting? Friday night? It's at the church hall. Seven-thirty. We can meet you outside if you prefer."

"I don't know, Maya. I mean, political congregation and all that... Wait... *at the church hall?*"

"The cleric's a friend of Lawrence's. He's cool with it."

"How're we going to get past the Neighbourhood Watchers? And the drones?"

She holds up her hands. "They have a plan, Ess. They're not that naïve. Anyway, Watchers and drones don't bother with the church. It's all Unity, isn't it?"

I purse my lips at her.

"Ess." Brian points at his watch.

"I'm done," I say to Maya.

"Please." She takes my hands in her own. "Please come. Please, please."

"Maybe." I sigh, getting up from the table. "But if I'm not there, just pop in and save the world for me. Promise I'll bail you out if it all goes to hell."

Chapter Two

There's a face. No one I recognise, but he looks angry. His hands are raised and clenched, his features twisted up to the heavens. In the jittery light, his fists appear to be shaking, his eyes wild and flashing. Sprawled across the background—splintered trees, a torrent of water, broken windows and buildings, broken bodies.

The whirling spout of a tornado begins to spin and cleave the charcoal sky—

A ping as a private message hits my Vixie inbox. I drop the pencil, relieved to turn away from my sketch.

FractalEyes: *Hey.*
Vixie44: *Hey.*
FractalEyes: *No forums tonight, I hope.*
Vixie44: *Nope—just delusional artwork.*

There's a pause, and I glance at my drawing again. It seems to move by the gaslight that falls on the table. I bought a shedload of gas lamps a few months ago, when the power cuts kicked up a gear, and now I prefer them to the electrics. Gaslight has an apt Dickensian aura. I can pass a whole night in my living room, seated on a cushion here, sketching. Lately my pictures have been more disturbing than ever. Charcoal. Random and spiky, like nightmares... This angry man I don't know.

FractalEyes: *Excellent. Can you send me a pic of it?*
Vixie44: *Nope. It'd scare you. Scares me. What you up to?*
FractalEyes: *Working late again. Biiig project.*
Vixie44: *Big chemistry?*

FractalEyes: *Big, enormous chemistry.*

Vixie44: *Ooh… flame tests??*

FractalEyes: *Hahahahah. Yeah, baby. Just lit up the lithium.*

Vixie44: *You've got lithium? DON'T BURN IT!*

FractalEyes: *Fiend… I'm a chemist—if you want drugs, I can get hold of anything. So, I'm doing high school Bunsen burner stuff. Tell me about this artwork.*

Vixie44: *Well, according to this evening's offering, I'm channelling the destruction of the planet…*

FractalEyes: *Oooh, sexy.*

Vixie44: *Not from where I'm sitting.*

FractalEyes: *Oops gotta go—potassium's lively. Stay off PolitiWorld, okay?*

He signs off. My finger twitches over the PolitiWorld app, and pauses. Not tonight. I'm off-centre enough—the pain of the anniversary, the heat, this creepy drawing... Fractal's right, I don't need a textual battering from strangers to go with it.

He first piped up two years ago, a few months after the attack. That was after the digital purge but before Masking was a thing. Anyone could reach your inbox then, so thank God I had the sense to invent Vixie44. I didn't care what I posted, or who I upset as Vixie. Luckily, Fractal only wanted to check if I was okay. He says he's a chemist, so he must be a little older than me. He's not far away, only Worcester. We've chatted on loads of subjects. Politics mostly, but other things too—books, films, art, music… love. But we've never met.

I go into the grease-stained kitchen and switch on the radio. The room fills with the melodic twang of Sally Starling.

"As part of his campaign to end fuel poverty, Home Secretary Oliver Foster-Pugh visited Worcester today for the announcement of a new renewable energy venture at the head office of ConservUnity, a company at the forefront of green technology."

A chiding, aristocratic voice chimes out over the speakers.

"I'm delighted to be here today on the banks of the beautiful River Severn at the launch of this inspiring new venture. I'm sure my honourable colleague Dr. Kerry Tyler, the MP for Worcester, would want me to thank the dedicated team at CU for their endeavours. None of this would be possible, of course, without the considerable investment of time and money by Sir Alex Langford OBE..."

Blah blah blah.... well, it's hotter than hell in my kitchen, so they'd better hurry.

Maybe this meeting Maya was on about yesterday is a good idea.

"In the United States, hurricane Dylan has made landfall on the North Carolina coast, causing widespread devastation and loss of life." There's a respectful pause, but it's never long enough. "The death toll stands at 632, but is expected to rise in the coming days..."

Oh, man. It's getting worse.

I raid the fridge for cider, pop ice-cubes in a tumbler, and pour. When I rub the glass across my forehead, the delicious, cold trail evaporates slowly from my skin. The usual chippy smell creeps through the window, and a group of teenagers laugh nearby.

You're a teenager too, Ess.

But oh, my bones ache, my eyes itch with exhaustion.

The cider doesn't calm me down. The only thing that will is cigarettes, and hang the expense. My trainers and anorak go on right over my pyjamas. I grab my purse and walk down Potter Road towards the river.

It's busy in town, and there's an abundant police presence. On River Street, a crowd of middle-aged men gather outside a bar and explode with laughter at something I can't make

17

out. Underneath the revelry, their bodies are tense and primed for action.

There's a fizz in the air, like there used to be before a fight at school. A teenager clambers up an alley wall, his friends egging him on from the ground. A string of rainbow-painted girls queue outside *Kiss*, the only nightclub in town. Their clothes are marginally less gaudy than the pink neon sign over the door, but their fingernails match it photon for photon.

The newsagent next to the club is open as always, so I brave the hard, stilettoed stares in the line and squeeze past to the shop. The guy behind the counter smiles at me. He clearly doesn't mind my pyjamas. I bet he's seen stranger sights after closing time at *Kiss*. All the same, he has an orange Neighbourhood Watchers badge on his lapel, so I try not to act too eccentric.

I buy two packets of cigarettes and, on a whim, a cheese-and-onion pasty, and step outside. The stiletto girls are cat-walking in past the blocky bouncer. I don't want to go home yet and a perverse part of me wants to turn right, into the club dressed like this—give them something to stare at.

Thinking better of it, I go left towards the roundabout. The Braai is a little up the road straight ahead, and for a moment I want to see Brian, have a drink with him and his pals. Brian's easy company when my head's a mess. He's the only person I've met since the attack who has never asked me about my family. I can tell he knows about me by the extra care he takes. If I work a late shift, there's a fully paid taxi to take me home. His leftover specials frequently make their way into my bag somehow.

I was all over the news when the attack happened. Struck a perfect note for the media spectacle: the tragedy, my youth. Sixteen-year-old girl loses her entire family; watches her little sister slip away with tubes in her arms. It was hard for them to resist. When Darya died in hospital days later, the press soon forgot about me, and that's how I liked it. But how do you outrun the curiosity of everyday people? Brian's unusual because he doesn't push like that.

Instead of going into the Braai, and confirming Bri's worst fear that I'm the sort to wonder around town in pyjamas, I turn right onto Bank Lane towards the river. I forgot to go back yesterday and see about Merrie after his dog died. Half of the rough sleepers have already bedded down for the night. The other half mill around, keeping a respectful hush for their comrades. Living on the streets must be exhausting.

"Essie," says a voice from one of the sleeping bags behind me. A pallid, bearded face peeps out of the nearest pile, pale blue eyes creased up in greeting.

"Andy. Sorry, didn't see you there." I turn back and plonk myself next to him.

We've come to know each other since he's been sleeping on Bank Lane. If he's here, I always stop for a chat.

An idea strikes me. "Want a pasty?"

Andy takes it from me and tears into the wrapper. After a huge bite on it, he offers it to me, and I shake my head.

"How's things?" I light two cigarettes, offering him one which he takes and smokes through half-chewed pastry.

"Bit sad today. Merrie got into a fight last night. Got stabbed."

"Oh, my God, is he okay?" I think of the empty vodka bottle, Merrie's dead dog.

Merrie and Andy are best mates among the crowd here.

"Dead."

A tight band of shock and guilt presses on my chest. "I'm sorry, Andy, that's awful."

Andy shrugs, but it turns into a wounded huddle and his eyes flicker. We sit hunched in silence as a drone passes overhead with an abrasive buzz.

"Where you going all dolled up like that, anyway?" he says when it's gone, trying to straighten his back.

"Cheeky git." I laugh at my bean-stained top. "These are my best PJs."

He chuckles and finishes the pasty in one mouthful. There's a whistle from down the road toward the river, and Andy snaps his head up.

"You'd better go," he says. "The coppers are coming. You

19

look more like one of us than I do. You'd be the first to get arrested."

Neither of us moves.

He tips his chin away. "Go."

"You'll be okay?"

"Yeah, course," he says, flapping his hands in a shooing motion.

Maybe it's the news about Merrie that inspires the rush of rebellion. My feet turn away from home, down Bank Lane. I march toward the river where a few steps lead up onto the path. Side-by-side at the top, two policemen block my way like sentinels. When I peer up at them, the rifles strapped across their chests twitch, level with my face.

Why did you come this way, you idiot?

"All right, love?" says one copper. "Going for a walk, are we?"

Brows drawn in an angry slash, he moves closer, forcing me to step back. I eye the weapons they carry before them like talismans, and my heart hammers.

"Yeah," I say with a tense smile. "Just going for a walk. Needed air."

The first copper checks out my pyjamas and grimaces. A glance at the other one gives me a jolt. I know him: Charlie.

He was only two years above me at school. God, he must be just out of police training. If he remembers me, he shows no sign. The stare is blank and ice-cold. My throat tightens.

"You'll need to put that ciggie out, then," says the first cop. "We don't want any accidents along the river."

I narrow my eyes at him. There's no law against smoking on the river path. He knows that, and judging by his smirk, doesn't care if I do too. The cigarette falls from my fingers, and I grind it out with my trainer.

The copper clears his throat. "I hope you're not going to be a litterbug."

His eyes glint and jaw tenses as he snatches the gun. There are about a thousand cigarette ends down there already, but he's dead serious. Conquering a sigh, I bend and pick up a filter tip that looks like it could be mine. The cop gestures with his gun to the bin on the path behind him. I brush past them and dispose of the cigarette end.

"Good," he says. "Now, if I see you drop any more crap, you'll be back here cleaning up the rest of them. One at a time. Got it?"

I nod, keeping my expression neutral.

"And try making more of an effort. You'll never get a fella looking like that," says Charlie.

I glare at him, but keep silent.

"Get lost," he says.

As I walk away along the river, their eyes burn into my back. Guts twisted with unspent anger, I keep going. A minute later, when I venture a glance behind, they're gone.

I exhale sharply with relief. It's lucky the police didn't find me that interesting. There's still a cramp of worry in my stomach for Andy, but I can't do anything to help him.

Despite this, it's good to be by the river. Its wild, silty smell revives me. There's an iron bench along the path near the bridge—one of those dedicated to a deceased resident. This one was donated by the family of Lila Etheridge, who died on 31st October 2016. That's the day I was born. How come I've never noticed this plaque?

Feeling obliged under the circumstances, I sit on the bench. After a quick glance back for the coppers, I light a cigarette and inhale it deeply, feeling my heartbeat as it slows. Another drone passes overhead, but it doesn't lock in on me. The moonlight skips across the water, the river flowing so fast its blackened surface looks as if it's scattered with sequins. The stream echoes under the bridge where it emerges from darkness.

Officer Charlie. He went out with my friend Beth three years ago. His eyes were clear and warm, then. I wonder what could have made them so cold, and what Beth would think of Charlie being a copper now.

Above the chatter of the river is a scuttling noise, scraping on rock. There's a movement on the bridge. In the shadow of

21

the overhanging trees on the bank, a dark figure clambers over the sandstone wall onto Bridge Road. He grunts as he lands, then scampers over the bridge and away to the west.

The guy has draped something white across the bridge. It looks like a bedsheet or a tarpaulin and it's splashed in erratic red and black lettering:

CHANGE HERE

I laugh. Maybe it's a surreal comment on the poor quality of the trains. *Change here for a replacement bus service to….*

Wait. If the coppers are still nearby, they'll see it too. The man would have narrowly missed running into them—or he didn't miss them at all. But if he's gone, they'll think I did it. Arrest me for vandalism, and political dissent into the bargain.

There's a shout from the cusp of Bank Lane and Officer Harassment sprints along the path towards me. He slows down and reaches for his gun. I yelp and dodge away, plunging into the darkness under the bridge, heart hammering, eyes bulging. Harassment wheezes as he closes the distance to the bridge.

As I reach the end of the tunnel, the grass bank emerges as a brief escape from his line of fire. My chest burns as the clouds cover the moon. If I can get up to the bridge, it might be possible to jump and dive over the wall. At the top of the bank, I risk a pause and glance back. He's there, gun trained on me.

"Get down here right now, or I'll *shoot* you down."

I look up at the sheer stone wall of the bridge ahead. It's over five feet tall, almost as big as me. And the ground beneath me is soft, too yielding. Do I have the strength to get over the wall and onto the road beyond? A miscalculation would mean a fall, a broken neck.

Come on, Ess. Unless you fancy a few nights in jail being pushed around by this guy.

My eyes snap back to Officer Harassment. He stands motionless, feet planted, gun steady and pointed at my face. Our gazes meet down the barrel.

Chapter Three

Expecting a shot to ring out, or an impact, I turn and launch myself at the bridge. My fingers fight for purchase on the crumbling rock as my feet scramble... and find a toehold. The ancient sandstone gives way underneath as I push off. Enough of my weight thrusts upward for me to balance my chest, then my hips on the top of the wall.

I dive over the other side to the road. It's a shorter, three-foot drop, but my face and shoulder crash into the concrete, rubble scraping against my cheek. I hiss as it stings, and for a moment lie dazed and panting, unable to command my limbs, or feel anything except the warmth of the blood trickling down my face.

A scuffling noise below alerts me it isn't over.

He's coming.

With a colossal act of will, I struggle to my feet, ignoring the stabbing pain in my shoulder.

Officer Harassment swears as I duck below the wall and lurch away along Bridge Road. Did he lose his nerve? There's no time to ponder. Before he can regroup, I straighten into a sprint. All I can do is hope Charlie hasn't come around this way to cut me off.

I slow my pace, and glance around, taking shaky breaths. An idea comes to me and I dodge up the first possible side road to avoid the main strip of River Street. There are no cops on the quieter lanes and I see no civilians either. After tracing a wide circle round it, I reach my flat on Potter Road, slip inside and lock the door behind me, then collapse on my sofa, panting. Gradually my heart rate slows, but my eyes dart around the room at every creak. I sit up for a long time before I even try to sleep. When I do drift off on the sofa, it's fitful and invaded by images of Harassment's livid face as he aimed the gun.

***

The next morning I call in sick.

"Is everything all right?" Brian's fretting because I'm never off.

"Fine. Dodgy tummy, that's all." And shoulder... and face.

I hate to miss the rough-sleepers breakfast service—I need to know if they picked Andy up last night. All the same, I hunch behind my half-drawn purple curtains and wait, watching the downpour beat into the glass. The air is oppressive. I open the window, close my eyes and let the rain drive the smell of wet turf into my face, clearing the haze in my head.

Nobody comes, and by the afternoon, hiding in my flat seems pointless. I go in to work.

"What are you doing here, silly mare?" Bri says. "Go home, you look proper rough. What have you done to your face?"

"It's only a hangover, Bri."

He nods in sympathy and offers no challenge, which makes me flush with shame.

"Was Andy in this morning?"

"Yeah, he was here."

"Was he okay?" I try to sound casual.

"Seemed fine to me."

I drop the guilt I've been carrying around since last night. Brian frowns, peering at my face, but doesn't comment.

There's talk in the Braai of the *Change Here* banner on the bridge, although nobody appears to understand its meaning. Maya comes in on my tea break and I plop down in the seat opposite her, grateful for the rest. My throat is sore and my head is pounding. Great—getting sick for real now. Why the hell did I come into work?

"What happened to your face?" Maya peers at me.

It won't wait any longer. Like Maya's spy act from

yesterday, I glance around me. "I saw him. Last night. The bloke at the bridge."

"Huh?"

Did she not hear, or not understand? "I went for a walk by the river. He was hanging the banner when I got there."

"Why didn't you call me before?" asks Maya. "That's so cool."

"Well, no it wasn't, actually. It was bloody scary." I tell her about Officer Harassment and the chase on the path, being brief and quiet.

"Wow," she whispers, raising her eyebrows. "You're quite the renegade these days."

"I didn't do anything. Except lose my shit. Did you hear me say he was gonna shoot me?"

Her mouth forgets its sexy pout and drops open. "Christ, Essie."

"I know." I take another furtive peek around the Braai. Two middle-aged men in business suits have taken the table next to us. I don't know them, and my heart pounds hard enough to ripple my Braai apron.

Stop it, Ess. They're just suits.

Something strikes me. "Is this your boyfriend's thing?" I whisper. "This activism you were on about?"

She looks blank, which after my experience on the river last night, only irritates me.

***

It's the next day, and Maya's activist meeting is tonight. It'd be crazy to take any risks after the chase at the river, like tempting fate. And besides, this virus gets worse as the day wears on. Though I try to rest, every time I lie down a raspy cough overcomes me.

But I've run out of cider. I crave distraction, so perhaps a flying visit to the meeting, just to say hi, would be okay. Then I'll get a smidge more medicinal booze and go home.

It's nearly seven-thirty by the time I leave the flat.

The meeting hall is a neat-gabled brick building on the opposite side of the road to Unity church itself. A few deep breaths, and I push through the heavy doors. At the other end of a parquet porch, a sign on the inner doors reads:

Do Not Disturb.
Balmford Mental Wellbeing meeting in progress.

Has Maya conned me into attending some counselling group? Confident I can defeat any therapist, I move into the room.

Despite my lateness, nothing has happened yet—there's just an old protest song playing. A sleek, black-haired girl sitting inside the door looks up from a tablet screen with dark eyes painted even darker. She forms a tight, intimidating smile around a pierced lower lip. I feel my shoulders hunch, aware of my pale, sweaty face and red nose.

"Can I take your name, please?" The lip-ring gives her a slight, muffled lisp.

"Er... Essie Glass."

She nods and looks at her device again. "Just need to check a photo ID, please Essie."

I glance around for Maya. At first, I can't see her among the smattering of people, and a suffocating, tight-chested sensation threatens to overwhelm me. I shoot a glance to the side and Maya's there, making herself a drink from a tea urn.

My bus pass is out of date, but it's all I have.

The door girl inspects it, taps on her tablet. "And a picture." Without waiting for permission, she holds up her phone.

I frown. "Why?"

"Precautions."

This is a weird therapy group. "If I say no?"

She shrugs. "No photo, no entry."

She snaps a head shot as I fix a tense, lopsided smile.

In five shaky steps, I'm at Maya's side. "I'll have one of those."

She jumps, inhales a sharp breath. "Jesus, Essie, you scared me." She pours me a drink all the same, giving me a gentle shoulder barge. "Glad you came."

Maya gestures to the front of the hall and a dusty, wooden stage. The obligatory drowning hands of the Unity sign loom against a green-curtained backdrop. She pulls me forward, making me spill hot tea on my arm. A pair of twenty-somethings talk with bowed heads by the stage.

As we pass, Maya grabs one of their hands and squeezes it. Lawrence, I assume. He winks at her, tipping his head towards hers for a moment. Broad and sort of handsome, in a misshapen, rugby player way, he reaches for a slim, silver laptop perched on the edge of the stage. The movement has dislodged an earpiece and he presses it back into his ear. As he turns with the laptop, I notice the screensaver:

CHANGE HERE

It flashes across the screen in alternating black and red lettering. The same design as the flag on the river bridge. The connection locks in my brain, and my heartbeat kicks up a gear. This isn't therapy.

We sit, and the twenty-something that isn't Lawrence leaps onto the stage with a microphone. His safety boots clump on the hollow wood. A mesh of red-blond hair waves atop intelligent green eyes, freckles and lean shoulders. He's wearing a beaded bracelet that makes me picture him labouring for a South American environmentalist guerrilla faction.

"Thanks for coming, everyone," he says in a strong Birmingham accent. He moves around the stage with a firm grace. "Let's get started."

Lawrence taps on his laptop and the music dies. There are perhaps a dozen people, and at least as many empty chairs. The black-haired girl from the door joins an older woman with red-rimmed eyes on the front row, a few seats away from us. They have a brief, murmured conversation, and the black-haired girl flicks her fringe back, staring ahead.

28

From the stage: "Welcome to the inaugural meeting of *Change Here*. So let's get to know each other first. For those I've yet to meet, my name is Gabe. I think we should start by saying a few words about why we're all here tonight." He gestures to the black-haired girl. "This is my partner Hallie, and her mum Martha. Hallie, would you kick us off, please?"

Hallie rises from her seat as Gabe dismounts the stage and approaches her. He kisses the top of her head as she takes the mic from him with a shaky hand.

The fingers of her other hand hook themselves around the bottom of her black Filibusta tour t-shirt as she turns towards us and clears her throat. "Hi, everyone." Her voice is quivering and thin, the brashness she had at the door gone. "I'm here because they killed my brother Francis in a police raid in Birmingham last year."

Hallie looks at her mum in the front row. Amid the stillness of the rest of us, Martha's shoulders slump, and her head drops. A sob emanates from the curtain of her grey-laced dark bob.

"They said he was growing pot in his attic, but he wasn't." Hallie's t-shirt twisting has become feverish. "Said he threatened them with a gun. It's not true. Francis hated violence."

Martha shakes and sobs louder. Looking stranded on the stage, Hallie's face cramps with concern for her mum. Gabe takes the seat on the other side of Martha, and squeezes her shoulder. As he turns to her, his jaw clenches.

Hallie sniffs. "The only rebellious thing he did was to publish a couple of articles in his university magazine, one about climate change conspiracies and another calling on students to march against the Education Community Contribution Act."

I remember something in the news about that law. Twelve-year-olds working on fruit farms to pay for their education. They started it this month, in time for the raspberry harvest. Half of them got heat exhaustion, but the government wouldn't stop the scheme.

"That's all it took," Hallie continues in a quivering tone.

"They said it was reasonable force, but they shot him four times. He..." She looks at the floor, swallows. "We can't go on like this."

It feels like the air pressure has dropped in here. Hallie scampers off-stage, then collapses into her seat, and the comfort of her mum.

Gabe stands and takes the mic. When he speaks, his voice is quieter, shaking from an emotion it takes me a moment to understand is anger. "Hallie's right. This is serious. We have to act. Now."

He lets out a sharp breath. "Would anybody else like to say something about why they're here?"

An older couple, perhaps in their sixties, bustle forward and take the mic from Gabe.

"I'm Sophie. This is my husband, Mark." Mark nods, his stony expression folding into a tight smile behind wire glasses.

"I'm retired now," says Sophie. "But I used to work for an environmental charity—until they blacklisted us. The things I've seen. We've all seen. I mean, you only have to look out the window.... And then we're all supposed to sweep it under the carpet and just live with it? Well, fuck that."

Even Mark raises his eyebrows, but Sophie ignores him. "Hearing Hallie's story just makes me more determined. I'm so sorry." Sophie's kind blue eyes glisten down at Hallie. "It's ages since I've heard talk like this. We can't wait any longer, we have to act."

"Thank you, Sophie. I couldn't agree more." Gabe retrieves the mic from her.

Sophie and Mark hold hands as they sit down and a young couple from the back shuffle forward and speak next. They introduce themselves as Paul and Agata.

"They let me stay because I'm married to an English man," says Agata, nodding at Paul. "But they deported my parents to Poland last Christmas, though they had lived here all their lives." She looks down at the bump in her belly. "The baby's due in July. How will I cope without Mama?"

"Someone spray-painted *'Go home, Polish scum'* on our

front door," says Paul, with a rage that looks so long-held it steams out of his eyes. He passes a hand over his shaved crown. Agata drops her head and her pale, tired hair trails over glassy eyes.

We lapse into silence. What is there to say?

Before I've collected myself, Maya springs up and takes the mic from Paul as he passes. "This is my best friend Essie."

My head whips up, a swoon of dread in my stomach. "What..?"

"She has a good reason to be here."

She shoves the microphone under my nose and closes in on me with her high-eyebrowed expression. I glare back, hating her for the betrayal, but the microphone doesn't move away.

"Maya." I try to make it sound like a warning.

But when she reclaims the mic, it's only to say, "Essie lost her whole family."

I'm furious with her, but I can't run away this time. After shooting a *we'll talk later* glance, I grab the microphone. Unable to face the others, I half-turn and end up staring at the green fire escape sign high on the right-hand wall. It flickers while I talk.

"My family were all killed two years ago."

There are intakes of breath, and it feels like they're inhaling a part of me. My sore throat constricts as if I'm choking. My cheeks burn.

"It was a terrorist attack... I was all over the news at the time, and they used it to…"

Maya nods, her eyes damp with tears too.

"There were immigration crackdowns after that. The Foreign National Register, the English First policy. I was like their poster girl for a while, and I didn't stop them." My voice catches, and oh, my head hurts. "I should have stopped them."

Maya mouths *'No'*, but the thing that was choking me has gone, and I'm purged. I flop down in my seat, my legs numb.

When Maya puts an arm around me, my head dips to rest

31

against her. Maybe she was right. I'm so tired, I can't figure it out.

"Thank you, Essie," says Gabe, touching my arm. "So here we are. Ten of us. Not many. Yet. We all have at least one good reason to be here though."

When I lift my head from Maya's shoulder to look around, everyone is nodding.

"We're all worried about the same things: injustice, greed and poverty, our dying planet, everyday abuse of the powerless. But what can we do about it? Nothing. Because we're *all* powerless.

"In the twenties, just like a century before, division spread through Europe, then beyond. For leaders, trade was the priority, not humanity. Not our world, our only home. What came next…?"

"Violence," says Hallie, staring at her hands.

"Everyone was angry," says Gabe, with an anguished nod. "We shook ourselves apart. The forgotten became the majority: the poor, the homeless, the disabled and disenfranchised. They couldn't hold that much fury back." He paces left to right, right to left, gripping the mic. "Around that time, we reached another milestone in our history. Anybody remember?"

"The tipping point," says Sophie.

"Yes," says Gabe. "Sophie, could you tell us what a tipping point is, please?"

"When an ecosystem transitions to a new state. So it can never go back to the way it was."

"Never go back," says Gabe through gritted teeth. There's a dense quiet now, like we're all confronting the truth we try hard not to think about. "Debate over whether the tipping point was real raged on right up until it happened. And if we thought everyone was angry before… The people, failed by their leaders, turned on them. Especially here.

"We live the rest of the story every day. After the crackdowns, rampant police power, the Dissent and Congregation Act, control of the media. The government monitor every word we post online for seditious content,

Masked or not."

I shift in my seat. I've wondered if my name is on a watch-list somewhere. It doesn't feel risky sitting in my living room typing under a Mask. I'm not daft, I'm aware they can identify us all, but how could they monitor everybody?

"This is England, though," Gabe continues. "So it's all done with a polite smile. Unless you're poor or homeless. Or, God forbid, call people to action." He glances down at Hallie, and she bows her head. "It gets more brutal then."

Gabe looks at the floor, but when he looks up his eyes shine.

"There's an enormous task ahead. We'll have to start again from the beginning, build something better than this. We begin with acts of disobedience. Expose them for what they really are."

Acts that change the world without being punished? Seriously?

Maybe I'm not the only one thinking that, because Agata asks, "How?"

"Well, as you know, I've already made a start this week, with the banner at the river. A small gesture, but it proves we can act. We'll be able to share more details soon."

Well, somebody damn near got punished for that stunt, mate.

"We tear it down first, then build... then escalate. The word will spread. Censorship laws, even the Neighbourhood Watchers can't stop communities talking to each other in private. We'll inspire people to follow, and take action. That's how we remind them they're supposed to work for us."

There's an empty rattle in the hall as ten people applaud.

"However, be aware we're talking about breaking the law. By meeting tonight, we've already broken the law."

With perfect timing, the power goes down. The room

darkens. We wait in silence until the generator kicks in.

As the lights flicker back on, Gabe continues. "Not to sound too distrustful, but we've got pictures of you all here. So, if you don't want to get involved, we'll say goodnight and you're free to go. Forget this evening's conversation and never speak to anyone about it, and we can remain friends." He's trying to keep it light but there's a sheathed sword of a threat underneath. When I look closer into his eyes there's cold steel behind the passion that makes my breathing rapid and shallow.

No one moves. Tension grips my neck, and I swallow down the urge to cough.

"But let's not dwell on that." Gabe smiles. "We start in earnest next week. For tonight, I want to thank you all for coming."

When the meeting's over, Maya's buzzing as we wander to the back of the hall. "Gabe's great, isn't he? Inspiring. Lawrence says he's got connections high up in the scientific world. He can get us access."

"Yeah, he's okay. That was out of order, what you did."

She's decent enough to lower her eyes. "I know. I'm sorry. S'pose I did get a bit carried away."

"A *bit*?" My jaw juts. "As if I haven't had enough people prying into my life."

"I'm sorry. I thought it would be good for you to talk about it." She tries to put her hand on my arm, but I step back.

"To a room full of strangers? God, Maya, when I saw the sign on the door I thought you'd brought me to a support group or something. I wish you had now. Would have been less humiliating."

She flushes. "Well, from where I was sitting, it looked like it did you good."

I hate that she's right. The rational part of me wants to walk out. Yet talking about my family, tonight, with these people... it's opened something in me. A box that's been closed since they died. I need to see where this goes.

"Do you think it's worth the risk?" I keep my voice low.

"Two nights ago, they nearly shot me for just being *near* Gabe's banner."

"Come on. You're forever ranting online about how rubbish things are. I know it's dangerous, but here's a chance to do something about it. It's better than going on those stupid forums anyway."

"Let's not have that conversation again, okay?"

Maya holds up her hands. "Fine, you go ahead with your cyber self-harm trip, love. Fill your boots. Leave it to the rest of us to sort everything out."

"That's not fair."

Her lips twist in a grimace. "You're wasting your life getting angry on Politiworld. Meanwhile, here's an actual *thing* we could do."

My face grows hot, my throat prickles. "How could I *not* be angry? You would be too if—"

"I *am* angry. How do you think it goes for me, every day? Being brazenly Muslim and female out in the world? The police harassment, the morons..."

In the half-empty hall, everyone can hear us and I feel a sting of embarrassment. "It hardly compares. That's a different thing entirely."

"It's the *same* thing, Essie." When I glare at her, she steps back from me a little. "Look, I'm not minimising what happened to you, of course I'm not. You know how I feel about that. I'm just saying we're all hurting."

I sigh, my fury spent. "Maybe you're right."

"You know I am." I haven't seen her eyes this weary and mournful before, even at Darya's funeral. "Is this how you want to live the rest of your life?"

Maybe not. But what else is there?

The others have gathered at the back of the hall to make tea and coffee. The muted clanks of crockery, the low hum of conversation make me so tired. I want cider, not tea anyway. Tea's not going to sooth this raw throat.

For a moment, I cling to Maya's arm. "I need to go. Want

to come back to mine for some premium quality cider you're about to purchase? You owe me."

"Sorry, babe. Lawrence and Gabe want to hash out the details for next week's meeting now. Can we catch up another time? Go home and get some sleep, you look terrible."

No kidding.

Chapter Four

Officer Harassment raises his gun to shoot Darya in the head. I move towards her, but a flash blinds me and shock pulls me to my knees. There's no noise, just silent rain, then a high-pitched hum. Like the dial tone in hell.

Darya...

But... my little sister has no head. Has he already fired the shot? I smell smoke. No sound but this infernal ringing, which must be in my brain. The rest of Darya's body drops to the ground, crumples on itself like someone has cut all her tendons. Harassment laughs, and, cruelly, I can hear that just fine. I—

I strain against a mute scream. The barbs of it needle my throat, and I'm burning up. Breath frozen, I listen to the raindrops pelt my window and the deeper thud of my heart.

Breathe...
Just a nightmare.

Damn weather. The heat and rain will be the death of me. This crappy virus loves the damp.

And the nightmares... Haven't had them this bad since the months after the attack, but sickness has reopened the wound. It's conceivable that all the events of last week were a fever dream. Is it possible to hallucinate a cop aiming a gun at you?

I haven't seen or spoken to Maya. She's been stuck in Worcester most of the week because the trains aren't running, and the Worcester Road was closed until yesterday. My phone has no signal—probably just the weather, but it doesn't help my confusion.

Going back to sleep isn't an option, so I climb out of bed and stumble to the sink for a glass of water. Down one, pour another, and take it through to the dingy lounge.

Shut up in my little box and so poorly, I miss my family more. My old home. I was born in the house I sold—right on the kitchen tiles. Mum once told me Willow saw the whole event, loitering horrified in the doorway. She couldn't sleep for months, kept waking up screaming. That idea used to make me snigger: my ferocious, sharp-angled, big sister Willow having nightmares and crying for 'Mummy'.

Our house was chaotic, rowdy, petulant—but a proper home. When I look around this lonely shed, it chokes me to think about what I had. All the laughter and secrets. Even the bitching. Yeah, I was born in that house, but it was in this grim flat I grew up….

Sleep must have come eventually, because I wake on the sofa, cold and rigid. It's morning and mushroom-coloured light seeps through the curtains. At least there were no more dreams, or none remembered. The fever has broken, and my head isn't pounding so hard, so I disentangle myself and slowly put my life back together.

***

That evening I debate whether to go to the *Change Here* meeting. And if there really is a meeting or I just dreamt it.

As I gaze at the rain, Maya appears and bangs at my living room window. A surprised yelp escapes my throat.

"Let me in," she mouths then, as she strides into my flat, says, "Didn't want you bailing out on me."

She's wearing old-fashioned rubber galoshes and a clear plastic poncho which teems with glittering raindrops. Inside the hood, her hair is untouched.

"Jesus. You made me jump, you clown. As if I would bail out." A coughing fit ambushes me. At least the meeting wasn't a hallucination.

"Where the hell have you been? I've been trying to call

you for days." She taps her foot.

"Like it's my fault the phone service is down. Has Gabe or Lawrence said anything to you about the banner situation? Stop dripping on my carpet—come into the kitchen."

"Hmm. House proud." She eyes my dusty, threadbare living room as I shove her through the door to stand on the lino. "Banner situation? Oh… the banner. Yeah, well, we've talked a bit. How're you feeling, by the way?"

"Do you think we could get Gabe to warn us when he's going to strike in future? Might give me an outside chance of making it to my nineteenth birthday without getting my head blown off."

She performs a few rapid blinks. "Wow, you've been rehearsing that, haven't you?"

"Oh, God. You know what? I forgot to tell you—the other copper. The slightly less psychotic one? Guess who it was."

"No idea."

"Remember Charlie from school?"

"*Charlie* Charlie?" She squints. "Beth's ex, Charlie? He's a cop now? Wow, I always knew he was a wrong'un. Wait until I tell Beth."

Beth and I fell out in the aftermath of the attacks over some stupid thing I can't even remember. Toby, probably. She kept telling me to dump him. I wish I'd listened now. A moment of uncomfortable silence follows.

Maya chews her lip. "Well, we don't want to be late..."

I suit and boot up, and we set off. It's a ten-minute walk, but it takes longer to navigate the slicks and drain deltas of rainwater. The *Balmford Mental Wellbeing* sign hangs on the church hall door again.

Everyone has made it through the weather this week: Lawrence, obviously. Sophie, Mark, Paul and Agata are there too, soggy and steaming. As we pass by, I catch a few of Paul's words.

"The police battered my cousin on the spot. For 'back chat', they called it. He's only fourteen. What the hell?"

We sit at the front again, next to Lawrence, who greets us and then bustles about with his laptop. The hall smells of wood polish and the mildew on the window frames.

Sophie and Mark are behind us on the second row, and I turn to say hi. They're drinking homemade nettle wine from a flask and give me several generous nips. It soothes my raw throat and makes my head buzz a little.

Gabe fizzes into the room at the back, and we give a smattering of applause. He waves to us and smiles as he approaches the dais at the front.

"Sorry I'm late. Great to see you all back again. Thanks for braving the weather."

He bounces up onto the stage, wearing the same khaki shorts as last week, with a quilted vest over a white t-shirt.

"Now you're all fully inducted members, we can talk openly. So... we've sort of announced ourselves. The inaugural *Change Here* banner remained in place at the river until last Friday morning which is good going. Guess the police were too busy hassling homeless people to get it removed until then." He takes a swig of water to the tune of a couple of cynical snorts from the group.

"We got a buzz around town with our first shot. People are talking—wondering what *Change Here* could mean. Now we work on creating a bigger noise. So." He cracks his knuckles. "On to phase two."

Lawrence stands, clutching a stack of brown envelopes. He hands one to Maya who glances at it, then raises her eyebrows and shows me our names on the front. While Lawrence moves among the group distributing envelopes, Maya opens ours. She takes an age fumbling with the paper, and then sits with the note held up to her face. An inscrutable smirk plays on her lips.

Eventually I grab the paper. In blocky typeface, it reads:

THU 10th MAY
TOWN HALL

I'm not sure what it means, but I don't think *Town Hall* bodes well.

"So, you know when and where. As for the what, it's

40

simple." Gabe scoops up Lawrence's laptop from the edge of the stage and shows us the *Change Here* screensaver. "You need to make your own banner like this. Then hang it visibly in your location. We've selected the locations for maximum impact."

No kidding.

"So," he continues. "It would make sense to choose a quiet time to hang, as it were. And tell no one about what we're doing here—post nothing online, say nothing to anyone."

Paul clears his throat. "Er… Gabe. How are we meant to avoid the drones?"

"Good question, Paul. Lawrence?"

Face flushed, Lawrence stands and holds his laptop awkwardly aloft, screen facing the group. We're such a small band, so close together, we can all see what's displayed. It's an aerial picture of River Street, and it's moving. The roof of the post office passes right to left, the wrought iron clock over the door swinging on its bracket, seemingly in a gust of wind. There's a synchronized creaking around the hall, as the same wind smacks into the old bricks and wood here. The footage of River Street is live. It's a live drone. Oh Christ. Several breaths, in and out, sound in the hall.

"You've hacked a drone? Bloody hell." Paul whistles.

Lawrence grins. "That's not all." He turns the laptop screen towards himself, taps a few keys. When he twists it back the picture is pixilated, corrupted beyond recognition. We could be looking at anything. "We can scramble it. Or…" He hits another key, and the scene reappears. Sort of. It's River Street, but faint, low sunlight plays on the roofs of the buildings. "Splice it. This is footage from the last pass of the same drone, an hour ago." Lawrence is grinning and while I look at Maya, she levels a misty gaze at him.

There's an awed silence in the room. At least *I'm* awed, in its truest sense. I'm keen to see more, but I want him to disconnect from the drone—what if they trace him? This must have occurred to Gabe, because he touches Lawrence's

41

arm, prompting him to shut the connection down.

"Lawrence is finishing up a program we can download to our phones. If you need to, you'll be able to disable a drone while you carry out your mission."

No one makes a sound. If it was meant to comfort us, it has only brought the risk into sharper focus.

Gabe continues, undeterred by our stillness. "A couple more requests: Please tell no one else in the group your assigned location. That way, should you get caught, you're not tempted to give anything away."

That strikes me as kind of martial, which gives me a queasy sensation in the pit of my stomach. Maya has a grim set to her jaw, but when I glance around at Sophie and Mark their eyes are sparkling with excitement.

"And my second request: Don't get caught."

***

The black coffee wobbles as I set it down in front of Sophie, sending it sloshing over the side of the cup. It lands on the biscuits I've piled on the saucer, though there's no need to sneak them really—Brian gives away enough food at the Braai.

She winks and squeezes my hand. In return I flash her a nervous smile. We weren't supposed to talk, but Maya and I are the last to go anyway, so what's the harm? As our day has approached, more doubt has clouded my mind about this whole idea. Although I can't deny the effect has been remarkable.

Someone draped the first banner over the front of the nightclub, the next one appeared around the top of the church's sandstone steeple on Sunday morning. It was hard to read—you had to circumnavigate the little graveyard and gardens to see it all. But most people got the general idea. Then it was the school, the supermarket, and someone redecorated the bridge. That was a feat because the river burst its banks on Tuesday and the water was up to the brick curves of the arches. You could see the bottom of the banner eddying with the flow.

Police are all over the place—there's been a steady increase since the first banner went up Saturday night. You're lucky to get ten minutes between drone passes. They rarely bother with frequent flying this far from the big cities, but we've drawn their attention.

The *Change Here* lettering at the nightclub matched the lurid pink-and-gold Kiss sign on the front of the building. There it hung, on a huge sheet of white tarpaulin with its sparkly arrow pointing down towards the door of the club. Like it meant *Change this nightclub*.

When the breakfast crowd thinned, Brian and I closed the Braai for a spell and went to see it. Around twenty people gathered outside *Kiss,* murmuring to each other. Frowns creased most of the faces, but there were one or two discreet smirks, too. When I glanced at Brian, his features were smooth and blank so I couldn't see on which side of the fence he fell. When he glanced at me, I chewed my lip, trying to keep my face neutral.

A few minutes later, a burly man in a Hi-Viz vest was atop a ladder ripping the banner down while a mousey stuffed suit from the council muttered to a cop on the ground. Thankfully it wasn't Officer Harassment, or he'd have no doubt hauled me in for questioning. It's a small town, but being at the scene of two of these things in a fortnight wouldn't have looked good. Seeing the uniform gave my heart a little jump-start that it would soon be my turn.

And now it is.

"You'll be fine," says Sophie, as Maya floats into the Braai.

There's a council meeting at the town hall at seven-thirty tonight so we need to get our sign in place by then. It's four-fifteen now and I still don't know how we're going to access the building. Everyone who's been in the Braai today has been full of theories about where the next banner will appear. A few have guessed the town hall, which is not helping my nerves.

Maya comes up to Sophie's table and play-punches me on

the shoulder.

"Comrade." She nods, deadpan.

"Shhh." I glance around at the packed, steamy café. "You'll get us arrested before we've even begun."

"Way to act natural, Essie. Listen, I've got this. Relax. It'll be fine."

"That's what I told her," says Sophie over her coffee.

"Well, thank you both. That's confidence inspiring," I say, my voice shaking. "Only, I wonder if either of you could help me out with how we're supposed to scale an eighty-foot building with our bare hands in broad daylight, with drones and cops crawling all over the joint."

Maya rolls her eyes. "I have a plan. Just listen—"

But I'm not stopping. "With a fifteen-foot banner. Without breaking our necks, ideally."

There's a pause, then, "You're a downer," says Maya.

***

My shift is over at six-thirty, which only gives us an hour to get this done before the council sits. Maya insisted we had to wait 'til now. Muttered something about Lawrence helping. Before we leave the Braai, she hands me a baseball cap and dons one herself. We pull them low, shrouding our faces in shadow.

The town hall is on Unity Street, past the church and the huddle of shops. When I was a kid, its name was Eustace Street and the church was St. Eustace's. In the late twenties, they decided we should rename all *Enlightening Institutions* for Unity.

Well, jackpot: Eustace Street had a church, a town hall and a college. They rechristened all of them. Unity Street is one of those flukes that make some people believe in fate.

The sandstone hall stands apart among the Tudor buildings that flank it. A dense blanket of cloud sits above a shining red sun. The rain has stopped, but through the steam that rises from the roof-tops, the sky looks like a bonfire with glowing embers glinting off windows.

It's quiet, but a few people are still making their way home from work as Maya glances at the sky. My heart pounds as she pulls me down Unity Street and sharply into the arch leading under the town hall. In the centre of the courtyard beyond, the bronze figure of St. Eustace dominates a fountain, his burble echoing around the mossy sandstone space.

I listen for drones, my chest tight, my lips stuck to my teeth. Maya is flushed, her dark eyes bubbling with bright sparks.

She snaps her head around and pulls me off to the left of the arch, covering my mouth with her hand. A cop strides down Unity Street on the other side of the archway. We freeze. I'm afraid to breathe until his footsteps have faded towards the river.

"Come on," she whispers, crossing the courtyard past St. Eustace to a window on the opposite end of the quadrangle.

When she taps on the glass, a face slides into view. By the time I make out Lawrence, his outline has disappeared. There's a rattle at the adjacent door as it opens and Lawrence stands behind it with a set of keys.

Maya darts inside, turns and beckons me through the door. In the dim, paper-cluttered office beyond, she unshoulders her backpack and rips open the zip. Out comes our crumpled banner fashioned from a white bedsheet. The words *Change Here* stand out in stark red dye, painted to resemble blood dripping onto the scene below.

The lower third of the sheet contains a depiction of a police officer beating a man in a sleeping bag, made from oil paints I found at the back of a kitchen cupboard. His partner is pocketing the money from the man's begging bowl. The whole time we were making it, I thought of Andy, and I had to keep stopping to wipe the fog from my eyes.

"That looks ace," says Lawrence, and we nod. I painted it, and even I think it's good.

"Maya said you'd get us in," I say to Lawrence. "Didn't believe her, if I'm honest." It's hard to speak when I can hardly catch my breath. Maya's folds the banner, then checks inside her rucksack again.

"I'm a tech contractor for the Council." Lawrence has his laptop out. Lines of incomprehensible code are white on black across the screen. "We get passes to the buildings for projects."

So *that's* why Maya said we had to wait until after hours. "Won't they know you were here, then?"

Lawrence holds up the swipe card between middle and forefinger. "I pilfered the spare team pass. No name recorded against this one. And guess who's got the passcodes for all the CCTV and access records?"

"Genius," says Maya.

I don't like the sound of it. What if they have back-up files? Think I'd rather have taken my chances up a drainpipe, drones or no drones. But we're here now.

We ascend a wide, plush staircase to the first floor, along a corridor and up a second flight of dusty, uncarpeted stairs. Maya wrestles with the banner as it trails awkwardly behind her. To prevent her tripping and breaking her neck, I pick up the slack, feeling like a frazzled bridesmaid in her wake. At the top, Lawrence opens a heavy, wooden door and we enter a dark chamber. The doorway is set in a long wall of a rectangular room.

A mahogany table dominates the space, giving off an aroma of beeswax. Leather chairs border the table and two windows at either end of the opposite wall stretch from the ceiling to three feet shy of the floor. Red-orange light spills through them and glints off the brass microphone holders embedded in the desk. It lights the Unity sign at the head of the room, making it look to me like the hands are bleeding. This is where the council is due to sit tonight.

Lawrence checks his watch, a chunky black bracelet on his broad wrist that displays the time when he moves. "You've got fifteen minutes. The chairperson arrives in twenty. I'm gonna go and wipe the records now. Before you're visible from the outside, remember to activate the drone scrambler, okay? I didn't do all this hacking for nothing. I'll meet you downstairs. Good luck." He kisses the top of Maya's head, runs his hand over his cropped hair, and leaves us to it.

Maya crosses the room, dips into the rucksack, and comes out with a pile of black rods, connected by elastic string running through their centres. Tentpoles. The *Change Here* members raided their attics to donate them.

With trembling hands, she passes me a little bundle of the sticks, then shakes the banner out and I grab the other end. It billows as we spread it out on the floor along the wall, spanning the gap between the windows.

Next, we assemble the tent poles, the small sections snapping together like sorcery to form long rods. With a yellow duster plucked from her bag, Maya wipes the rods clean of prints, sweeping firmly and slowly. Why didn't I think to bring some gloves?

All those sticks have made just three poles, two for Maya and one for me. Holding the end with the cloth, she shove-threads the first one inside a narrow fabric tunnel we sewed along the top of the banner. Covering my hand with my shirt, I do the same at the opposite end as Maya follows up with her second pole. When we're finished, the rod at Maya's end sticks out a foot or more. She purses her lips. Nothing we can do about it now.

Maya darts left and I go right, to the windows. We heave up the wooden sashes, so synchronised it seems like a dance. They open at the front of the hall on Unity Street. I peer up and down the road, but I can't see anyone out in the dim early evening. It's that in-between time you get in small towns but not in cities, where the after-work crowd are home for tea and the night-timers aren't out yet. There's no shadow or buzz of a drone, but I swear lately they've made them quieter. They sneak up on you like muted hornets.

On my phone, I call up Lawrence's software. He's called it ShoppingApp, for reasons best known to himself. When you open it, there are two labelled buttons, nothing more: *Basket* for scrambling, *Trolley* for splicing. Splicing's risky, so Gabe says to do it only as a last resort. With a shaking finger, I press *Basket*.

I squint through the glass, up at the sky again. "Ready?"

My phone display tells me we have nine minutes until the chairperson arrives. What if he's early?

Maya scoops the banner off the floor, but it's buckling in the middle, the three rods shifting position. "Wish we'd thought of something to secure these things better."

I sigh. "Can't be helped. Let's just do it and get out of here."

"You go first." She dodges round the hulk of the banner and approaches me.

"Maya…" She's thinner than me, but I'm stronger. I'd cope with hanging out of a window better, if it came to that. If it's left to her to pick up the hanging end, she'll probably fall and break her neck.

"Stop wasting time." Her eyebrows rise above the line of her glossy fringe. We've attached a rope to each end of the banner and she thrusts one at me.

With jittery fingers, I drag the contraption over to the window with the rope. The trailing ridgepole scrapes on the floorboards as I tie a knot round the catch at the bottom of the wooden frame. The other end swings away from the wall, clattering against the table behind us. That's the end Maya's going to have to catch once I throw it out of the window.

"Go on, Ess." Maya is back at the other end of the room.

A deep breath, and I lift the banner and try to cram it outside. It's too long and rigid to go easily. Despite the height of the gap, I have to bend the poles in a bow shape, the leading curve poking out of the window, the fabric of the banner flapping in my face. God, we should have thought this through.

One more shove, and with a brittle twang the banner catapults through the window, nearly taking me with it. I throw myself backwards, a fiery jab hits my hip as I collide with the table. By the time I dive back, the banner is hanging limply down the front of the building. The sequential clatter of the tent poles echoes as they land on the pavement.

Twelve feet away, Maya stares at the sheet, bereft of its scaffolding.

"They fell out." Her voice is flat with shock.

We look at each other through our open windows, then down at the banner swaying with its own momentum. Maya's end dangles out of reach.

What the hell do we do now?

I check my phone. Four minutes to go. My heart squeezes into a little ball and a trickle of sweat runs down my temple. Maya's face is tight. She's gnawing her lip. I hope that means she's thinking, not panicking.

A car engine approaches and Maya must have heard it too. We look down Unity Street towards the river. A white car rounds the bend in the road. As the vehicle draws nearer, I make out a light bar on the roof. Maya swears at the same moment I realise it's the police.

Chapter Five

Panic makes me inventive. With a hoarse yelp, I lean out of my window and seize the rope tied to the catch. A ripple passes through twelve foot of paint-crusted sheet below.

"Maya, grab it!" I swing the sign that way as her head pokes out of the other window.

The banner sways from side to side, but with the other rope weighing it down, I can't get it high enough for Maya to reach.

The police car is about a hundred yards away now, crawling towards the crossing, where they'll surely spot us. I swing again, arms stiff with terror. Maya leans dangerously far out of the window, and stretches her fingers desperately. Still nowhere near enough.

We pull ourselves back in.

"Shit!" Maya slaps the wall in frustration.

There's a movement and a clattering. She looks down on the floor.

At first I think she's broken the window frame, but lying on the carpet, its brass hook glinting, is a wooden window pole. It was propped against the wall. Maya's eyes widen. She beams at me, grabs the pole, and thrusts one end out of the window as I go back to swinging my rope.

One swing.

Two.

On the third, the hook snags the sheet. Maya snatches the pole back through the gap, grabbing the rope and tying it to her window in a flurry of frantic movements. We slam down our windows, fixing the banner in place.

From behind a sliver of undrawn blind, I peek down at the street again. The police car draws level with the town hall…

and slowly passes us.

I let out a gasp of relief and grin at Maya. She's still staring out of her window, her mouth forming a tense *O* shape. As I follow her gaze, my relief evaporates. The car has stopped just beyond the hall. It reverses twenty yards towards us and squeals to a halt. Two cops get out and glance in our direction. Maya darts back behind the wall, but I'm frozen. One of them is Officer Harassment, and he must have spotted me standing here like an idiot.

The tent poles, scattered in segments all over the pavement, draw his eye. He kicks at them, spits, and draws his gun. Maya and I dive onto the floor out of sight. I've lost all sensation in my legs. The skin on my arms prickles.

Oh, God, did he see me?

Maya's eyes bulge. She gasps as I stumble to the door, rip it open, then run straight into a dark-clothed man.

He's in already?

When I look up from the chest, it's Lawrence's face in a twist of fear.

"Police—" is all he gets out before Maya grabs him.

"Come on," she says, and we tear down the stairs.

As we reach the bottom, there's a bang on the door ahead. Officer Harassment's voice barks out, "Police. Open up!"

"Basement." Lawrence pushes us both towards the back of the building.

I start to argue that running into the basement would surely trap us. A gunshot thuds into the door. My body contracts at the sound, squeezing the breath out of me as Maya squeals. Someone is kicking the door. Its frame shudders. In moments, they'll be inside.

Lawrence swears. "Just go," he says, grabbing Maya's arm.

With no better option, we run to the rear of the building. Our feet skid on the Minton tiles. We round the corner to a service lift. Lawrence hits the B button as we dart in. The door closes to the thump of another kick from the outside. A terrifying crack of splintering wood reverberates in the hall. As the lift descends, our own rasping breath envelopes us.

In the basement, Lawrence sprints to the left, grabbing the security pass from his belt loop. He lets us into a room labelled '*Comms*'. The door closes behind us, and we slump with momentary relief. We've bought ourselves a little time.

The room is sweltering, and dark save for row upon row of flashing lights. The air smells of heat on metal.

"Door." Lawrence points the way to the back of the room, gasping for breath.

There's a smaller room at the back. He opens another metal door by pressing something on the wall. We burst out into pelting rain. The door clangs shut.

Seconds later, the power goes down and all the lights are out, even the streetlamps. Maya and Lawrence have disappeared in front of me. I freeze on the spot, staring into the black void. No movement sounds, just the relentless patter of rain on the tarmac of the carpark. I hope that means the others have stopped too, but I daren't cry out to them. Maya vents a wobbly breath from a few feet away, and I relax a little.

The lights come back on as the generator kicks in. Maya's in front of me, Lawrence a little ahead of her. A moment later, a security alarm wails, and we all start.

"Come on," says Lawrence.

We're soaked through in minutes. Even with the power back on, the heavy cloud cover offers near-darkness. Good. We'll be able to spot drones easier, with their hellish winking red lights. We scamper across the small, empty carpark and then push through a gap in the chain-link fence. I'm guessing police backup hasn't arrived yet because no one is searching the rear of the building. We slip away.

"Christ. That was lucky," says Lawrence when we're clear of the premises. "Two seconds slower, and the power cut would have locked us in."

I gape at him, mouth dry and vision blurring with shock.

We have no time to freak out before a soft buzzing above us.

"Drone." I duck uselessly, as if I can hide.

A litter-soiled alleyway leads from the rear of the town hall and comes out on Church Lane. Hedgerows on either side meet overhead to form a thorny tunnel, and cover. Lawrence pulls out his phone as we flee down it, and prods the screen.

"Scrambled. But we don't have long." He sighs. "Come on."

We troop down the alley like shell-shocked veterans and turn right.

"Where're we going?" I ask.

"Church," says Lawrence.

"Jesus, Essie," Maya keeps repeating in a croaky voice. As we approach the church, I nudge her to stop.

We near the soot-sullied sandstone building, glancing around nervously. The door is open and orange light spills out onto the bowed stone steps in the front as we mount them.

It's warm and tranquil inside the church. The cleric, I think his name is Fielding, has dressed comfortably in a checked shirt and jeans. He's raking a hand through his dark, curly hair as he talks to two damp, shabby men just inside the entrance. I recognise them from the sleeping bags on Bank Lane.

Cleric Fielding hands them blankets and points towards the altar. A gaggle of people have already settled on cushions and prayer mats, gathered around a cluster of lit candles in pewter holders. Despite their number, only a murmuring of conversation drifts our way. The church smells paradoxically of dust and polish. Cleric Fielding smiles as we approach, and it seems he's about to offer us blankets, but then he greets Lawrence with a big bear hug. After some flustered introductions, he welcomes Maya and me with a smile.

"Please call me Seth," he says. "I can't get used to being called Cleric."

Lawrence puts a hand on Seth's arm. "Can we talk?"

Seth gestures with his head towards the vestry and we

53

follow him down the chessboard-tiled nave.

"Lawrence went to school with him," says Maya in a sibilant whisper, nodding at Seth as we move. "They used to hack together. Pair of geeks."

"He's incredibly young to be a cleric," I say.

"Hmm... fast-track training. Unity needed new blood to sell the combined scriptures. Maybe they thought it would calm things down and stop everyone blowing stuff up. "

I glance at her. "You know a lot about it for a heathen."

She shrugs. "My dad's really into it. Unity, I mean. Not blowing stuff up."

Andy is there, reclining on a mattress and I wave as we go by. He smiles through a mouthful of chocolate cake. Seth ushers us into his office and closes the door gently. It smells of old books and the same floral furniture polish as the church.

After Lawrence flops onto a long, red sofa in the far corner, Maya and I follow. Stuffed bookshelves occupy every inch of wall, with the exception of a kitchenette to one side. Seth leans back against the door with his arms crossed, and regards us for a moment.

"Tea," he mutters, and busies himself with that for a while.

Safe for now, we're all dealing with what just happened in our own way. Lawrence is staring at the floor with gritted teeth. Maya jiggles her legs and breathes too fast.

My heart is taking its time to slow down, and I'm still sticky with sweat despite the soaking rain. But also... I don't know, kind of buzzed. I'm glad it was Officer Harassment who lost us—it feels like I got him back somehow for the crap he gave me at the river. I'd do it all over again—even though it's only Harassment and his partner who will ever see the banner in place. *We* know we did it.

With all their weapons and drones, they couldn't get to us. If we can do this, what's to stop us doing bigger stuff?

Seth brings a tray of mugs and sits opposite on a swivel chair purloined from his desk. He looks at each of us with a grave frown. I grip my mug. Has Lawrence told him about *Change Here*? And if he has, wouldn't Seth have to tell the police? He's Unity, and they have rules—codes to obey.

"I hope you all know what you're doing," Seth says.

For a tense moment, I silently concur. Then Seth's face creases in a smile, dimples opening in his cheeks. "Lawrence, you're a nut job, but good on you. Good on all of you. Been ages since we had some old-fashioned sedition going down."

This makes me chuckle.

Lawrence rolls his eyes. "You're supposed to be a man of the cloth mate, not Che Guevara."

"Can't I be both? Seriously though, you need to be more careful. One of the lads was trying to settle in a doorway opposite the town hall. The damned place flooded, so he took refuge here. But not before he saw the whole escapade."

Maya and I exchange a glance.

"Don't freak out, it'll go no further. But he heard you shouting out of the windows. He thought it was some kind of weird double suicide at first. Wouldn't be the first time. But then he saw the banner." He screws his face up. "Sounded a bit Laurel and Hardy to be honest."

That does it—I collapse into laughter. It's the thought of me and Maya frantically trying to land the thing, tilting out of the windows like clowns. I cover my face with my hands, hysterical. Then Maya starts up too, giggling like a loon while Lawrence stares at us both. Even Seth is sniggering, and he wasn't there.

"Stop it, guys," says Lawrence, looking concerned now.

Maybe he thinks we've lost our minds. Perhaps we have, but we can't stop. Maya snorts and I slap my knees to sober myself. The hysteria eases down into giggles. Seth reaches up into a cupboard behind us and comes out with some holy wine in an enormous bottle.

"Well." Seth shrugs. "Nobody ever turns up to communion now, anyway."

I start up giggling again. As I try to regain control of myself, Seth grabs more mugs from the kitchenette, pours us each some wine and raises his.

"To the revolution," he announces with a grin. We all drink deeply to that and Seth refills our mugs. The wine tastes like raisins and is too acidic, but it hits the spot. Even Lawrence relaxes a little.

It could be the danger and alcohol making me bold when I say, "Can I ask you something, Seth? Do you actually believe in God?"

Maya jabs me with her elbow, but Seth seems unperturbed.

"Honestly? I don't know," he says, settling his steady, green eyes on me. "But does it matter what I believe? To the people who come here, I mean."

I don't know the answer to that. Would it matter to me if I came here?

But you did come here, Ess.

"If there's a God, he's had his feet up for a while, hasn't he?" I say, mug halfway to mouth.

Seth presses his lips together, then sighs out a nod.

I swig wine. "And we have science, why would anybody need God?"

"We have science, yes," he says. "But people still come. I don't know… maybe we're filling a different hole here. Maybe science doesn't work for everything."

"But you said nobody ever turns up."

"Yeah, I did." Seth laughs. "Some still do. The eternally hopeful ones."

"How nice to be eternally hopeful." My voice sounds solemn, wistful. Not cynical as I intended.

"Amen to that." It strikes me as flippant for a cleric. "Most of my customers are Unity followers these days, not your traditional Christians. But I'm no purist. I like it that way."

"My dad's Unity," says Maya. "Says the only way the West will accept Muslims is if we stop calling ourselves Muslims."

"He's got a point." Seth takes a swig of holy wine. "Feels like surrender, though, some would say. Is he local, your dad?"

"Liverpool."

"Seth," says Lawrence, his face rigid. "We need your

help."

"Yes. You do," says Seth. Maya and I look up at him, confused. "The police were here."

"What... when?" Lawrence jumps up from the sofa.

"Sunday. And Monday... And this morning."

Maya puts her hand to her mouth.

"Asking about the support group that meets in my church hall on Fridays."

Lawrence swears under his breath.

"Yeah, I know," says Seth. "Good job I had cover for you. I run a counselling course here sometimes. I've got training materials, workbooks and stuff."

"Did they ask for names?" Lawrence paces around the vestry.

Seth nods. "But I said I didn't have any. Confidentiality and all that. I don't think they believed me, but it's a stretch to accuse a cleric of lying with no evidence. Even for the police. They'll be back, no doubt."

"We'll have to move the meeting place," Lawrence says.

"I think we'd be better off becoming experts in psychoanalysis," I say.

"It's not funny, Essie," snaps Maya. "We've broken the law. A lot. They could have shot us."

Well, look who's changed their tune.

"No, Essie's right," says Seth. "It's the perfect cover."

Lawrence's gaze bounces round the room. "I'll talk to Gabe." He looks at Seth. "Thanks, mate, we really appreciate it. We'd have been in deep trouble without you."

"Damn right, you would." He winks. "Now tell me you don't believe in miracles."

Chapter Six

We have less than twenty-four hours to recuperate. The following evening, Maya and I are pushing through a swarm of some godforsaken flying insects, like giant gnats, on the way to the meeting. We're both riddled with bites, so I guess that's their thing, these bugs.

The hall is in semi-darkness, and a sign on the inside door says:

Balmford Mental Wellbeing group cancelled this week.
Please ask at church for details.

Maya glances at me, sticks out her bottom lip. "Lawrence didn't say anything."

We exit the hall and cross the road to the church. Seth stands just inside the door. He winks at us, pointing wordlessly to a wooden door beyond the altar. A flight of bowed stone steps leads downwards between crumbling walls that mute our footfalls.

It's blessedly cool down here, with a damp earth smell that reminds me of the river, though we're half a mile away from its banks. The steadying hand I brace on the wall comes away clammy with sandstone and moss.

Everyone is huddled together twenty yards off at one end of the crypt, murmuring among themselves inside a circle of gas lamps. The orange flicker and the smell of damp feel like home. Paul and Sophie sit on deep red, velvety prayer mats. Agata and Mark perch on a carved stone structure against the far wall that might be a sarcophagus. As we approach, it's clear they've fought through the swarm too. All are sporting the same rash of red lumps as me and Maya. Paul's face is one big, angry bug bite. With our footsteps grinding on ancient dust, faces turn to us and there's a clatter of applause which makes me giggle.

"Town Hall ninjas," says Hallie, snapping a salute from a plastic chair, the laptop wobbling on her lap.

"Banner didn't stay up for long, though." I scratch at my hand. "Ten-minute ninjas." Chuckles ripple around the crypt.

"Doesn't matter," says Gabe from a shadowy corner. "I sneaked past and got a photo before they ripped it down."

Lawrence hands him a phone and he shows us the picture. The light is dim, but the banner looks good against the sandstone frontage.

"Bit risky, taking that." Maya nods at the phone.

Gabe shrugs. "Not as risky as hanging it."

"You got that right," I say.

There are nervy laughs all round. Gabe's eyes sparkle with pride as he gazes at us.

Seth appears at the top of the stone steps. The giant gnat things seem to have left him alone. Maybe God's protecting his own. "You've got an hour, Gabe. I can't pretend to be polishing the lectern much longer than that."

"Thanks, mate," says Gabe. "Appreciate the lookout service."

"My pleasure." Seth's silhouette disappears.

Gabe pockets his phone. "Glad you all made it through the end-of-days plague of locusts. And sorry about the sneaky change of venue. We figured it was wise after Seth's conversations with the police."

He looks around the room, a smile for each of us. "Guys, I'm impressed. We did it. I'll be honest, I thought it was a risky venture at first."

Now you tell us.

"But you came through, big time. You amaze me, all of you. And Lawrence, your drone app… genius, man." He claps Lawrence on the shoulder. "Now, we concentrate on momentum. We need to get the press to cover us. There's word around town but nothing in the media. It's a blackout, is what it is. They don't want others to follow, so they're covering it up. We have to escalate. Make ourselves heard. Watch this space."

As he speaks, my heart thumps. I can't remember ever feeling this way—that what I believe and what I do could make a difference. My life is small and usually occupied with the business of existing. Gabe can see something bigger. Survival yes, but more. And I need it.

Gabe picks up a tray of glasses as Hallie pops the cork off a bottle of sparkling wine, the report ricocheting off the sandstone. "But tonight, we celebrate."

When drinks are in hands, Gabe toasts, "To victory! And the revolution."

Our returning call is tangled, but enthusiastic. The fizz tickles my throat and warms my belly.

We spend the rest of the hour revelling in our audacity, exchanging crazy stories of our banner hangings, and speculating wildly about the next campaign.

On the way home, Maya gives my arm a goodbye squeeze at the bus stop, and I turn towards Potter Road with an optimistic bounce. The gnat things seem to have gone to bed at last, presumably happy-drunk on human blood. The evening has a fresh warmth and a breeze that smells of honeysuckle.

At the flat, I switch on the laptop, meaning to check the forums. But the meeting has cheered me so much that, full of ideas for sketching, I go to the trestle table instead.

I used to draw pictures of my family all the time, but after the attack I couldn't do it anymore. Tonight, I push my charcoal sketches aside, and sketch my mum's face in pastels. I have a print of all of us on my wall—one of those shots from a studio session we bought for my mum's birthday. It was only a few months ago that I could bring myself to hang it. Until then, it lay at the back of a kitchen cupboard.

That photo shoot was three weeks before the attack so it's the last picture of us all together. Darya's in the same t-shirt she was wearing on the train when the bomb went off—red and white stripes with red daisies around the neckline. The hospital returned it with her other clothes, bloodied and torn, in a yellow clinical waste bag. I remember thinking two things at once—why would they reckon I'd want them; and wasn't there a more dignified way of returning them?

We mostly look daft in the photo—I felt like an idiot posing with elbows on the white plinths they dragged out for us. Still, I love my mum's face in that picture. It's not a beaming smile, but a little one playing around the corners of her mouth, hinting at her dimples. Still, she looks so vibrant in that weird, pokey studio. I draw her like that, fizzing with life. And though I'm crying all the way through, the pastel I make is beautiful too.

There's the ping of a message. My gaze lingers for a moment on my mum's face, then I open my laptop and read.

You're going to die.

I rub my eyes. It's possible the tears are blurring my vision and my brain is filling in the wrong blanks. The words don't change:

You're going to die.

The handle is *TheOtherOne32*. Not one I recognise from PolitiWorld, or any of the other forums. It's been a couple of days since I've been online, so how could I have rattled anyone's cage that much?

Toby?

He could have found me on here. But then he knows where I live, so he could come here and mess with me in real life if he wanted to. And he has—but not for a while. Someone told me he's got a new girlfriend in Leicester, poor cow, so why would he bother with me now?

I've decided it must be a forum nut when another message pings.

I can get to you anytime. Just waiting for the right opportunity. Maybe on the way home from the Braai.

He knows me. Or maybe I've mentioned the Braai in a post somewhere. My heart pounds, my stomach knots. My eyes flick around my flat as if he might be hiding behind the sofa.

I know I'm supposed to ignore this stuff, but that's harder than I imagined. Probably I should report it, but the police have other things on their minds these days. And I don't need their attention.

Mostly, I want to reply with a stream of swear words. The other urge is to smash the laptop against the wall and hide under my duvet.

A third message arrives.

In the end, you'll beg for death.

I pace into the kitchen, sick to the pit of my stomach. There are no cigarettes in the house, so I pour myself a cider and sit on the floor, trying to slow my breathing and racing pulse. The screen, visible through the open door, draws my eyes as if I expect it to jump at me.

The next message comes. I don't want to read it but I'm compelled to. This one is far more descriptive about what will happen when he gets to me. I grab the screen as tears blur the words.

I should call Maya.

There's another ping. I groan, about to give in and trash the laptop. It's not *TheOtherOne32*. My breath squeezes out in relief.

FractalEyes: *Hey.*
Vixie44: *Hey.*
FractalEyes: *How's you?*

I can't do this now.

Vixie44: *Good thanks. Sketching.*
FractalEyes: *Not more planet wrecking...?*
Vixie44: *Nope. Nice ones.*
FractalEyes: *You okay? You seem tight?*

A long pause. I type a reply and hover over the button. Delete. Retype... send.

Vixie44: *Had one of those crazies message me tonight.*
FractalEyes: *From the forums? Christ. I knew this would happen. What did he say?*

I can't bring myself to type his disgusting words—only copy and paste a section of it and send. Before it goes, my eye catches some of it: *"... cut your throat, and watch you bleed...."*
I stare at the ceiling until it has disappeared. There's no reply for a minute.

FractalEyes: *Essie, you need to report this.*
Vixie44: *Who to? Who cares?*
FractalEyes: *Well, I need to see you, then. To make sure you're okay.*
Vixie44: *I'm fine. He's just an idiot. I'm gonna ignore him and when he realises I'm not scared, he'll give up and go away.*

Not scared? Really?

FractalEyes: *Please. I need to see you. Come on—we've been talking nearly two years now. You're not curious to meet me?*

Of course I'm curious, and that's what seals it. It's not that I reckon FractalEyes can help me. I can't imagine how that would work. Unless he's Batman.

Vixie44: *Okay, but somewhere public.*

He's late, and I'm starting to think this was a mistake.

Essie, this was never a good idea and you know it.

The Cuckoo Bar on Worcester Road is almost always busy early evening, which is why I suggested it. Not that he's a danger. It just makes sense.

This place is popular with the students at Unity, who are nothing if not eclectic in their drinking habits. As tradition dictates, it's their first stop on the college pub crawl, already in full, sweaty swing.

Inside, the walls are a warm, dark orange and overrun with a flock of cuckoo clocks which all go off on the hour. They turn the music down in the bar to honour the event and get everyone to join in with their own noises at last orders. Great for any tourists wandering in from the more attractive towns up- and down-stream; a source of ironic amusement for the Unity students; quite irritating for almost everybody else. Usually, I like the absurdity. Tonight, all it does is shred my nerves. I'm sitting at the pitted oak bar, in my green dress as agreed, when the seven o'clock cuckoo cacophony kicks off.

Ten minutes go by, and I've nearly finished my coke. Josie the barmaid has already shot me a couple of pitying looks, like she knows I've been stood up.

More threatening messages have arrived in the few days since we arranged this—not as numerous, but just as vile. Each time one dropped, I didn't want to read it. Every nerve was telling me not to open it, but there was no resisting. I've been in a daze all week. At work yesterday, I nearly burnt Brian's hand off while draining pasta.

"Vixie44?"

I turn. He's not Batman. He looks like a giant, undernourished red panda, with soft, reddish-brown hair and round, clear eyes that seem to quiz everything around him.

"That's me," I say.

He blows a *phew* into his fringe.

Early thirties perhaps. He makes an awkward, upward movement with his arms and it seems he's going to go in for a hug. Thankfully, he doesn't.

"Are you always this late?" There's a blunt edge of irritation in my voice.

"I'm so sorry," he says, pressing his lips together. "I got caught up at work."

"Biiig chemistry?"

"Yeah. Biiiiig chemistry. Enormous chemistry." His voice has the soft, rural twang of a local.

I give a nervous laugh, and there's a short, shy silence. A rush of belated gaucheness hits me as he glances at my fingernails, painted purple for tonight, to match my boots.

"Can I get you a drink?" he says.

"Oh, yeah. I'll have a… cider, please."

"Hmm. Cheap date," he says, and blushes, which makes him look rodent-cute.

He perches on a stool, orders a cider for me and a beer for himself. Josie puts them down, lingering a little too long, inspecting him with narrow eyes.

When she moves on, I say, "So… shall we do real names? Bit weird calling you FractalEyes."

He laughs, rakes his hair back from his forehead. "Good point. I'm Jack."

"Essie," I say. "Short for Estella. But don't call me that."

"Okay, agreed."

"So," I launch. "I'm really okay. I don't need anyone to protect me. This guy's just another pitchforker who doesn't like my opinions, that's all. He's not alone there. I'm not worried."

"You're not worried." He nods with an upward tick of the chin.

Unsure whether it's a question, I don't reply. He inspects his beer. There's another pause while I struggle to bridge the gap between his online wit and the person in front of me. Probably, he's thinking the same about me. My face grows hot, my jaw tense.

"Essie…" he says. His mouth looks like it's working itself

65

into a stutter, but no sound comes out. It's embarrassing to watch.

I take a breath and say, "You're paying, right?" When he nods, I catch Josie's eye behind the bar. "Jos, can we have a bottle of tequila and two shot glasses, please?"

Josie raises an eyebrow, but fetches them without comment. Jack tries to protest as I push my cider aside and pour us each a large measure. Right to the rim it goes.

"Bottoms up," I say, and gulp mine down.

Jack hesitates, bites the inside of his lip, then gives in and swallows his shot with a grimace. "You've got to be more careful online. There are nutters everywhere out there."

"Tell me about it."

"I'm serious." He leans towards me. "You don't know who's reading your stuff."

I laugh. "Sadly, I do. Only too well."

He shakes his head and holds it on one side. "It's no joke. It's not only the nutters. There are rational people who could be watching you too."

I thought *I* was paranoid. "Okay, I get it. I'll be careful."

He unhunches his shoulders. "Thank you."

The atmosphere's less awkward now, and more like an amusing social experiment. I decide to loosen the mood.

"So, Jack." Leaning on the bar, I cock my head. "What gives? Why is a thirty-something-year-old man chatting online with teenagers?"

"Teena*ger*. Singular."

A wave of my hand dismisses this. We fidget with our glasses, probably both wanting to top up, wondering if we can risk it so soon. I can't stand the suspense, so I refill both and empty mine almost as quickly while he watches. The crowd is thinning out as the Unity students move on to the next pub. With their departure, the noise and the energy drop a gear.

"Shall we find a booth somewhere?" There's a slight slur in my words already. I should have eaten something before I came.

Once we're settled in a discreet corner, his shoulders relax a little more. He pours this time.

"Tell me about this big chemistry," I say, trying to sound sophisticated.

"Not much to tell," he says. "Environmental research. Bit boring really." He grins. "It's not all lithium and Bunsen burners."

"Got any family?"

"Mum and Dad moved to Devon a few years ago. My sister lives in Dubai."

"No wife?"

Jack puts down his glass. "I wouldn't be here. I'm not that guy," he says, his eyes bright and wide open, locked on mine. Oh… those eyes are rather nice. "I just want to make sure you're okay. There's no agenda."

I peer closer at his face, but I can't find any clues, so I nod.

After a brief hesitation, he says, "Tell me about your family."

This is tricky. I've had a lot of tequila so it's impossible to talk about them without a few potholes in the road. "What do you want to know?"

In a soft voice: "What happened to them?"

"You don't remember the news coverage?"

He gives a little flick of the head, which I take as a no.

I pull in a slow breath and blink my blurry eyes. "They were on the train home from Manchester, pulling into New Street station, when it exploded. They told me Mum, Dad and Willow were killed instantly because they were in the same carriage as the bomb. But Darya wasn't with them because she'd gone to the loo."

Jack's eyebrows draw down, his neck craning stiffly towards me.

"That's where they found her. She had a massive head injury and…" I swallow. "Well, she was unconscious, bleeding. It seemed lucky at the time that they found her and got her to hospital before the convulsions started, so they could treat her quickly."

"Christ…" says Jack.

I've told that bit of the story so many times I've become fluent in its language. It's lost some of its venom. None of the numerous accounts in the past two years have been as painful as the one at that inquest.

"They were so busy treating the head injury they missed the sepsis. By the time they diagnosed her, it was too late." I stare at a knot in the woodwork of the table, covering and uncovering it with my glass. Feels like there's another knot in my chest and I stop short at the border between the endurable and not. As though they don't belong to me, my hands pour us another tequila. Not that I need it. I knock mine back like medicine. Aside from us, the room is almost empty, and Jack is matching it for stillness.

"You weren't with them that day?"

I knew it would come up because it always does. But I'm never prepared for it, and tonight is no different.

The tequila bottle lies between us. Yellow label, blown glass design on the neck.

"I'm sorry. You don't have to talk about it. I shouldn't have asked."

"No, it's okay. I would have been. On the train, I mean. It was a wedding in Manchester. A family friend's daughter, and I should've gone. Except, being an arsehole, I decided I didn't want to. So, I faked a migraine." My forehead leans on my palm, to stem the old, imaginary headache and the new, real one. "God knows what Mum and Dad were thinking. I never even got migraines."

"They were probably thinking you were pretending to have a migraine because you didn't want to go. Who wants a moody teenager at their wedding anyway?" he says, then probably realizes that was a little flippant. He clears his throat. "You can't give yourself a hard time about that. Nobody could have known what would happen."

I've heard the platitude many times before, so my only response is a vague twitch of the mouth. Goosebumps ripple on my arms. This conversation doesn't feel right anymore. I hardly know the man. Taking an unsteady breath, I check the tequila bottle again and share another measure between our glasses. The cuckoos start their eight o'clock shindig. Jack jumps and emits a cry.

"What is this place?" he says, looking about him like he's landed on an alien planet. It's so boyish, it makes me giggle.

"Tell me more about your biiig chemistry job."

He shrugs. "I work for ConservUnity."

He swigs his tequila. I follow suit, and squint at him. "In Worcester?"

"Yup."

"It was on the radio the other day," I say. "You had a big event there. Green tech and such. Some politician?"

"Yeah."

"That's your project? Hang on... Aren't you the ones with the Judgement Day Plan? It's all over the forums. When it all goes tits up on Earth, you lot are going to save yourselves with your own tech."

Jack jerks his chin to the side, eyeing me. "Sounds like rumours propagated by cyber-nutters."

"Like me." I chuckle. "That's what I thought. So, what's the tech you're working on? That politician was acting like it's going to change the world."

"I'm not really allowed to talk about it. It's…" I expect him to say classified, but no: "… sensitive."

"What is it, then?"

He shifts in his seat and rubs at a spot on the table.

"Come on. We're virtually on the same side. You can tell me. I promise it'll go no further."

"I can't." His voice is firm, and a little too loud. He takes in a quick breath and blows it out. "What do you mean 'same side'?"

Ah, I probably shouldn't have said that.

Oh, what the hell.

"I'm in an environmental group. We've started a campaign. To change things. Make them see sense and stop this race to oblivion."

His nose twitches, like a rabbit, and his eyes narrow as he

inspects my face. "That doesn't sound very… legal."

"Well… it's not, strictly. We haven't done anything bad. We've only hung a few banners, so far. But we have to do something. They've taken our rights away, so how are we supposed to act without breaking the law?"

He rubs a hand up his cheek. "I don't disagree. But that's risky. Someone in your position, no family to look out for you. The police would have a field day."

A flippant reply stalls on my tongue. It seems I'm not much of a match for the tequila. The room is uncomfortably hot and there's an echoing burn in my chest. I lower my head for a moment and close my eyes. When I glance up, he's watching me again. I hold his gaze, and perhaps it's the tequila, but we seem stuck that way. He leans forward and I mirror him, examining his smooth, round features.

"Essie…"

"Hmm?"

"I should get you home." He settles up with Josie, who peers at him then glances at me, brow creased despite my attempt at a smile.

As we weave up River Street, he takes my hand, but something has changed in his posture. He's stiff and aloof. Tequila and muggy air is a heady mix, making it easy to relax enough for the both of us. I keep up a steady stream of drivel on our brisk hike up the steep incline on Potter Road, and then we're outside my building.

"This is me," I puff, turning to face him.

He gives me a little smile. "Look after yourself, Essie. Stop taking risks. Please. I don't want to see you in trouble."

It's so long since someone showed concern for me like this. I mean, apart from Brian and Maya. Someone this cute. It's like my heart is softening in my chest. I lean into him and whisper, "Come in."

He pulls away, gaping at me. Then he reaches out and strokes my cheek while I gaze blearily at his chocolate eyes. A soft buzz of a drone draws his eyes upward for a moment.

Before I lose my nerve, I grab his face with both hands, pull it down towards me and kiss him with parted lips. His mouth opens against mine and I taste the tequila on his tongue, smell his spicy sweat. My fingers and toes are tingling, and an eager heat grows between my legs.

He pushes me gently away with a gasp. "It was really nice to meet you."

Not waiting for me to respond, he scuttles down Potter Road, leaving me panting. Dismayed at the embarrassment that'll greet me when the tequila wears off.

***

Jumpy and irritable, I pace round my flat. It's after midnight. The sound of a crowd of kids laughing and shouting seeps through the window.

My humiliation hits me again and I pass my hand over my face. Kneeling at my trestle table, I pick up my charcoals and sketch whatever comes to me. There's no discernible form, only lines and shading. Maybe shapes of windows.

I didn't even tell Jack the worst of that day.

After they were all safely away to Manchester—Mum, Dad, Willow and Darya—Toby and his mates came over and had a party in the house. It was his idea, but I was up for it. I guess I wanted to please him. He was difficult to please, so I would go along with most things he wanted. What an idiot...

They arrive at the house, about twelve lads with cans of beer. I call Maya but she won't come. She doesn't like Toby or his mates. We exchange a few tense words about that, and I hang up. The lads get really drunk on beer, then vodka and gin from the drinks cabinet. Trash the place, eat all the food, smash up the kitchen, pee in the flower beds. I'm pretty drunk myself so I storm off upstairs in a temper.

None of them notice except Toby. He comes after me, and it starts off okay. He gives me a cuddle, kisses my forehead, tells me he'll get rid of them and help me put the house back together. But I stay angry too long, and he's livid with me. He hits me for the first time—a back-hander that makes my nose bleed.

He keeps his promise though—clears his mates out while I hide in the bedroom. It sounds like there's a fight but don't dare go down to find out. When Toby makes it upstairs maybe half an hour later the house is quiet again. He's sobbing, saying sorry, saying he's a drunken idiot, to forgive him. We both cry, and I do forgive him then. By the time we fall unconscious on my bed, it's close to five in the morning, and grey light seeps through a gap in my curtains.

When we wake up later that day, it has already happened. But it isn't until Toby turns on the TV that I realise anything is wrong. The newsreader is listing the locations of the bombs, precisely running south to north: Bristol Temple Meads... Cardiff Central... Birmingham New Street... Liverpool Lime Street... Manchester Piccadilly... Leeds... Newcastle. Thousands dead, probably tens of thousands injured. They keep saying how much worse it would be had it been a weekday, but it's awful enough.

We watch the screen in remote shock as the pictures come in—shaky phone footage to begin with, then the camera crews arrive. Dazed and bloodied faces, people crying, flashing lights, warped iron, smoke everywhere. Toby and I sit there with our cups of tea and watch, still half-asleep and hung over. The whole rail network is suspended and here's what's in my head: 'They'll have to get a coach home now, and it'll take them ages'. How stupid.

I want to ring Mum to see what their plan is, but can't find my phone. Later it turns out one of Toby's scabby mates has stolen it. We've just started clearing the bottles and food strewn everywhere when the doorbell rings.

There must be a nasty little kernel in the pit of my mind by now, because as soon as I see the cops on the doorstep, there's no question. I slam the door closed then sit on the hall floor pushed up against it. No words or cries come out. Toby appears at the kitchen door just as one of the coppers peeps in through the letterbox.

"Estella? Estella Glass?"

There's no avoiding it—I have to let them in.

Chapter Seven

Less than two weeks after my humiliation with Jack, there's something to celebrate. A dozen bottles of champagne line the bar. Brian ordered them for Maya, and she plants a wet kiss full on his lips, leaving him a little discombobulated.

"Bri, you are a darling." Her eyes fizz as she looks around the Braai. The *Change Here* crew have decorated it with balloons and foil confetti on the tables.

Everyone's come out tonight. We've even organised a cake with a print of Marilyn Monroe iced onto the top. I can't say I see the parallel with Maya, but it was Bri's idea and no one had the heart to take it away from him. The Braai's closed for the night, the shutters pulled down to give us the place to celebrate. On a Friday. Bri's busiest night. He dotes on Maya that much.

Maya laughs when she sees the cake. "Guys, it's only a bit part. I've got one line in the first episode. That's it."

"What's the line again?" asks Lawrence. There's no way he's forgotten.

"Leave it, Grandad, he's not worth it," we all repeat together, in varyingly accurate cockney accents.

"Yes, thank you." Maya rolls her eyes. "It'll probably be cut anyway, so I don't know what all the fuss is about."

"I'll have your champagne, then." Gabe fumbles his empty glass onto the bar and reaches for hers.

As he grabs for it, Maya squeals and snatches it away, spilling wine on my dress.

Amid the kerfuffle, Lawrence leans in close to Maya. "I'm proud of you, babe. You're already a star."

Gabe mimes a violent vomit, and receives an elbow in the chest from Hallie. He fakes a stagger, but then trips over a chair, sprawling on the floor.

As I watch him scramble to his feet, the bubbles hit my brain and I giggle. "Someone's had a head start."

Hallie raises her eyebrows, tips her chin to the side. "Oh, yeah."

"Come on, pal," says Lawrence, helping him to his feet. "Time for a cup of something strong and black, I think."

"A brandy, perhaps?" Gabe winks at me as Lawrence and Hallie lead him away to the bar to straighten out. Maya and I plop into a brown leather sofa by the loo. Andy appears and huffs down in the armchair opposite. It seems he got ready at the vicarage because he's wearing one of Seth's denim shirts and smells of Seth's sagey cologne. He's clipped his beard and it makes him seem younger, no more than forty. I always thought he was in his fifties at least.

"Essie Glass." His eyes shine at us through their champagne mist as he lifts his drink. "And Maya Taheri."

"Andy Barker," I say as we clink glasses.

Andy drains his bubbly and snorts out a laugh. "This morning I was picking a sandwich out of the bin. Now... living the dream." There's no bitterness in his voice. Seth told me he was an artist before his breakdown, a sculptor, but I've never been able to ask him. If I couldn't sketch anymore, I wouldn't ever want to talk about it.

Andy puts his glass down with a quaky hand. "I saw Merrie today."

For a few seconds, neither I nor Maya know how to respond.

"Not actually Merrie," he says, his head on the side, and I can't deny my relief. "He's dead, I know that. I'm not mental. Just a guy who looked like him coming off the river path. Had a dog like Merrie's CeeCee too."

If ever a man needed a hug. We clash heads as I stumble into him. His stubbly beard grazes against my neck as he pats my back like you would a child. When he pulls away his eyes are heavy-lidded, head lolling.

"I'm made up for you, Maya," Andy says, then falls asleep in his chair, hugging a cushion.

74

"I'm made up, too," I say to her over Andy's raspy snores.

Maya gives me a fierce squeeze and kisses me on the cheek. "Thanks, babe." She glances around at Lawrence, who's thrusting a glass of water under Gabe's nose while Brian works the coffee machine behind the bar. "Thought I'd proper screwed up the audition. Lawrence might not be too happy with me though."

I must appear confused because she goes on. "We're going to have to take it easy on all this," she says gesturing expansively round the Braai. "I mean, this is the first episode of a serial. There's no guarantee but it might lead to something more, and that's not going to happen if I get myself a criminal record, is it?"

"You can't…"

"This is my career. I've been waiting two years for this break. I'm talented–"

"Yes, you are, but–"

"But if I don't make it, it has to be because I'm not good enough, not because I got arrested for some stunt."

I switch my gaze away, frowning, unable to wrap my head round what she's saying. And it's not just the champagne.

Brian must be back in the kitchen. Gabe's slurping his coffee, flanked by Lawrence and Hallie, who eye him warily.

"You think this is just stunts, what we're doing here?" I ask Maya.

"You know what I mean."

Andy smacks his lips in his sleep, like he's dreaming about pasties.

"This whole protest thing was your idea." Part of me gets it, even as I shake my head. Telling Jack about it was a reality check for me. Like a grownup has just come into the room and asked me why I'm crayoning on the walls.

Maya doesn't know about Jack. The day after I met him in the Cuckoo bar, she found out she got the part and it wasn't the right time. She'd only freak out about me meeting up with strange men. Anyway, I'm too embarrassed. My cheeks burn when I remember what an idiot I made of myself. I haven't replied to any of Jack's messages since. I don't need his pity.

"Maya…" I say, but there's a scraping sound as Gabe climbs onto the bar.

"Okay folks," he shouts.

Everybody stops talking and turns towards him. We cancelled the *Change Here* meeting in honour of Maya's success, so we weren't expecting Gabe to speak tonight. Especially with Brian here. As she tugs at his trouser leg, Hallie tries to talk him down, but he ignores her pleas. I glance at the kitchen door as Brian appears, his usually affable demeanour stiff and watchful as Gabe stumbles over a beer tap.

"Soo-onwards," says Gabe, the words colliding with each other.

Maya glances at me and shrugs. Brian's face flushes and contracts as he heads towards Gabe.

"There's annn event. In Worcshester. Next week. They're calling it a celebration-of-our-community." He holds his fingers up as quotation marks and sniggers. The movement sends him off-balance, and he sways perilously close to the edge of the bar.

Brian reaches Gabe and grasps his ankle. "Come on, mate."

Gabe shakes his caught leg like a dog up a lamppost. But it's ambitious for the state he's in. This time he falls off and thumps to the floor. Hallie screams, and there's a whoop of surprise around the room. Gabe crumples on the flagstones, all miraculously unbroken limbs and red-gold hair.

"But what it really is, iss demonstr'on of their power," comes a muffled voice from the bottom of the Gabe-heap. His head pops up from the ruins, his face somehow unmarked. He looks like a wackamole.

"This's what they do. They see rebellion, it's hold a sshamm event." Gabe climbs to his feet and peers around the room, his eyes feverish. "We have to show 'm we're not-sscared. Not gonna sstop."

Nobody moves.

"We're going to have a rally." This bit is clear as a tuning fork.

Christ. I can't believe Gabe's spouting off like this. After lecturing us all about discretion.

"Oh, man," says Paul softly from behind. I turn towards them as he murmurs to Agata.

Quietly, with rapid, small movements, they gather themselves and move towards the door. Paul opens it and gestures Agata to go first. She hesitates and turns back to the room. I catch her eye and her mouth gives the slightest of upward twitches, but her eyes are glistening. Her hand cradles her belly as the first tear spills down a flushed cheek. I give her a tiny nod, a mournful smile as Paul tugs gently at her arm.

"A rally. Yeah," Gabe says. His bleary gaze is on the door, so he must have seen them leave. "Crash the phoney celebration. Can't get to us all."

There's no sound in the room—it feels as if no-one is breathing. This is rambling insanity. They could shoot us on the spot for such a display of rebellion. Press or no press, they can do it and make it look any way they want. I look at Maya, whose face is heavy-browed, a mirror of my anxiety.

"Look, I know 's'dangerous. But we're a crossroads. We're a…. That's where we are. They wan' crush us. Schtop us beating them. Blink now, 's over. Can't fail. Can't."

Brian is peering at Gabe like a naturalist who's discovered a new species. When I turn around to see how Sophie and Mark are taking this, they've slipped away, too. Hallie and Lawrence just look grim.

Oh crap, this can't be happening.

Lawrence takes Gabe's arm and leads him to a table in the corner, talking earnestly while Gabe's head droops.

I raise my eyebrows at Maya. "If you want out, you'd better have that conversation with Lawrence now."

***

"It was just the drink talking." Gabe switches his earnest gaze between the four of us—Hallie, Maya, Lawrence and me. It's the morning after, and we're on a purifying walk along the river, pale-faced and stale in the bright sunshine. "There's no need for the intervention. I'm not completely insane."

"You sounded serious, mate," Lawrence says. "Drunk… but serious."

"Too much champagne. And brandy… vodka." Gabe squeezes Hallie's hand and gazes at her with wide, earnest eyes. "That's all. Sure, I'm angry. But I'm not suicidal. Besides, at least we know we got to them."

"You scared us," says Maya. "You scared the others even more."

Gabe nods, his eyes downcast. "I know. And I'll talk to them. Persuade them to come back. I promise. I'll calm it down, we'll go slow. Just… stay with me. Please? We've got so much more to do."

We exchange a flurry of glances. Nobody seems sure what to do next.

"Okay," Lawrence says eventually. "But let's take a break. Have a think about our next move. We've got to be clever about this, now, or it's all over."

Gabe flashes a tired smile at Lawrence. "Thanks, mate. I knew you wouldn't let me down."

***

But a week later the phone jolts me awake.

"Maya?" I pull my phone away from my ear and check the time on the screen. Just after six. Maya's never up this early.

She doesn't even say hello. "Gabe's going to do it. Hallie just called. He left her flat last night mumbling about standing up to them, and she hasn't seen him since. She's frantic. Convinced he's going to show up for the rally. She's going after him. Alone. We have to help her."

No one has mentioned the rally idea since our conversation at the river last week. Gabe seemed to have forgotten the whole thing.

But now… this dawn call from Maya. On the day of the event.

Gabe's going to do it?

I close my eyes. "Hold on, Maya. What are you talking about?"

I try to free my feet from the duvet, but it's all twisted round them.

She sighs, then intones, "Gabe's disappeared. He got drunk last night. Told Hallie we had to 'stand up to them'. Then he left her flat and he won't answer his phone. She thinks he's going to stage a protest. Alone."

"Oh, crap. What?" I know that's not helpful, but I'm still sleepy.

"Hallie's going. To try to stop him doing whatever he's planning to do. We can't let her go alone. We have to help her stop him."

"Maya, I've got work. I can't come now."

"Rally starts at two. We'll meet at the fountain and track him down." She closes the call without saying goodbye.

So later, after my shift I'm crammed into the tiny, humid toilet at the Braai changing into unremarkable jeans and a t-shirt.

"Essie, can I have a word?" says Brian as I come out of the tiny cubicle and into the bar. He jerks his head to the kitchen door and I follow him. It smells of roast lamb and carrots in here.

"What are you doing?" His eyes bore into mine.

"Eh?"

"Don't *eh* me. What's going on? You've been like a cat on a hot tin roof all morning, then you tell me you're leaving early. Then you get changed out of your usual crazy hippie get-up into these?" He flaps a hand at my jeans.

"It's not hippie get-up. Nothing wrong with a bit of colour."

"And now you're deliberately evading my point."

I sigh and turn my innocent starc on him. "Nothing's going on. I've got an appointment. Woman's stuff." It's worth

79

a try.

"You're going to crash that event."

"No."

"Crap."

I shift my weight onto one hip, looking at the floor.

"Do you know how stupid that is? Have you any idea of the risk you're taking?"

"I know what I'm doing. It's not—"

"No, love, you really don't," he says. "What if they find out your gang met here? Have you thought of that?"

"But—"

"When they catch you—which they will—if they don't shoot you dead on the spot, they'll question you. They'll make you tell them all about your little band of rebels. What you did, where you went, who helped you. You work for me. And you sneaked in a meeting at my place of business. I'll be on their list."

Though he's got it wrong about the rally, none of this has occurred to me before. I don't think it's occurred to Gabe either. Or he doesn't care.

"I'm a foreigner, Essie," Brian whispers. "I've spent years getting to Good Citizen, but that won't matter. One wrong move and it's all gone. *I'm* gone. Back to South Africa."

My face feels numb. He grips my shoulders, and I've never seen Brian looking so fierce. His eyes are blazing, lips flattened and tense.

"That can't happen. Do you understand?"

"I'm not going for the rally, I'm—"

"Essie. *Do you understand?*"

What's the point in explaining? He won't believe me, anyway. "I'll stay."

Brian leans away and sighs. "Okay. Good."

"Do you want a coffee?" I say, pushing through the door to the bar.

"Now you're talking."

The moment the door closes behind me, I grab my bag from under the beer taps, sprint across the room and out onto the street, heading for the bus stop to Worcester.

80

Chapter Eight

The river is wider in the city, the water darker. Along the path drift the aromas of mud, cigar smoke and something sweet, like candyfloss. I hustle past the highest flood marker, a slate plaque nailed to the wall of a pub, about ten feet from ground level, dated March 2020. Even though I must've only been about four, I remember so clearly asking my dad when I would be tall enough to reach that mark and him laughing and tickling me under my chin, making me squeal.

Today it's busy on Unity Green, bright and hot. Stalls line the perimeter, creeping right up to the pink sandstone of the cathedral. Each one is decorated in the colours of the flag, touting various patriotic tat or games of hook-a-duck, coconut shies and tombola. They've projected the Hands of Kinship onto the cathedral wall against a red and white background. I spare them a disgusted nose wrinkle.

The Council have built a huge bonfire twenty yards from Worcester's Unity fountain in the centre of a lawn burnt brown and crisp by the sun.

Draped over the enormous chipped woodpile: Our banners.

From where I stand, my painting of the copper stealing the begging bowl is visible. Drones skitter back and forth, painted in red and white for the occasion, but no less needling.

A face painter is daubing the English flag on the flushed cheeks of children who babble like tributaries of the river. The smell of frying onions wafts from a burger van parked in the corner. To the left, opposite the cathedral, a sound stage is in the latter phase of construction with a huge red felt backdrop, banks of amps placed on either side. Unity Green is teeming with coppers, clad in dark, probably bullet-proof jackets, each with a rifle in hand.

A tidal wave of nausea and fear runs through me as reality hits home.

You don't know how to keep your head down, do you Ess?

And this time I've probably landed Brian in trouble too. But I'm only here for Maya's sake. I'd never forgive myself if something went wrong and I'd bailed on her.

Like you bailed on Mum and Dad? On Willow and Darya?

I collapse on the lip of the fountain, our meeting place, and wipe the sweat off my forehead. The platform is finished, sound equipment hooked up and a microphone is placed centre-stage. A banner hangs on the red backdrop now:

CELEBRATE HERE

It has the same colour scheme and lettering as Gabe's original banner on the bridge and there's no doubt it's a taunt aimed at us.

A hand touches my shoulder.

I cry out, spring up and whirl as Maya entwines me with a hug.

"Thought you weren't coming," she says into my ear. When she pulls back, she looks pale and high-shouldered.

"Me too, for a while. Where's Lawrence?"

"Meeting Hallie coming off the bus." Her eyes skitter around the crowd, which is thick now, choking and sweaty. "No sign of Gabe, yet."

A spindly, spidery-looking man scuttles onto the sound stage, a patriotic brass band blaring through the speakers. He stands stiffly at the mic.

I spot Lawrence waving across the Green. "There they are."

As they approach, Hallie is red-eyed and her usually sleek,

black hair hangs in sticky clumps. Instead of reflecting the sunlight, it consumes it like a black hole.

"Thanks for coming, guys. I don't know what's got into Gabe. All week since the Braai he's been a picture of rationality. Then last night...." She mimes her head exploding.

"We'll have to split up," says Lawrence. "He'll—"

The spidery man at the mic drowns out the rest of Lawrence's sentence. "Thank you, thank you everyone. Welcome one, welcome all. I'm delighted to see so many of you could make it today for our very own Worcester Day of Celebration."

Lawrence scowls at the stage, then back to us. "Ess, you go left, check around the stage. Maya go right to the stalls. Hallie and I will check out the cathedral. There's half a chance Gabe'll mount a protest from up the tower. If you get collared by a drone, use the app."

We split up, and I head towards the stage as Spider Guy continues. "My name is David, and I'm the chair of the council here in Worcester. I'm so proud of our patriotic, beautiful city—look at the sun shining down on us. It's as though God Himself has come along to share our joy."

There's a vibrant cheer from the crowd gathering at the front, and my gaze turns that way.

What the hell is the matter with these people? *God Himself*? How can they fall for this crap? There must be people who see through it, but then I suppose they wouldn't turn up to this charade. I close my eyes in frustration.

When I open them again, Gabe's thirty yards away, striding towards the back of the stage where Spider Guy is spouting. I turn back to shout to the others, but they're already out of sight. If I try to contact them, I'll lose Gabe and it'll be too late. It's up to me.

Gabe's moving fast, a rucksack straining at his shoulder. He disappears behind the backdrop of the stage. I glance around. Nothing but rapt faces in the crowd, smiling up at Spider Guy in a misty daze. No one's paying attention to us. I inhale a steeling breath that squeezes my pounding heart and follow Gabe.

There's only a three-foot gap between the rear of the stage and the high, Victorian brick wall behind it. Surprisingly, there are no cops back here. No drones hover this far away from the horde out front. The sheer cliff-faces we're trapped between make my head spin. Beyond the far end of the back of the stage, there's a wooden gate painted bottle green. Gabe walks along the rear towards it. I linger at the other end, frozen on numb legs, watching. He peers at the plywood of the backdrop, puts his hand up and pushes it, then grabs one of the bracing beams and pulls hard. There's a little movement, but only a little. Gabe gives a satisfied nod.

At the far end, he drops to his knees and unshoulders the bag. Slowly, silently, I creep towards him. I've no idea what I'm going to do... something.

"We have so much for you to enjoy today," says Spider Guy on the other side of the divide. "Music and dance from some of our most talented Good Citizens. We have exciting local produce to buy and souvenirs to help you remember the day."

"You're all crapping yourselves," Gabe mutters to himself.

"Stop," I whisper.

Gabe jumps up and whips round. I shrink back against the partition. We gaze at each other as if we've never met.

"But before all that, I'm afraid we have some unpleasant business to take care of," continues Spider Guy. "And who better to guide us through it than Worcestershire's brightest star in parliament, Kerry Tyler MP?"

Gabe rolls his eyes. "Jesus. That woman's a right piece of work. Homeland Environment minister, my arse. Half the country can't afford power, and she's burning banners."

There's more cheering and a little off-mic murmuring on the other side of the partition.

I swallow the lump in my throat. I don't like hanging around back here one bit. "Gabe…"

He puts a finger up. "Shhh."

A well-spoken woman's voice drifts over the backdrop. "… And I'm afraid we have some criminals who conceal themselves behind banners and anonymity. They will not come forward to make their case. They don't care about our community. They don't want to be Good Citizens. They prefer to use asinine stunts to draw attention to themselves."

Gabe huffs at this and yanks a bundle of white fabric from his bag. He unfolds it just enough for me to read:

PROTEST... RESIST

"Glad you came." He winks, then delves into his bag again. Out comes a keyring with no keys attached. He shoves it into my hand. Crudely taped to the other end of the chain is a black plastic box the size of my little finger.

"What's this?"

"Open it."

Slipping my nail into the tiny crack, I prise the thing open on its hinge, like a locket. Inside is a single grey button embedded in the base. "What...?"

"Detonator. A little surprise for them." Gabe grins at me, a gleam in his eyes. "You can press it if you like, when we're done here."

My face grows hot, spiky electric currents race up my legs from my toes. "No. Gabe... I didn't come here for that." I flip the box closed and slip it into my pocket out of his reach.

"It's just a little display, Ess. Like fireworks, really. No one will get hurt. Well... Tyler, maybe."

I take the banner, trying to fold it back up on itself. "Not today, Gabe. Come on. Please. Let's put this away. Go home, yeah? We can talk about our next move then. Make a proper plan."

He glares at me and snatches at the fabric. "No. You signed up to this, Essie. Remember? You had your chance to walk away at the start. It's too late to decide you want out now."

I gape at him, then glance behind me, along the backdrop. Surely it won't be long before a cop comes around to check here?

Gabe holds up the banner. "I'm prepping this, then I'll

take that button back. Don't move." He marches past me and back to the other end while the MP's voice sings on. He starts to climb, a corner of the banner held in his teeth. I look up at the sky, breath almost sobbing out of me.

How can this be happening?

I glance back at Gabe, in the desperate hope he's come to his senses. No chance—he's nearing the top of the backdrop now six feet above the ground and ducking his head below the top. The banner drapes on the ground below him.

Just beyond him, there's a rapid movement. A dark figure.

Oh, Christ. A cop.

Pure instinct drives me around the corner, out of sight and into a no man's land of cables and chipboard at the side of the stage. By some mercy, a white van shields me from sight of the crowd. I lean back against it and check for drones.

There's an anguished cry from Gabe's direction. I peep anxiously round the back of the stage to where Gabe is climbing. My limbs are shaking, my forehead numb and cold.

Two cops have hold of the banner. They yank it, hard. The banner's rope entwines with Gabe's arms, and he falls with a shriek.

He's face first in the rubble. A copper leaps on top of him, yanking his arms back, trying to cuff his wrists. The other one smacks him on the back of the head with his rifle, and he screams into the ground, bucking the first copper off him.

There's a surge of adrenaline so powerful a spasm passes through my legs. I stagger back, tripping on a stray plank of wood, and sprawl on the floor. My head slams into the brick wall behind me. Spots of light spray across my vision, closing it down. There's an abrasive ringing in my ears.

When my head clears, it's the MP's voice I hear first, exclaiming words I can't comprehend. There's a stench of smoke and I impress myself by deducing they're burning the banners now.

A crowd cheering. Gabe screaming. I turn towards the sound. He must have put up a fight because although he's down, the policemen are kicking him. Of course, they've made sure to do it behind the backdrop, out of sight of the crowd.

Have they seen me? It's a distant question, with no emotion attached. Like a Sunday crossword clue. Gabe turns towards me, his face a mask of blood. They haven't cuffed him yet, and he gestures the way behind me.

One of the coppers grabs his arm and yanks. A nauseating crack echoes down the backstage alley.

That shatters the paralysis. I scramble to my feet and dive away from the cops towards the gate. One desperate thought: is it locked?

There's a rasping shout behind me, the metallic rattle of a rifle. Now they've seen me. If that exit is locked, I'm dead.

But it's not locked. I yank it wide and dart out of the line of fire. A bullet tears into the brickwork behind me.

Life number three gone, Ess.

Following the river breeze, I turn left down a passageway. I can't catch my breath. It's like my lungs are pierced with tiny holes and won't inflate. My sobbing slows me down, but I can't help it. Heavy footsteps pound behind. I daren't risk looking. The footsteps pause. The rifle rattles again. Every moment I expect a shot. But I'm at the river now, and turn mindlessly towards the bridge, past the crowds outside the pub. The drinkers' bemused faces whip past me. I don't know if the cop's still behind, but I hope that he won't risk firing into a crowd.

Out of sight beyond the arch of the bridge, I take the detonator out and throw it at the river. I finally heed my burning lungs and dodge behind a hawthorn bush, bent double, panting. The movement riles my stomach and I throw up, spitting into the weeds. My legs give way and drop me to the ground. Crawling behind the shrubbery, I know I can't linger, but I can't go on either. I curl into a ball in the dirt, hands over my face, mouth stretched in a silent scream of horror. Shocked tears course down my cheeks.

There's shouting from the direction of the Green. The MP's voice has halted now, and Spider Guy's voice chimes

87

out over the PA, "Please, everybody. Just stay calm. Let the police do their job and nobody will get hurt." There's a crackle and a pop and Spider Guy goes silent.

Oh, God, Maya. Where's Maya?

Heavy footfalls approach, slapping on the concrete path. I snap into a tight ball like a hedgehog, and close my eyes. The hawthorn is huge and leafy, but there's no way this copper will miss me. They can probably smell fear. They can definitely smell sick. But still I hold my breath and freeze in hope.

The bridge marks this cop's breaking point. The footsteps halt under its cool arch, and a frustrated wheeze takes their place. A few moments later, they sound again, slowly receding.

Four lives down. Time to retire, Ess.

As my legs unfurl from their knot, a buzz sounds up high and I hunch low.

A drone follows the curve of the river towards me and swoops like a sparrow hawk. Looking for me, maybe. The humming raises pitch, as if in irritation. My heart lifts its tempo in response, and an iron band fixes across my chest. It's close, but I daren't look up to see how close. I think of Lawrence's app languishing on my phone, but I can't even move a hand to my pocket for it.

The drone pauses over the bridge… then veers off towards the Green.

After an achingly tense wait, I unfold myself from the dirt, brush off my jeans and scramble down the bank. Worcester is quite drunk on patriotism this afternoon, so no one pays me any attention. With filthy jeans, vomit-stained t-shirt and sweaty hair, I pick my way to the bus station. All the drones, it seems, are busy on the Green.

It's an eternity before I reach the safety of home. Glancing around to check I'm not being followed, I slip inside the front door, whip my curtains closed and collapse on my sofa, breathing raggedly, sweating and shaking. My head is pounding.

When the shuddering subsides, I snap on my laptop. Desperate to call Maya, to see if she's okay, I know I can't risk it in case they took her too. Maybe she's sent me a message, though. Images of them battering her the way they did Gabe keep coming at me. It feels like I'm bouncing off the walls as I pace around the flat.

I steel myself and check my inbox. It's a couple of weeks since the last death threat, but I still get the same dread in the pit of my stomach in case he comes back.

There's another email from Jack, but I can't deal with it now. He's been trying to reach me since the night we met, but I can't bring myself to respond or even read them. He's taken to writing short messages in the subject line so I can't avoid them. This one says, *'Are you okay? Please talk to me'*.

I can't stay in my flat, I'll lose my mind. And since I'm probably fired from the Braai, there's only one other place I can think of to go.

In the rippling heat of River Street, it occurs to me I didn't actually see that detonator sink.

Or even if it landed in the river.

***

Seth isn't inside, but I see him through the vestry window, tending one of the newer graves at the back. My movement must have caught his eye because he glances up, waves and disappears round the side.

Moments later, he reappears at the vestry door. "Essie."

"I got away," is all I say, without expecting him to make sense of it.

"Lawrence called me from the square. He thought they must have caught you with Gabe." He takes his gardening gloves off and drops into his armchair. "Sit down, woman, before you fall down."

I flop onto the sofa. "Do you know what happened? Did

89

they get out?"

"Don't know," he says. "We got cut off and I still can't reach him."

No… no, no. Please.

"They got Gabe." I close my eyes. "They broke his arm. They were bashing his head… Maya…" And then the tears come. "Seth. I'm scared in the flat. Can I stay here?"

He scoots over and squeezes my shoulders. "Course. I'll get some blankets and pillows. Everyone from Bank Lane is out in the open air tonight because of the heat, so you'll have the place to yourself."

I put my head in my hands, exhausted and desolate.

"Essie, they'll be okay," he says. "I'll bet the others got out. And they'll just rough Gabe up a bit then let him go."

I search his face for some reason to think he's right. He can't quite hide the cloud of doubt in his eyes.

Chapter Nine

I wake up to reddish sunlight on my face, and that's weird because my bedroom gets evening sun. Have I slept all day?

Someone has mullioned my window. When did that happen? The pillow is too hard, and at an awkward angle. Then I remember I'm in the vestry, on Seth's red sofa, surrounded by his books. Every inch of my limbs aches from my narrow escape yesterday.

Maya. The detonator. Christ.

Upright in a second, I cast about for my phone. It's fallen on the floor. Before my thoughts can disentangle themselves, my fingers have last-number redialled. By the time I realise Maya's phone could be in police custody, it's too late.

The call connects.

"Essie." She's hoarse.

"Maya, where are you? Are you okay?"

"Worcester. Home, I mean. You okay?"

"Yeah. The rally." The only words I can form with numb lips.

"We think they arrested Gabe. Hallie's in a right state." The phone rustles, as if against her ear. "So are we."

Something bites in my brain and my limbs ice over. "We can't talk on here."

"Not a problem. Lawrence secured the line. I'll send you the app."

I blow out a sigh. "Okay... I saw it. Gabe. They were battering him." My chest constricts, squeezing the breath out of me. "Is he still in custody?"

"Must be. His phone's off, anyway."

"Do you think he'll give us up?" There's a catch in my voice. I'm pacing in the vestry now, in yesterday's mud-crusted jeans and sicky t-shirt.

"Lawrence says no way."

"They might come for me, anyway." I screw my eyes up, willing myself to remember the plunk of the detonator sinking into the river. But I can't. They'd have my fingerprints.

"Have you seen the news?" she says.

"No. What?"

"Full-scale riot on the Green. It started getting weird before we left. There was a kerfuffle in the front row. Was that you...? No, 'course not. The police tried to contain it, but it got out of hand. Fire bombs, looting, the lot. They shot into the crowd. They haven't reported any deaths, but... they wouldn't, would they?"

My heart is kicking. "Gabe didn't even get a chance to do anything. What were they rioting about?"

"Yeah. Me and Lawrence talked about it. Guess they didn't need Gabe to rile them. Why the crowd had to trash the place is beyond me. That's where stiff upper lip gets you. One-way ticket to Moronsville. Look, we're coming over."

"I'm not at home."

"Eh? Where—?"

"Don't panic. I'm at Seth's. Well, the church."

"Oh. Okay. We'll come there, then. Be about half an hour."

I venture into the vicarage across the little courtyard at the back of the church. Seth's in his office, so I knock on the window. He springs up and smiles, pointing to his left. We meet at the door.

"Morning," he says. "How you feeling?"

Better now I've seen him. "Achy. And I stink of sick."

"Yes. Yes, you do. Come in. You can use my shower, and I'll find you some clothes."

"I won't wear anything with a dog collar."

Seth gives a bass chuckle. "I get charity donations for Unity. Keep them here until I can get them cleaned and pressed. Should be able find you something without a dog collar. Can't guarantee it'll be as striking as your usual selections, but it's better than a cassock."

Why does everyone think I dress weird?

"I just like a bit of colour, okay?" I call as he leaves.

He returns with a pair of jeans and a checked shirt. They're musty, but I'll take musty over vomit any day.

When I come down twenty minutes later with my wet hair soaking through the shoulders of the shirt, Maya and Lawrence are waiting in the office with Seth. They all wear serious frowns.

Seth stands up to give me his chair. I wave him to sit back down but he says, "I've gotta go, anyway. I just got a call. Andy's in hospital. I'm taking him some bits and bobs."

"Hospital?" I don't move towards the seat.

"They think it's pneumonia."

"Oh, no." Is there ever any good news? "Tell him he has to get better soon." My head spins, and I have to lean against the door to steady myself.

Seth gives a tight-lipped smile, his eyes bloodshot. "Will do."

When Seth's gone, Maya gives me a hug, and even Lawrence squeezes my shoulder. We sit—Maya and me on the sofa, Lawrence on the fake leather office chair.

"Glad you're okay," says Lawrence.

"How'd you get out?" I switch my gaze from Maya to Lawrence and back again.

"Hallie got to the top of the tower first," says Lawrence. "When I caught up to her, she was watching Gabe below, at the back of the stage. We saw you talking to him and the coppers pull him down. Then we ran."

Maya looks at me, eyes hooded by a creased brow. "Lawrence called me. But we couldn't risk phoning you, Ess. In case. We didn't have the security app installed 'til this morning, and…"

"It's okay." I put my hand on her arm. "Lawrence, did you know about the explosives?"

Two sets of eyes bulge so wide they could pop.

"He was going to blow up the stage. Like fireworks, he said."

"Shit." Lawrence springs up from his chair and paces the office. "He's lost the plot."

"How did *you* get out?" asks Maya.

"I still don't understand how. They didn't see me at first. Too busy beating Gabe, I guess. I got a head start." I can't admit I don't know what happened to the detonator, because that would mean it was real. It must've gone in the river. Must have.

"I'm sorry," says Maya. "That's terrifying."

"Yeah. I threw up all over myself."

She winces. "Ew."

"Yeah, well. You would have, too," I say, feeling a sting of irritation like a paper cut. "Lawrence, what about Gabe?"

Lawrence takes in a long breath. "More beating. If he survives, I suppose they'll question him."

"Will they jail him?"

"Possibly. Did they see your face? Could they identify you?"

All I can do is shake my head and hope not. It's midday, and the office is stuffy. I twist behind me and open the window, letting in the scent of gardenias, though the air is heavy and still.

"We're finished with this," says Maya, glancing at Lawrence. There's that *we* again.

"Yeah, me too." I try to shake the sensation of things sliding off course. "I've got enough to worry about."

Maya snaps her head around at me. "What's that mean?"

I still haven't told her about the death threats, but they stopped anyway. The last thing I need is her freaking out about me meeting Jack. I shrug, shuffle my feet. "You know. Life."

"Estella Glass," she says. "Spill it."

My full name always breaks me. "I was getting stupid messages from someone," I say, barely opening my mouth to shape the words. My legs jiggle. "But I haven't had one for two weeks now, so it's no biggie."

"Stupid messages?"

"Yeah."

"By stupid you mean abusive." Is that anger, or impatience in her voice?

"Well, yeah. You might say."

"Well, who could have seen that coming? Essie, you're an idiot."

"Probably am." I can't look at her, just down at my twitching feet. Well, when you're knee deep in it, keep wading. "Then I met this guy I've been chatting to."

"From the forums? Are you determined to get strangled in an alley or something?"

"No. This wasn't a nut, just a guy I've been chatting to online. Jack. He's nice."

"How long have you been chatting?"

I glance up. "Couple of years."

She tries to peer into my eyes but I point them back at the floor.

"You've never said."

"Because I knew you'd freak out, that's why."

"I wonder why that is," she says, folding her arms like a teacher. "What's he like, this Jack?"

"Nice. A bit older." No way am I going to tell her how much older. "You know what? You've got Lawrence, what's wrong with me wanting someone too? Should I be on my own my whole life?"

"No, of course not. But there are better ways to meet people."

"For you, perhaps there are." I glance at Lawrence, but he won't meet my eyes. He looks like he's trying to push himself into the fabric of the chair. Maya's face is flushed as we glare at each other.

"It's so easy for you," I say before I can stop myself. "You're pretty. You've got—"

"You're pretty. Just… Most guys like straightforward. But there's someone out there—"

"Oh, spare me the soulmate crap. I'm not like you. You've got everything. A family that loves you."

"That's not fair." She shakes her head, looks at Lawrence, and that makes it worse. She could be right, but I don't care.

95

"I don't want to talk about it anymore." Hot under her gaze, I rise from the sofa. "We met, and that's that."

"Are you going to see him again?" she asks, in the same tone of voice you might ask a dog *are you going to poo on the carpet again?*

My laugh sounds bitter. "You'll be relieved to hear I made a complete arse of myself. So, no, I won't be seeing him again."

Before she can stop herself, her jaw and shoulders drop, and she lets out a sigh. She looks pleased, and that guts me.

"I think you should go," I say, my voice flat and icy.

Maya gapes and tears up. When I continue to stare at her, she turns her wet eyes to Lawrence, then stands. They leave in a bustle of gathered bags and keys, but with no words. When they've gone, my legs give in and I fall back on the chair, finally letting out the sob that's been building all morning.

***

Days later, Hallie rings me. "Are you back at the flat?"

"Yeah." I couldn't stay at Seth's forever.

"Can we come over? Gabe's had a row with Lawrence. We need to talk to someone."

No!

"Hallie..."

"Please, Ess." She sobs in her hand. "He was four nights in jail. They... I've nowhere else to turn."

Gabe and Hallie arrive with a bottle of gin. He's bruised all over and walking with a limp. There's a brace on his arm up to the elbow. He must have fitted it himself, with its Velcro and straps akimbo. It can't be doing any good.

"It'll probably never heal properly because they wouldn't get him treated in custody," says Hallie in a quivering voice. We both look at Gabe huddling in my armchair. He's barely spoken since they arrived, won't answer any of my questions about the police or what they know. If they found the detonator. There's something lurking like a ghost in Gabe's eyes. What happened to him in jail?

"You should get that looked at," I say, more to Hallie than Gabe.

"Lawrence and Maya have bailed out," Gabe mutters, rocking himself. "Guess they never really believed in what we're doing."

Words won't come, so I offer a round of cigarettes and light each one as slowly as possible. Hallie pours us more gin. Nausea ambushes me, and I don't want to drink it.

"Who wants tea?" A little wobbly, I stand up and crush my cigarette in the ashtray.

"I'll help." Hallie springs up before I can protest.

In the kitchen, she glances back at the door then whispers, "I don't know what to do for him, Ess. They knocked seven bells out of him. You should see him underneath his shirt. They…" She shakes her head, and a tear slips from her eyelashes. "He's broken. What do we do now?"

"I've no idea." My hand trembles as I fill the kettle. Did she know about the explosives he planted?

"I can't do this anymore," she says, covering her eyes. "It's going to kill him. What did Maya say about the fight?"

So, that's why they're here. "Maya and I still aren't talking."

"What did you argue about, anyway?"

"I don't even know." Sick of crying, I swipe the tears from my cheeks so furiously the skin stretches.

Hallie puts a hand on my shoulder. When we hug, we leave snotty wet marks on each other's shoulders.

Gabe and Hallie stay all night. While Gabe drops into a heavy-breathing sleep in the armchair, Hallie and I drink tea and smoke in silence, watching his chest in its stuttering rise and fall. All the unasked questions float in the air above our cigarette smoke.

***

The next morning, we say a forlorn goodbye at my front door, and I run full throttle down River Street. Brian's still furious with me for ducking out on him the day of the rally and being late today will not improve matters.

Brian eyes me as I race into the kitchen.

"Forty minutes late, Essie. I reckon this is your final warning."

Unable to meet his eyes, I mutter, "Sorry, Brian. I wasn't well this morning."

"Guess not." He's doing his best to give me an angry scowl, but what I see most is concern. That's worse. "You trying to give me a heart attack, girl? Running off like that."

Guilt stabs my insides. "No. Sorry. Really I am."

"Pull any more of that shit, and I'll turn you in myself." The words are harsh, but his face softens at the edges. "Glad you didn't get yourself killed, anyway."

Several times during my shift, I overhear people talking about the riot last week, about the 'troublemakers' who started it. I feel like their eyes are following me as if they know something. I dodge into the loo, pull my hip flask out of my apron pocket and take a few steadying swigs. The gin soothes on the way down.

Closing my eyes, I lean my forehead on the cool mirror. It's a relief just to be out of their suspicious stares for a moment. Twice as many Neighbourhood Watcher badges shine on lapels this morning. Like they're trying to flush me out. Like they found the detonator and know it was me who threw it. Shaking all over, I take another nip from the flask before I face them again.

The walk home is frazzled and feverish. My mind is racing, but only traces the same confused circles. My legs and stomach ache, my skin itches with exhaustion.

Maya's standing outside the front door. Her eyes are wet as she sets her jaw in a grim clench. I halt a few yards away, drop my cigarette, and look her up and down.

"What do you want?" My heart pounds, but my voice flatlines. Despite my lingering bitterness and her tense manner, it's good to see her.

It's only two words, but her voice cracks in the middle. "Andy died."

Chapter Ten

The river thrusts blades of sunlight into my eyes as we shamble along the path. Seth clutches the black granite urn. Andy would have appreciated the indulgence. God knows the funeral was basic enough.

We stop the other side of the bridge. A handful each for Maya, Seth, Lawrence and me.

"See you again, mate," murmurs Seth. "Peace."

As we release the coarse grains, a gust of wind fires across the water, blowing Andy back at us. As the ashes catch in my eyelashes, Maya turns her face away and coughs. Andy clings to the skin of my cheek, as though he doesn't want to leave. I don't want him to go either.

Years on the streets left his lungs weak. Smoking won't have helped. Or malnutrition, so the doctors told Seth.

When the breeze settles, we try again. This time we watch his gritty remains swirl in the water's flow. We stand silent and still as they recede.

***

"Andy." Seth raises one of Bri's stained-glass champagne flutes. "You were awesome. Hope you get all the cheese pasties you want now."

With a sobbing cough, I take a swig.

Maya squeezes my shoulder and peers at me with glassy eyes. "Can we talk? Just the two of us?"

There's a lump in my throat so big I don't know how the champagne went down. "Yeah. That'd be nice."

We leave the blokes reminiscing about Andy at the Braai, and head home to my flat.

"These are amazing, Ess." Maya sets her cup of tea on my trestle table and sifts through the sketches there. "Psychotic. But amazing. You should do something with these." She holds one up to the light. "You're really talented."

"Yeah, well," I say. "That ship has sailed, hasn't it?"

Maya looks at me, head tilted, brow creased. She drops the sketches, comes over, and squashes next to me on the little sofa.

She hesitates, looking at her nails. "It's not too late. For either of us."

"It's not too late for you. You've more going for you than me."

Maya shakes her head. "Not true. Ess, we have to get out —this is getting mental now"

"Yes."

"Gabe's a mess. I'm scared he's going to snap and say something. Lawrence is scared too, but he's Gabe's best mate…" Her hands are fluttering in her lap.

"I know." I glance out the window, catching the movement of someone walking past.

Maya spots my laptop sitting on the arm of my chair. "I suppose you can say one thing. It's keeping you off those bloody forums." She emits a skittish giggle. "No more messages?"

"Nope."

I haven't been online since before Andy died. Jack has given up trying to get me to talk now, too. Though it's what I wanted, it makes me feel lonelier. If Maya and I weren't talking again, I'd have lost my mind.

"That's something," she says. "I don't trust that Jack, Ess."

"You've never even met him." My own whiny voice irritates me. "It's not like that. It wasn't him, it was me. I practically threw myself at him." I wince at the memory.

"Hmmm." She presses her lips together.

"It doesn't matter—he's gone now. And Crazy Death Threat Guy, too."

"That must have been Toby."

"What's life without a little bit of crazy ex?" I shrug, tired of the subject. "How are you and Lawrence doing?"

"Well." She chuckles. "Hasn't exactly been a standard romance so far."

I snort. "S'pose not. He's a good man, Maya."

"He is." She chews at her thumbnail. "He wants us to go away."

"Like a holiday? Great idea. Things might calm down while you're away."

She looks down, then painfully into my eyes. "Not a holiday. *Away* away. To live. Edinburgh. He's got a cousin there who's a Scottish citizen, so they'd let us in as residents."

She might as well have punched me in the gut. My lungs deflate in an instant. "What about acting? That part?"

"I can act in Scotland, too. And I can travel once I've got the visa."

It seems they have it all worked out. "That's great." Can't make it sound great, though. My voice is flat. "When?"

"A while. Lawrence has to get a job first or they won't let us stay. He's got a couple of interviews. We're up there next week for one of them and to have a mooch around. If one of the jobs comes off, Lawrence will tell Gabe. Please don't say anything. Lawrence'll kill me."

"I'm pleased for you. Really." My eyes sting with tears that make me blink.

"I'm sorry." She puts a shaky hand on my shoulder. "Maybe you could come with us."

"Don't be daft." Pushing my shoulders back, I try to give her a smile, but a tear breaks free from my eyelash before I can swipe it away. "You know I'm used to looking after myself. Have that going for me, at least."

Maya's tearing up now too. She grabs me, gives me a ferocious hug. We stay like that for a minute until I pull back to grab my drink.

"What will you do?" asks Maya.

I drain the last of the gin and waggle the glass for an answer. Another sob bursts out of her.

"Kidding." I laugh. "Just kidding. I'll figure something

out. Move to Birmingham, maybe."

"Don't lose the plot again. I couldn't bear the guilt."

She's sort of joking, sort of not. But where do I go now, without Maya to anchor me?

***

It's a weird thing. As much as it broke my heart, Maya's announcement snapped me awake. Guilt's been choking me every time I glance at that family portrait on the wall. The only damn one of us still alive, and I've been treating that like it's nothing.

The first step in the Essie Glass Rehab Plan is to stop drinking. So I clear out the mostly empty bottles of spirits and cider.

Next: get back on friendly terms with Brian. Enough of being a total loser at work. The sparkle he once had in his eyes when we spoke is gone. I want it back. Brian, and the Braai, are likely all I'll have left after Maya leaves.

The way back into Brian's heart is to volunteer for evening shifts. Sometimes he struggles to get anyone to do it because if there's a lock-in, you serve all night while he joins the party. So I do the late shifts for a week. Wednesday is our third late-night drinking session on the bounce. I'm exhausted, but it's worth it.

Gabe turns up on Thursday night and orders a beer. When I take it to his table, he grabs my hand.

"Haven't seen you around." He looks grey and flushed at the same time. I wonder if he's high on something.

"Sorry. It's been…" I swallow the lump. "Been trying to be a good girl here. Keeping my head down."

He stares at me, eyes red-rimmed but sharp. "Lawrence and Maya are leaving."

As he speaks, a storm breaks with a flash and a crack of thunder. We both switch our gaze to the window among the murmur of other customers.

I look back at Gabe. "I know."

He glances at the empty table behind him. "Things got out

of control before. But I'm finished with all that. I promise."
He's gripping my wrist hard, and when I look down my
fingers have gone white. Gabe releases his hold. "Don't rat
on me." The words could be a threat, except they sound more
like a plea. "Don't desert me."

Brian appears at the kitchen door, gives me a meaningful
stare.

My lips bend in a mournful smile for Gabe. "I've gotta
go."

"Can I trust you?" he whispers. His hand is twisting in his
matted hair.

Can I trust you, Gabe?

"Of course you can trust me."

When I come out of the kitchen ten minutes later, Gabe's
gone, out into the storm.

The Braai isn't busy tonight, and Brian isn't in the mood
for a lock-in, so he lets me go early. Since the complimentary
taxis home stopped a while back, I begin the fifteen-minute
walk home. The pavements are still glistening with rainwater,
but the storm took the sultry air with it. I'm relieved to step
out of the sweaty confines of the Braai into the relative
sharpness. It's quiet and still down here, but up by the moon
there must be a gale propelling the clouds across its glowing
face.

Soft, steady footsteps patter behind me. They settle in at
the corner of Church Lane, and there's an itch at the back of
my neck. My ears strain as I cross onto River Street. The
footsteps continue—a consistent twenty or so yards off.
Though carefully placed, they sound heavy. Probably a man.

River Street would often mean sanctuary, being busy with
drinkers and clubbers. But it's deserted tonight, as if the usual
bustle has only ever been window dressing for my false
assurance. The multitude of alleys and doorways makes me
jumpier still.

I pick up my pace and he matches it. My heart is pounding
now. How are my legs still moving with no nerves in them?

No drones are out, which is typical. Never there when you need them.

At the crossroads with Unity Street, I glance behind. The figure is loitering in the doorway of a betting shop, looking interested in the odds displayed in the window. The dim security light is enough to confirm it's a male, short hair, dark trousers, dark jumper.

Turning back towards home, I trot up the incline to my road. As if it's that easy to lose him. Briefly, I consider taking another turn to shake him off, but my feet refuse to take me away from sanctuary, only up Potter Road and home. Without looking back, I fumble the front door open and slam it shut behind me.

The hall window is frosted so I can only make out blurred light and a slight movement. I let myself into the flat and lunge the curtains closed. After a second or two, it seems worth the risk to snag one aside and peek out. He's across the road in the shadows, facing me. Emitting a little squeak, I dodge back against the wall. I didn't see him clearly enough to work out if I know him.

I gnaw at my lip, my heart kicking so high I might bite that too. The death threats, and now this.

Shit. What if Toby's back?

***

If he is back, then he's biding his time. It's been four days since I was followed home, and nothing. Or maybe I wasn't followed, and it was just Gabe-induced paranoia.

My penance at the Braai is over, and I'm back on early shifts this week. It means a dim, lonely walk to work in the morning, but I prefer it that way. At least then I'm not too tired to bolt if there's trouble. We're back on easy terms, Brian and I, and he's worried for me over the Gabe thing. If I told him about Toby, he'd go into overdrive and probably make me stay at the Braai. So he doesn't know. Nobody knows.

My shift is over at four, so town is still busy on the walk

home. For once it's a pleasant day—neither muggy nor raining. Fresh sunshine beams down and there's a happy buzz about the people browsing the shops. My shoulders relax as the heaviness of the past few weeks lifts.

There's the comforting mud-and-moss scent of the river. It's tempting to turn down Unity and walk along the river path for a spell. But a grain of unease remains. Instead, I lift my face to the sun and feel its steady beat on my skin. The rise of Potter Road doesn't feel as steep as usual. Maybe things will go okay now I'm straightened out. Toby will leave me alone. Gabe will move on, Maya will change her mind about Scotland and things will go back to the way they were.

Through the front door, a strong, spicy scent of cologne drifts in the hallway. Which is weird because the flat upstairs has been empty for months. Maybe I've got a new neighbour. That would be nice.

I unlock the door to the flat, wondering if I should pop up and say hi. The cologne must have followed me in, because I can smell it in the lounge too. I'll probably have to drop some subtle hints about the amount he uses, this new neighbour. Think I prefer the usual damp smell.

"Hello, Essie." A voice behind me.

With a scream, I spin. My limbs freeze, a shock like electricity punches my chest.

He's got more tattoos than the last time I saw him. And his head is shaved closer, shining above his handsome, mean face.

"Toby." My voice is weaker than it should be.

His eyes roam over me. "I always liked you in green."

I breathe for strength. "How the fuck did you get in here?"

Better.

But my heart is hammering its way out of my ribs.

He grins and holds up something shiny. "Spare keys." A chuckle. "Had them all this time. I just couldn't let you go, Ess."

"Don't call me Ess. Friends call me Ess. Not you."

He grunts, rises from the chair in the corner to block my exit, and starts towards me. Suffocating aftershave pulses from him, burning my nose and throat. It's stronger than he used to wear.

I back up on quaking legs, in moments against the wall. "What do you want?"

"That's not very friendly, Ess." His mouth twitches. "I only wanted to catch up. It's been a while."

"S'pose you split up with that girl, then. In Leicester. What, did she kick you out like I did? Smack her about, did you?"

He's right in my face now, almost touching me. Now he's this close, I can smell beer on him too, and his eyes are bloodshot, unfocussed.

I stare up at him defiantly. "Of course you did, you drunk fucking bully."

His fist closes around the keys.

There's no way I'm dropping my gaze. "Then you sent me those vile messages, didn't you?"

He swings for my face, but he's so drunk he doesn't adjust for my dodge. The fist slams into the wall. His knuckles crack.

The keys drop to the floor as he screams. While he stares at his injured hand, I send a hard knee into his groin, scoop up the keyring, and dart towards the door.

"Bitch." Bent over, he clutches his balls. Hope I popped one of them.

I snatch the door open. "Get out."

He takes a single step, then squeals like a little girl. "You stupid whore, you hurt me."

Inspiration strikes and I reach behind the chair he was sitting in to grab my old hockey stick. Living alone, it makes sense to keep something handy in case of nutters. Like Toby.

"Yeah, I did." I hold up the stick, my breath rasping. "Want more? I'm not scared of you, Toby. Get. The fuck. Out."

His eyes scorch into mine for a moment. He raises a clenched fist, drops it. Then he shambles the short distance across my living room, pausing inches away to glare at me. Face twisting with rage, he lunges towards me, and I dart back with a cry, crashing into the door. My cheeks burn with shame.

Toby sniggers. "Yeah. Still scared."

"Get out," I say between gasps.

His livid face lifts into a mocking smile. "Catch you later, Ess."

The moment he's out, I slam the door and lean against it. The front entrance bangs, and his unsteady footsteps recede. I let out the sob that's been trapped behind my hands.

As I open the bedroom door, it jams against something. Forcing it open reveals my clothes strewn across the floor. He's destroyed almost all of them—torn, slashed and scattered them. The room reeks of his beery urine, and something worse waiting for me under the bedsheets. On the mirror, he's scrawled the word *WHORE* in dusky red lipstick. He's smashed up the rest of my makeup, emptied it, smeared it on the carpet.

I sob, then retch, making it to the bathroom before the remnants of my Braai lunch come up.

It's more of an imperative to leave than a decision. The few clothes and effects he's left intact fit in a bin bag. Maya's in Edinburgh with Lawrence for a few days, and there's only one other place to go.

Seth's in the garden of his vicarage, clearing weeds from the path leading to the rear of the churchyard.

When he sees me, he pales. "Christ, Essie. What happened to you?"

I'm not crying or anything. But with no memory of the walk to the vicarage, I must be in a state.

"Can I come in?" My voice catches. The ground blurs when I look down so perhaps there are tears. "Th…there's nowhere else for me to go."

Chapter Eleven

Seth's vicarage has age-darkened wood everywhere, but it's clean and comfortable. It always smells of fabric softener or vanilla. Or coffee. He has the kind of towels I remember from home—proper home I mean, not my damp flat. They're thick and soft, with that same fresh scent like lemony Parma Violets.

It's hard to believe I've been here since the summer, cocooned inside Seth's kindness. I haven't been to the flat once. Toby could come back anytime. Perhaps he already has, and I don't care to find out.

Seth doesn't ask too many questions. He reminds me of Brian in that way, though he's easier on the eye. I come and go as I please—but the only going I do is to work. Maya's not been around much lately.

Tonight, I've cooked us a spicy tomato pasta, and he serves it up in the lounge with a bottle of red.

"Communion wine?"

Seth chuckles. "Sorry. Unholy plonk."

"Suits me better, anyway."

We eat in silence, together on the sofa in front of the TV news. The spice and wine give me a warm, fuzzy feeling. It softens the focus of the story about two kids that died in a subsidence accident in Norfolk. There's been another bomb in London. They're showing footage of a shopping centre, all twisted steel and rubble. This one was courtesy of Christian fundamentalists, but it's all the same pointless carnage in the end.

"How did Lawrence's interview go?" asks Seth, and I can't shake the feeling he's trying to distract me from the news. I wish he wouldn't.

"Really well, apparently. They're staying on in Edinburgh to celebrate." I ignore the compulsion to weep into my wineglass. Maya and Lawrence have been careering between here and Scotland, house- and job-hunting, and getting excited.

I wave my wine at the TV. "Guess Unity still has some way to go to persuade this lot to integrate."

Seth let slip once he's received dozens of death threats for working for Unity, but he doesn't talk about it much. Brushes them off as crazies, refuses Unity's offer of a security guard. I'm not convinced, because I know too well that crazies can do some real damage.

He gulps wine and scowls at the CCTV footage of the bombers on screen. "What are you thinking about the flat? I'm not saying leave—you can stay as long as you need."

"Not sure." It's clear I can't stay here forever, but the rest is beyond me. I've heard nothing from Toby since he trashed my place, but that doesn't mean he's gone for good.

"You should tell the police about Toby," says Seth for the thousandth time.

"Like I said: been there, done that. They weren't interested two years ago. No reason they would be now."

"It's harassment. Criminal damage."

Seth won't give up.

I sigh. "Yeah. Three months ago. Not gonna look like I'm that harassed, is it?"

He leans back in concession. "You never explained how you got mixed up with this guy. He's clearly a nutter."

Good question. "He wasn't always. And by the time he was, he was all I had. And I was a mess. I chucked him out in the end."

As I twist the linguini around my fork, I remember that day. Toby hammering on the door, kicking it, swearing. Me huddling in the bedroom, curtains closed, crying.

"I was terrified. Thought he was going to come back and... Stayed in the flat, though. S'pose I was braver then."

"You're brave now, Essie." His eyes flick up to mine, then away.

"I'm electronically brave. Analogue, not so much." My pasta's gone cold. I swig my wine. "Even then, that's where I disappeared to. Into the forums, where you can solve all your problems with a punchy paragraph."

"Hmm. I can see the attraction," he says. "Bit like Unity."

"In that neither has the answer? Or that's where you'll find all the nutters?"

He gives a mellow, melodic laugh. We've both eaten as much as we're going to, but we're not in a rush to clear up. Seth pours us some more wine. I'm supposed to be on the wagon, but drinking wine with a cleric doesn't count.

"Why are you a cleric?" I watch him twist the bottle to capture the drops.

"Why not?" Then seeing this doesn't satisfy me: "S'pose I wanted to help people. And I quite liked the Unity thing. It sounded... progressive."

"Really?" I raise an eyebrow at him.

"Yeah." He places the bottle on the coffee table, licks a drop of wine from his fingers. "To start with, it did. Universal faith and science. No more fighting over fossils and scriptures; different gods...the *same* God. I thought it might help us work it all out."

I've never considered it like that. We used to sneer at it when I was at school. A marketing ploy then, soon after, a way to keep us under control. Mould everyone into Good Citizens. Seth's only a couple of years older than me, but he must've started looking for answers before I had any questions to ask.

"But the GC points though, Seth? *Come to worship every week and get a fifty bonus.* You must have questioned your career choice then."

His mouth twitches to the side, the way it does when you hit home. "Yeah. It was a bit... desperate. But I can't really do anything else."

"Lawrence says you're an uber-hacking geek."

He snorts. "Try making a living out of that. Why do you go on the forums?"

I gaze at the wall, grab a lock of hair. "I started after my family were killed."

Most people flinch or get upset when I say things like that, but when I look him in the eye, he doesn't. So, I say more. "The forums were crawling with conspiracy theories afterwards, and I got a bit obsessed for a while. After that, it was just habit."

"Yeah, I remember the rumours." He swirls his glass and the wine swings alarmingly close to the rim. "Must have been tough, hearing all that."

"I couldn't get enough of it. Freaky, isn't it? I guess I was looking for a reason. The immigration theories were the best. They took off after the inquest."

"That coroner was an idiot," says Seth. "I heard he's a mate of the Home Secretary. Explains a lot."

"Yes. It does. But it doesn't really matter if it was a conspiracy, does it?"

"Doesn't it?" Seth is very still, his eyes focused on me. There's just the tick of his antique grandfather clock behind him.

"What I mean is, they got away with it. Nobody remembers all that talk now. Even I reckon it's a leap to suggest the government would blow up their own citizens just to pass a law, though."

Seth's silence unnerves me.

The inquest verdict was one of the worst days of my life. Me in my red, too-short dress. There were fourteen bombers, all but one from England. That coroner had no business connecting what happened to us with immigration laws. How could they use us like that?

"When you're ready," he says, "I'll come with you. To the flat."

"I should just woman up and do it." I stand, take his bowl and stack it with mine. "It's just my flat."

If I'm going to break out of the cocoon and go back to the flat, I need to start by checking messages—find out if Toby's still leeching around. So, later that night, I gather myself and switch on the laptop.

My heart pounds as my messages download.

But there's nothing from Toby. I sigh with relief. Perhaps trashing my stuff has satisfied his desire for revenge. My eyes flit to the PolitiWorld icon, and I consider diving in. Before I click, a new item, in bold *unread* italics, draws attention to my inbox.

FractalEyes is back.

I won't hassle you anymore, promise. Sorry about that night. There's a reason I was weird, but I can't explain it right now. I just need to meet with you. Just once. It's not about us or that night. You have no reason to trust me but please say you will. It's really, really important or I wouldn't ask. Anywhere you want—you name the time and place.

I close my eyes.

Oh, Jack.

What am I meant to do? I could ask Seth's advice, but I already know what he'd say. Stay a million miles away. The reason I don't want to ask Seth is that I don't like that answer. So, I have mine.

Before I change my mind, I type *Cuckoo, tomorrow night at 8*, and send.

***

On Friday afternoon, Seth helps me carry my stuff back to the flat. While I wait in the lounge, he tackles whatever has lain in my bed and all over my floor since Toby left it there months ago. He scrubs everything clean and bins the ruined clothes as I sit hunched on the sofa, trying not to think about what he's seeing.

"Come and have a look," he says from the doorway.

He's done a good job of disguising the smell, but to me there's still a trace of Toby's stink. I'll get some air fresheners. Or some cigarettes and smoke it out.

When he leaves, Seth kisses me on the forehead. "You can

come back anytime, Ess. I'm gonna miss having you around, in truth."

"Thanks, Seth." I give him a tight-lipped smile, so tempted to say yes my chest aches.

In the evening, the crowd at the Cuckoo is ebullient. I'm a little late, but Jack's not there. Josie nods at me from behind the bar and slides a neat gin on a coaster in front of me without comment. The coaster is a piece of folded notepaper.

His writing is small and spiky.

We can't talk here.
Drink the gin—casually. Don't down it.
Then take a scenic route to the river bridge.
Don't get followed.

My insides cramp. What the hell is this about? Does he know Toby followed me? I hurry my gin, trying not to look like I'm hurrying my gin. With no idea why, I glance around for people who might be watching me.

Glass drained, I clamber off the bar stool and wave goodbye to Josie, who shoots me a concerned frown, but says nothing as she pulls a pint.

Night has fallen, and my pulse flutters as I reach the river path. Jack is sitting on the bench dedicated to Lila Etheridge, who died the day I was born. His sweat-slicked face fixes on the dark water, and he doesn't seem to hear me approach until I say his name.

"Essie, Jesus, you scared me." He presses a hand to his chest and glances around him.

"Yeah. I have that effect." I plop onto the bench beside him.

He hesitates. "How have you been?" The tightness in his voice makes me feel bad.

"Good," I say. "Okay."

"Did anyone follow you here?"

"No."

"Thanks for coming. I realise you had no reason to."

"What's this cloak and dagger stuff about?"

113

He takes in a long, slow breath. "In a minute, I'm going to take an envelope out of my pocket and pass it to you. Put it into your bag quickly—I'll explain afterwards."

"What the hell?"

His agitation radiates across the warm gap between us. "Please just trust me. I will explain. Just need to make sure you get this first, in case anything happens."

"What... what's going to happen?"

"Please, Essie." His raised voice echoes under the bridge. He ducks his head down.

Even in the moonlight, he looks like he hasn't slept in days. His clothes are crumpled, his prairie dog eyes dark in shadow. "Please," he says quietly. "You don't owe me anything. But... this is really... I need you to help me do something. Will you help?"

It's a hard decision to make with nothing to go on. When I nod, a small, lumpy, brown envelope appears. I pluck it from his fingers and stuff it in my little shoulder bag.

"Thank you." He breathes deeply in the swampy air, giving me time to think.

"This isn't drugs is it? You're not stealing drugs?"

He laughs. "No. It's not drugs. It's probably worse."

I raise my eyes to the sky. Silver tipped clouds scuttle away from us as I wait.

"Your protest group. Can you trust them?"

"Eh?"

"You have a leader, right?"

"Yeah... G—"

He grabs my arm. "I don't want the name. Don't tell me the name, for God's sake. Just... can you trust them?"

"You're confusing me, now." I look at his hand, still gripping my wrist. "Not to mention hurting me."

He releases me. "Sorry."

A group of lads is crossing the bridge. One of them looks down at us and whistles salaciously as Jack turns his face away. The gang explode into laughter, but pay us no more attention as they move on.

I turn aside, to his shadowed face. "What's in the

114

envelope?"

A deep sigh. "It's the project I've been working on."

"The Biiig chemistry?"

Instead of laughing, he shakes his head. "Sorry, I don't have time to explain, but I need you to take it to your protest group. You guys need to find someone to help you process it."

Oh. "Jack…"

"It's a 3D printer file for a piece of kit we've designed."

"What kit?"

"Carbon capture. Bioenergy carbon capture."

"Okay… what?"

Slowly, as if to an idiot, he says, "You take biological material, from… waste and stuff, and extract the energy. And capture the carbon. The basic idea is one in every home and we reverse the warming and save the world. Well, it's more complicated than that, but…"

"Complicated how?"

"It doesn't matter right now. We just—"

"Anyway, that's not new, is it?"

"Not the thing itself, no." He shrugs. "But its power… There's never been a model that could absorb carbon dioxide so quickly, at such concentrations." He glances sideways at me, a proud smirk on his lips. "And that's not all. I've found a way to harness the energy that comes out of it. With the old models, you just had to bury the carbon, and lost it. But I reckon I can use it. Got to test that bit, but if I nail it, it's free electricity for everyone. Carbon neutral. In your own home."

Crikey. "No more power cuts?"

"No more power cuts," he nods. "And no more bills."

I gape at Jack. "Shit... the power companies won't like that."

"You think? Hence the cloak and dagger."

As my heart hammers, about twenty thoughts occur to me. If he can make a scrubber that powerful, have we cracked it, then? And this being the case, why is it now in my bag?

And am I safe?

"Why are you giving this to me?"

He shoves his hands deep into his pockets as another gang of teenagers crosses the bridge into town. "The project was government funded. The units would be cheap to make and free for everyone. But then, in the final phase, they cancelled it. No explanation given. Bastards."

"So how did this even come to exist?" I pat my bag.

He glances over, frowning. "We received considerable investment from a private source. The project moved from the university to ConservUnity last year, and my job moved with it. I was a lecturer at the uni, now I'm a CU research chemist. Okay. But then it turns out the units aren't going to be free. Or even cheap."

My brow creases. "Rich bastards get richer off other people's misery? So, what's new?"

"Nothing, really." he says. "Just…" He flaps a hand at the sky, meaning the state of things, I guess. "We're still doing this? Now?"

"Yeah, I see what you mean."

"Langford, my boss, didn't realise I was researching the power generation module at first. When he found out, he went bat shit. Told me to stop all activities related to that part of the project."

"Why?"

"Scared. In case he got shut down. Like you said, the power companies wouldn't like it. The government is pretty much owned by the power companies. And green tech firms like ours rely on the government for licences."

"You sure about this?"

"Oh yeah," he says with a slow nod. "Obviously, I carried on the research, anyway. I don't trust Langford as far as I can spit. He's probably cut a deal with the energy companies, or something."

"You carried on? Sounds risky. You could lose your job. Get in trouble."

He twists towards me on the bench. "Essie, if we can make clean energy for free… think about it. For free." His eyes are fierce, boring into me. "It would change the world as we know it. Famine, pollution, climate change… all gone.

116

Almost overnight. That's what they're throwing away. Without asking. On behalf of us all."

No wonder he's in such a state. "So, the plan is…?"

"Take the file to your people. Find someone who knows how to do this and produce it."

"Why do you need us?" A panic lights inside me. My hands clench, sweaty in my lap. How can I tell him *Change Here* has splintered? "You can do it yourself, can't you?"

He picks at the peeling paint of the bench. "It can't be me. I can't risk it, not yet. It's my job. And my life. Once the tech's out there, Langford can't stop it. Whatever he's planning, he'll be out of the equation. Then I can come out in the open and help with the testing."

"I don't know anyone who could do that."

"Your gang leader must. Just say you'll try. Please, Essie. This could be the end of us if you don't."

At first I imagine he means me and him, but he means everyone, I'm sure. What am I supposed to do? The state Gabe's in...

"I'll try." There's a lump in my throat. I need Maya. She's due back from Edinburgh tomorrow. Lawrence has agreed to start his training for the new job next week so she's coming back without him. Her text was jubilant, and a bit of my heart withered away when I read it.

"Thanks, Essie. I owe you everything. We all do." He stands. For a moment, it seems like he wants to say something else, but then he just gives a tight smile. Before I can mutter goodbye, he moves past me and slopes off down the path.

***

It's still early morning, but Brian's office is hotter than the kitchen at midday. Stuffed to the brim with receipts he never finds time to organise, the tiny room smells of warm paper. Brian himself is outside, taking a delivery of beer and quibbling over the invoice. I have a few more minutes to research Jack's boss.

The picture on Brian's screen is of two men in white tie

dress, one broad with a mound of hair swept back and slick, the other with a hook nose and wire glasses. Their mouths are wide in hilarity, champagne flutes in hand. Two nameless young women accompany them like bookends, their ball gowns dripping with privilege.

It's part of a double-page spread in a magazine I've never heard of—Our Life and Times, July 2005 edition. The caption reads: *'Close friends young entrepreneur Alex Langford and heir to global energy empire Oliver Foster-Pugh celebrate their graduation from Oxford University, both with First Class degrees. Well done, boys!'*

My mouth pulls into a sneer at the sycophancy.

There's a clang outside as the delivery driver starts to unload the barrels of beer. My heart spasms with guilt. It's a crap thing to do, using Brian's old computer to search this stuff. It's too risky to use my own laptop. The prototype lies at the bottom of the bag I always carry, inside the lining that I ripped months ago. I try to stop myself grabbing for it more than a hundred times a day.

With jittery fingers, I start a new search: *Oliver Foster-Pugh Alex Langford.*

Another picture, this one in the Worcestershire Echo, 25th April 2035. *Home Secretary Oliver Foster-Pugh attends a launch event at local green tech champions ConservUnity in Worcester.* It sparks a memory of a news report months ago. Foster-Pugh: the same hooked nose, different wire glasses.

These guys are lifelong friends.

Heir to global energy empire.

What kind of energy? Probably not the clean kind. Is that the reason Langford shut down Jack's research? His friendship with Foster-Pugh? Is he trying to help his friend stay rich?

Voices rumble in the bar. Sounds like Brian's supervising the delivery driver as he brings in the barrels. I close the browser, switch off the base unit, and spring out of Brian's chair.

The morning's shift is hot and draining. When I get outside for the walk home, it's barely any better. The river aroma floating up Bank Lane is heavy with mud, and I try not to think of Andy as I scurry past.

Though River Street is busy with shoppers, they drift like dandelion seeds in the treacly air. There's only me in a hurry, it seems, until I glance around.

He's wearing shades and, even in this heat, a suit jacket. And there's the familiar prickle on my arms. This guy is following me. And it's not Toby. Nausea twists my guts as I snap my head forward again and push on. At the bottom of Potter Road, I peek back. He's gone.

Or maybe he was never there.

You're losing it, Ess.

Then I see my front door kicked in. A whimper escapes me. Electric shocks fire along my limbs.

The flat is completely trashed. All the cupboards and drawers are empty, the contents scattered across the room. My sketches are torn into dozens of pieces. Some of the fragments are piled in the ashtray and burnt, others defaced with charcoal scribbles.

Gouged into the table top: *BITCH*

The knife that carved it is implanted in the table like an exclamation mark. My legs give up and I fold onto the floor for several minutes, staring at the word, the knife, breathing in gasps.

Oh, God. Toby again?

But apart from destroying the drawings, this is a little polite for him, isn't it?

I shamble back into the lounge and sit on the floor, clutching the outline of the prototype through the fabric of my bag.

Was it Toby? Or somebody else?

"Wait. Back up a bit." Gabe sits opposite Maya and me at one of the Braai's corner tables. "They have the technology to provide free energy *and* reverse the damage we've already done. And they won't make it?" He slaps the table with his good hand and swears, too loudly, drawing a stern look from Brian at the kitchen door. "Profits always first. Before the planet. Before our survival. They think they can do what the hell they like." He peers at his table-slapping palm, a frown creasing the top of his nose. "Let's face it, they're right."

Maya tucks her chin down and stares at me through her eyelashes. Classic *I told you so* Maya. She didn't want to meet with Gabe, but I spent days harassing her, then said I would do it alone. That scared her into coming along. She was right about the venue, though. What was I thinking? I suppose I wanted somewhere visible, in case Gabe lost it, but this is too public.

He's so volatile these days. And paranoid. Believes one of us is planning to turn him in. He's got Hallie walking on eggshells. I made Maya swear not to mention Jack's name, though she's still suspicious of him. Stopped her from calling Lawrence, too. He's training in Edinburgh. I'm one push away from her giving up on me. And Brian. I didn't dare tell him Gabe was coming, but now he knows something's going on.

"I told you, we have a plan," I whisper. "To stop them. We just need your help."

"Do you know anyone who can help us build it?" asks Maya.

Gabe barks out a laugh, making the couple on the next table glance our way. "For Christ's sake." He presses a shaky fist against his forehead. "There's maybe twelve people in the world who could do this stuff."

"Do you know any of them?" As I speak, Maya's eyes weigh on me.

He glances around and swears again, thankfully under his breath this time. We wait for him to continue as he fixes his gaze on the table top. He's rolling a paper napkin between his twitchy, intense fingers, then starts to tear it up.

Maya huffs. "Lawrence said that—"

"Lawrence will believe anything you tell him if you use big words." Gabe drops the fragments of napkin and sneers.

Maya's hands clench together. She looks like she wants to slap him. "He thinks you're his best friend."

Gabe shrugs. "I have no friends left."

"Oh, come on," I say. "It's not like that."

"Doesn't matter." He flops back in his chair. "I'm done, anyway."

"But you were all *'we're going to bring them down'* not so long ago." Maya spreads her palms, her jaw jutting forward. "What happened?"

Gabe holds up his arm, still encased in a support bandage, all straps and black Velcro.

"I never thought you'd give up that easily," says Maya. Is she trying to goad him into helping us?

"Yeah well, you weren't in that cell for four days, were you?" The lurking ghost in his eyes peeks out at us, making me turn away.

This is hopeless. With a hand on Maya's arm, I try to say *'leave it alone'* using my eyes. I think she gets it, because she leans back, a mirror of Gabe.

"And anyway, Maya," he says. "I'd be more likely to take that crap from someone who isn't buggering off to *Scotland.*"

"Okay," I say, hands up. "No stress. It's fine. J…" God, I nearly blurted out Jack's name. "My CU contact will just have to find someone else to build this thing. I'll message him." I pull out my phone.

"Wait. It's ConservUnity? You never mentioned CU before." Gabe's jaw is rigid as iron, and his eyes snap to mine. Then he closes them and huffs so deeply his chest seems to cave in. "Hang on." When he opens his eyes again, their ghost is hidden, but its aura still lurks in his pale irises. "I know exactly what to do about this."

"What?" Maya's voice is tight.

The old sparkle of optimism flashes in his eyes. But then

he whispers, "We're going to blow up the company. Blow it sky high. Let's see them try to screw us to the wall then."

Maya gasps as I put my hand to my forehead and close my eyes.

"Come on," I say. "That's not right. I didn't mean that."

"We have to stop them. Show them they can't get away with it."

It takes a minute to arrange this straight in my head. The Braai is packed out with lunchtime customers now, and there must have been a power cut, because the generators are on. I've been so wrapped up in our crisis I haven't noticed. Gabe is busy shredding his napkin again, making a pile of twisted paper on the table.

I put my hand on his to still it. "We will show them, Gabe. But not like that. We'll find someone to help us."

But Gabe's shaking his head. "Who? Technically, it's stolen property. We'd be in jail before the end of the day, with more broken limbs. No, we need to hit them where it hurts. Disable them."

"That's mental." Maya's eyes bear down on him. "Where does that leave us?"

"We'd still have the prototype." He nods at me. "And your CU mate."

"Who would be in jail," I say. "Or dead. These are powerful, dangerous people. We have to get out ahead of them. The only way is to find someone to make the prototype. Then they can't prove it's their property anymore."

Gaze fixed on me, Gabe takes a long inhale, releasing it through his nose. "Okay, fair point. Maybe I do know someone who could help."

While Gabe stirs his coffee, which must be cold by now, Maya and I side-eye each other.

"Who?" asks Maya.

"I have one condition, then you find out who." He pauses, looks at each of us. "One more gig."

I throw my head back, look at the ceiling.

Maya's eyes don't leave Gabe's face. "I thought you said —"

"Not ConservUnity. Something else."

"No more," says Maya, and it's more of a plea than anything.

"That's my condition," he says. "One more, no questions, no strings. And you're to tell no one. I'm serious. Not even Lawrence. Especially not Lawrence. Then I'll talk to my friend about your prototype."

I bite the inside of my cheek, searching for clues in his face. "How do we know you're telling the truth?"

"Don't think you have any choice. I mean, what if they find out you have the prototype some other way?"

I stare at him, not sure what he means.

"Stealing intellectual property, Essie. Industrial espionage." He picks up his damn spoon again, twirls it in his fingers. "Not certain what the punishment would be for that, but ConservUnity and their buddies have a lot at stake. They're bound to push for maximum jail time."

My cheeks flare with heat, and my chest tightens. Maya tenses beside me as the bustle of the Braai grows distant and echoes in my ears.

"Are you threatening me, Gabe?" I say. "Because if you are, you should know that goes both ways. I've got plenty on you, too. This whole *thing* was your idea. The banners... the rally. You led us here. No... worse. You let us lead *you*. Always a safe distance from the action in case anything kicked off."

He ducks his head low, eyes almost burning into me. "It wasn't very safe in that cell, Essie."

I scoff. "A broken arm. Is that all it took to break you? Some revolutionary. I should turn you in for cowardice."

As he glares at me, his twitchiness settles and he becomes eerily still. "Go down that road. I want you to."

My cheeks are hot. "You're a b—"

"Whoa... everybody relax," says Maya. "And keep your voices down or nobody's gonna *need* turning in. There's no reason for anyone to go down any road. We're on the same side, remember? Everybody's taking risks."

Gabe and I stare at each other for a while longer, neither

123

wanting to back down. It's not until Trudy, one of the other waitresses, comes to see if we want another coffee that the impasse ends.

Gabe's shoulders lower, and he tips his head to one side. "Come on, Ess. Let's help each other, yeah? You want to get that tech out there, don't you?"

It's not that I don't have reservations: There's no way to be certain Gabe's friend will help us, and I've no idea of his plan. It could be worth the risk: one last gig, tell no-one, and we get this thing made. But what does he want? Pictures flash through my mind of my trashed flat; Jack's face as he gave me the envelope.

I'll have to persuade Maya not to call Lawrence all over again. He'd only mouth off at Gabe, and we don't need a boy-fight on our hands. My gaze moves to the table, then back up. Gabe's face splits into a grin, so I guess he's received my concession.

"Two questions." I count them off on my thumb and forefinger. "What gig? And who's your friend?"

He taps the teaspoon against his cold cup. "All in good time."

Chapter Twelve

We left Balmford an hour ago, with its Halloween pumpkin bunting draped between the lampposts and inhabitants scurrying home in the deluge. The wind drives rain into our eyes and seems to change direction with us as we follow the bends in the lane, blurring my vision. We trek along the Worcester Road—Maya, Gabe and me. Three miles on, it wanes to a single track.

Beside me, Maya's breathing is strained. She sniffs and wipes her nose on the sleeve of her waterproof poncho. None of us have spoken since we passed the train station, which must have been half an hour ago. Before my legs went numb.

I have only the vaguest outline of Gabe's plan, which terrifies me. There's a place out here somewhere. He won't tell us anything else, least of all what's in his bag.

For now, Gabe doesn't know where I've stashed the prototype, but there aren't too many options to explore. You'd only need to watch me for a day, and the safe at Seth's vicarage is the first place you'd check.

I glare at Gabe's back, just visible on the muddy lane, and wish him to succumb to a pothole. Or fall down the ditch. I picture a truck slamming into him, his brains splashing into the puddles that line the road. But as much as I hate it, we need him now. If he knows someone who can make the prototype...

The road rises steeply and we trudge on, soaked through despite our plastic ponchos. Gabe's rucksack sheds rivers of water behind him. We must look like refugees.

A bank of clouds hangs low in the sky and gives only fleeting peeks at the moon. There are no streetlights here, so we switch on our flashlights. Tracks of sweat trickle down my face and spine and mingle with the rain as we plough on through the heat to who-knows-where. I glance up at the sky but there's no sign of drones. For now.

Gabe slows his pace, looking to the left. There's a ten-foot hedge along the track, and he peers through the gaps in the brambles.

"Yeah," he mutters to himself, then to us, "Switch off your torches."

Had there been any stars, we would have been afforded a spectacular view of them. Without the torch beams, it's dark and disorienting in the lane.

"Stay here." Gabe marches on.

Several paces ahead of us, he crouches low. My eyes adjust to the gloom and I watch him unshoulder the rucksack. He pulls out hedge shears, wiggles on a pair of gardening gloves and thrusts the blades into the hedgerow. There's a snipping sound and his head disappears into the hedge, then he peeps back out and gestures for us to join him.

Maya and I hesitate, neither keen to step up. Even in the dark, Gabe's eyes burn into mine, resonant with threat. It's a sharp push through the soaking hedge, and I have to wriggle to free myself from the more voracious thorns. I scramble to my feet on the other side and Maya follows.

Beyond the hedge, a ruthlessly trimmed lawn leads down to a curved drive. Apple trees line the way, lit up with yellow-white fairy lights.

"What is this place?" Maya swipes bits of foliage out of her hair.

Without an answer, Gabe leads us around the perimeter of the lawn, close to the hedge. As we near the driveway, the hulk of a square structure resolves out of the darkness. It could be a hotel. One of those exclusive ones that charges the price of a week's holiday for a night and has a famous chef. But I didn't think there was a hotel out here.

As we slink towards the edifice, Gabe keeps behind the screen of trees. Detail of the building emerges. Solid and angular in red brick, with stone columns. Neat rows of windows are all dark except two on the ground floor. My brain spits out the word Georgian and that seems to fit this place.

Gabe halts us about fifty yards from the house and turns. "Okay. You're doing this." He glances between us.

The back of my neck prickles. "What, exactly, are we doing Gabe?"

He reaches into his rucksack and pulls out two cans, handing us one each. From the chill and rattle I can tell it's spray paint before I see the label. It's red.

"Essie, you paint on the left of the porch: '*Murderers will*'. Maya, on the right, put '*face Judgement*'. Capital J. Big as you can manage, and high as you can."

In the glow from the fairy lights, Maya's eyes narrow. I feel mine do the same. This isn't a protest. It's a threat. Against someone we don't even know.

"Gabe," I say. "Where are we?"

"Deal was no questions, no strings. Remember?"

"Yeah, but you didn't say anything about..." I can't think of an appropriate word.

Gabe pulls his phone out of the bag. "I can call the police now, if you like, Essie. Reckon you can run fast enough to get to the vicarage before them?"

Before I realise what I'm doing, I've slapped Gabe hard in the face. He grabs my wrists and squeezes them, shoving me back into one of the apple trees. A low fairy light catches in my soaked hair. We glare at each other. Silence except for the rattle of rain on leaves.

I jerk my hands, but he grips tighter, burning my skin, and draws a yelp from me.

Maya thumps him on the back, spraying raindrops into her eyes. "Let her go, you arsehole," she hisses. "Now."

Gabe releases me with a pull and another shove. I look from Maya's tense face to Gabe's sneering one and rub my wrists. How did we get here?

Through gritted teeth, I say, "I came to you for help, you bastard."

Gabe's mouth twitches as he rubs his flaring cheek.

Maya looks at me. "You can smack him around all you

want when it's done." Turning to Gabe, her gaze grows stony. "Let's get on with it."

Maya's right—there's no choice now. He'll turn us in if we don't do this. We're trapped. So we creep towards the house along the treeline. Gabe lets us lead this time. Hanging back to watch us for signs of mutiny, I imagine. He hisses instructions to us to keep us on the right path. At any moment, I expect the glare of a security light, the blare of an alarm. If they exist, Gabe seems to know how to avoid their range because we remain concealed by night and silence. When we could reach out and touch the brick of the house, Gabe halts us.

Up close, it's clear this is a private residence. No curtains shield the ground-floor windows, and I am close enough to see into two of them. Both rooms are in darkness. I can make out a cosy space I imagine they call a snug, and a dining room with a slab of a table. The driveway sweeps around to the left to a parking area at the side of the building. It's occupied by a single, expensive-looking car.

"Who lives here, Gabe?" I could offer a speculation. Peering at the blank sky, I wonder if whoever it is can afford a fleet of their own drones.

"Okay," he says, ignoring my question. "Get it done."

He backs away to the screen of trees where he bends down to open his rucksack again.

Maya shifts her eyes: a glare at Gabe, a worried frown at me. "Come on." She pushes me towards the left of the door as she ducks to the right.

The two lit windows illuminate her tense face. She crawls underneath their glare and takes her position on the right. We gape at each other across the rain-sodden chasm, and she nods in the light from the windows. There's a raised platform abutting the foot of the wall a few feet away from me, which turns out to be a hatch, like a coal chute. I point down to it, and Maya looks for something similar on her side. She finds nothing, shrugs, takes out her spray can and stretches up on tiptoe. The platform gives a dull *thunk* and moves a little as I step onto it, holding up my can.

The spray makes a dangerously loud noise to my ears as I form the letter M. Surely someone in the house will hear it. Rain catches hold of the paint so the lettering is awkward and drips at the bottom, making it look like blood. Gabe will love that effect. I glance back in time to see him holding something bulky up to his face. A camera, a long-range lens. That double-crossing... he's taking pictures of us. I should have taken his head off with that slap. When this is over, I will.

I look to see if Maya's clocked him, but she's engrossed in her work. From the extent of her stretching, my guess is she's trying to form the capital J. I don't know what else to do, so I turn back to my '*Murderers*'.

The loud bark of a dog sounds from inside the house on my left. I start and drop the can on the coal chute cover with a clunk which sets off another bark volley from a window the other side of me. I spin and turn over on my ankle, slamming into the wooden hatch.

"Essie," Maya hisses in the distance.

I open my mouth to reply I'm okay, but the screech of an alarm drowns out my voice. My whole body jerks in panic. Maya screams my name.

We run. Gabe bolts up the driveway. I follow him, wincing at the pain in my ankle. Instinct makes me veer away to the right. Maybe it's a desire to get away from him as well as the house. I head across another expanse of lawn, towards a dark wooded area beyond. The barking is outside. I turn to check on Maya. A whimper escapes me: she's too far behind. The dogs are gaining ground, slobber flying from their snarling mouths.

A silhouetted male figure appears at the porch, followed by another. The second man steps in front of the first and hunches his shoulders. He's holding something up to his face with both hands. Aiming a rifle at Maya.

"Maya, run!" I yell, but I don't know if she hears me and she's running, anyway.

There's a flash from the gun. A shot echoes out across the darkness.

Maya hits the ground.

We both scream and I dart back towards her. There's another shot. A bullet thumps into the grass at my feet. Another scream bursts from me as a third shot fires.

I freeze.

The dogs catch up to Maya. They snap at her as she tries to get up, and she collapses again. Did the first shot hit her, or did she go down for cover? Either way, they have her now. I sob, call her name again, turning in a horrible circle of indecision. Do I run? Can I help her?

The man with the gun runs to check Maya. The dogs retreat to a guard position, growling. He jabs her with a foot. A gurgling cry escapes her and I utter my own. My head whips around. There's no sign of Gabe, or any other possibility of help. It's just us.

He looks up at me. We freeze like that for a moment while the second man approaches Maya and drags her backwards towards the house. She's unconscious, or playing it.

Or dead.

"No," I moan. The gunman races at me, rifle in hand. I dive into the trees.

The only thing I know is the need to run. It's so dark in the woods I can barely make out the trunks. I stumble over fallen branches and undergrowth, trying to find a path. He does the same behind me. There's no shooting, so he probably doesn't want to risk his head being ripped off by a ricochet. He whistles for the dogs, so I push myself to sprint faster, though my lungs burn. I sob, then inhale the rain that scatters from the branches, and cough. It's a waste of precious energy to cry, but I can't stop it.

My foot hits a tree root, tipping me headfirst down an incline. The ground disappears and I fall, landing hard in a pile of leaves. I lie in the mud, unable to move or breathe.

As my mind and vision clear, I squint into the darkness.

I'm on a narrow rock-littered path, facing the ridge I fell down. The gunman appears uphill between the trees as I scramble to my feet. When I try to run, my knee buckles and

I'm down again. He starts towards me, but must realise it's too steep and slick with mud.

There's nothing but another rocky precipice behind, a steeper fall than the first. I try to crawl away from him down the muddy track. He calls the dogs, but they don't fancy coming down either.

He lifts his rifle and aims at me. "Don't move!"

"Wait. Please." I hold my hands up, and force myself to stand again, as if that will make me safer.

The rifle clicks. Nothing happens.

He swears. Begging is beyond me now, and there's no way I can run with this knee. He aims again, and pulls the trigger. Tears squeeze out of my eyes as I shut them tight and turn my face away, my breath trapped in my throat.

Another click. He picks his way towards the escarpment above me as though reconsidering a descent. When one of the dogs comes in range, he grabs it by the collar and tries to force it down to get me. It snaps at him, and he utters another curse as he snatches his hand away.

While he snarls at the dogs, I stumble further left along the footpath, curving behind a clump of holly trees that would cover me.

"I said don't move!"

A shot cleaves the air. I scream and jerk backwards. My foot slips. The ground gives way and I'm falling again, this time with a landslide. Rocks thump into me, stinging.

The gunman and dogs have gone and there's only a tumult of leaves and rubble. It's no more than ten feet down, but it feels like I'm falling forever, over, around, down…

I land full-force and face-down onto tarmac. A blade of pain shoots the length of my spine. What seem like boulders pelt my back, my head. My leg twists and jams underneath me. What little I can see pulses and shifts as though my brain is being pried out of my skull.

When my senses clear, the rain has slowed to a drizzle. I turn over to let it fall on my face, trying to revive myself. There's no sound except the gentle patter of water on the leaves I'm lying on.

My pursuer might break out onto the road anytime, but I can't make my limbs do anything. Every time I try, pain paralyses me.

A splash of headlights bounces off the slick road. The word *cops* rings in my brain. Moaning at the bolts of pain in my head and leg, I roll over into the gully until the car passes. I feel like roadkill as the beams sweep over me indifferently and move on down the track.

I can't stay here any longer. With more strength than I thought possible, I force my limbs to support me. This must be Worcester Road, so I struggle to my feet and limp away, hopefully towards town. There's a warm tickle on my temple, and I swipe at it with the sleeve of my poncho. Blood mingles with the mud and raindrops that still cling there. Everything slips sideways and I stagger, a rough-barked tree the only thing that prevents another fall.

The shock is subsiding, lucid thought coming back.

Maya. Oh, God, what have they done to Maya?

They shot her. They took her. I don't even know who they are, what they'll do.

There's no sign of Gabe on the road, nobody to help. I can't call the police.

Seth.

But when I pull my phone from my pocket, it's cracked, the screen blank. I'm on my own. I stagger in the direction that might be home.

What have I done? How could I be so stupid? They'll kill Maya. I've killed her.

I wish I'd let them take me. Then this would all be over.

***

When I get to the vicarage, filthy, bleeding and babbling Maya's name, Seth comes out to help me up the steps. It's

132

after midnight.

He brings me tea with painkillers, a bowl of warm water, cotton wool and a mirror and watches me clean up. My hand shakes as I wipe my swollen face. Sitting at the kitchen table, he waits for me to tell him about it. Which I do. Everything. Including what he's been hiding in his safe for me.

"Jesus," is all he says after I'm done. He springs up from his chair, grabs his phone.

"What are you doing?" My voice has a sharp edge of panic.

"I'm calling the police. This has gone far enough."

"No!" I grab for the phone, but he jerks it away and holds me back with his other hand. It doesn't take much, I'm as weak as a newborn.

"You can't. Please Seth, you can't." The hoarse plea in my words makes me feel more desperate than ever.

He shoots me a tight-jawed look which could be anger. Or disgust. "Do you have any idea how serious this is?"

"Yes." I glare at him. How dare he? "Yes, I do. Seth, everything you're thinking now I've already thought. A million times on the way home."

He gapes at me, phone in hand, finger poised over the call button.

"It's my fault. Whatever has happened to Maya is my fault." My voice cracks. I clear my throat, angry at myself. What good is this anguish now? "I went along with Gabe's plan. I made her do it. She wanted to tell Lawrence, call the police. But I wouldn't let her."

"You—"

"I'm a stupid, reckless, arrogant..." I rest my hand on my head, behind my bleeding temple. "I'm going to turn myself in. But not yet."

Seth has put down his phone now, and that's good. His eyes are wide and glassy with horror. "Okay let's think about this," he says slowly. "There'll be a way to do this. We need to work out a story. How can we get them to find Maya without giving away...?"

"No more lies. I want Gabe to face this with me. He

133

started it all."

"But giving them the whole story? That's not just Gabe. It's you and the others. Brian. Me. Your CU mate."

It's the sum of consequences of what I've done. All of them flash through my head now, making my stomach rile. They don't shine as brightly as Maya's face, though. On the lawn of that house, screaming.

"It has to stop." My voice is quiet but firm. "But there are a couple of things I have to sort out first."

"That file in my safe?"

"That's one of them."

Seth squeezes my shoulder. "Essie. I want to help. Tell me how I can help you."

***

There's been little sleep overnight for either of us. I must have dozed off on the sofa though, because the gentle scrapes of Seth making toast in the kitchen awaken me.

"You need to let your ConservUnity mate know what's happened." Seth puts a mug of tea on the coffee table in front of me. We don't say 'good morning'.

"He won't answer my messages." I borrowed Seth's phone and tried again and again last night before I finally fell into a doze. I rang Maya's phone too. Over and over. But all I got was a whiny out-of-service tone.

"What about Lawrence?"

"No answer. He's training in Edinburgh this week."

God, the thought of telling him what happened to Maya. Her parents... A black spiral of despair threatens to overwhelm me. My vision shuts down and I expel a sob. Seth puts a hand on my arm, and the darkness lifts a little.

There's only one other person who can help. I grab Seth's phone from the table, drag the number from the back of my brain.

"Hello?" She sounds as rough as me, and her breathing is agitated.

"Hallie."

134

"Essie."

"Have you seen Gabe?" I can't keep the dread out of my voice.

"Yeah. Well... no. I had a call from him around midnight. What happened last night?"

"Where is he?" I clutch the phone so hard my earlobe is numb.

"He's gone."

Is that good or bad news for us? "Where?"

"I don't know. He sounded like he was on a night bus or something, but he wouldn't tell me where to. He just said he was getting out, goodbye, and cut me off." She sniffs. "Now he won't answer my calls. Ess, what the hell's going on?"

"I can't talk on the phone. I'll meet you at the river bridge. About an hour?"

Hallie gives a shaky sigh. "Okay," she says, and hangs up.

Chapter Thirteen

Yesterday's storm has left the river path mired in mud and fallen leaves. The air is tranquil and dry, peppered with the scent of damp moss baked by the sun. I pull in a steadying breath as I limp down Bank Lane, trying not to think of Maya, alone, frightened, in pain…

Dead?

Hallie's already there, pacing under the sandstone arch of the bridge. Her hands are in her pockets, but through the fabric it's clear they're clenched into fists. She freezes, watching me approach as if I'm a wounded animal. We exchange a short, shaky hug. I check up and down the river. It doesn't appear we're being watched, and the last drone swept overhead just before I mounted the path. We should be safe for a while.

"Christ, Ess. You look like you've been ten rounds with Teddy Franks."

She's not wrong. Besides the limp, my forehead is bruised and swollen, raw from the fall. There's a gash on my forearm I don't even remember getting.

"Did Gabe do that?" Her mouth clamps shut, and she plays her teeth against the silver stud in her lip.

"Not exactly."

"What's this about? What happened?" Her face, normally dark like her eyes, is pale and taut.

As we squelch along the river away from Balmford, the story bleeds out of me. Skirting Jack's identity and the CU conspiracy, I tell her how I confided in Gabe, his blackmailing us; the disastrous attack on the house.

Hallie stops, puts her cold hands on my shoulders, and turns me. "Big old Georgian pile on the Worcester Road?"

"Yeah." I squint at watery, frightened eyes below her furrowed brows. "You know it?"

"Oh, yeah. I know it."

"Who lives in that house, Hal? What did Gabe mean, '*Murderers will face Judgment*'?"

She looks down.

"Hallie…?"

"His name's Alex Langford."

Oh, shit.

Though, I expected something like that, didn't I?

"He's the Chief Exec of ConservUnity."

"I know who he is."

"The tech you stole and the house share the same owner. And he's going to be really, really pissed off." She paces ahead, then back to me, her hands twisting her t-shirt, making little stretched lumps in it. "Essie, that guy is bad news. He's meant to be this respectable entrepreneur, but I've heard things. He—"

My heart folds itself into a painful cramp. "He took Maya. I think they shot her." My voice cracks. "I don't even know if she's still alive."

Hallie bends double, as if she's about to throw up in the river. A couple of wheezing retches burst out of her. Her bloodshot eyes emerge from under her hair. "You can't go to the police."

"I know. I thought about it all night. They'll take Langford's side—"

"It'll finish Gabe."

What the hell?

"You don't know the half of what they did to him in that cell, Ess." She stares out across the water. "They didn't just refuse to treat his arm, they broke it again. And again. They

137

tortured him." A shaky hand rakes through her fringe. "He said in the end, they weren't even asking questions. Just trying to get in his head. When he came out, he thought everyone was going to turn on him. Took me days to convince him it was all lies."

I think of his eyes, burning into me in that sodden lane. "You didn't. Convince him."

"Essie, I know he's done some awful stuff—"

"You think?"

"But he's still Gabe." She covers her mouth with the back of her hand. "You don't know him like I do. He's amazing. He sees connections in things no one's ever thought of. He could do this, Ess. Beat them. Everything he talked about, he can do it. I need him back. We all do."

You'd better hope you see him first, then. Because if I get the chance…

I close my pulsing eyes, trying to clear my mind of Gabe's face.

"So, have you still got this thing, then?" Hallie's voice is casual, but there's a gnawing feeling in my brain.

"It's safe." My fingers close around the envelope in my pocket.

"I'd be tempted to throw it in there." She nods at the river. Does she know I've got it with me?

"I am tempted. But I can't. My friend put a lot of faith in me." All the same, my eyes find the water. "And what if it *is* the answer? If this thing can turn it all around..." I wave at the scorching sun.

Hallie frowns. We keep walking. I'm not eager to go home, and neither is she, it seems.

Far off to the north, there's a faint sound of sirens. We approach the old boat club on the far side of the river. Two teenage boys lounge on its concrete steps in the momentary glare of the sun. Their cigarette smoke drifts across the water, mingling with the autumnal scent of bonfires, making me crave nicotine. Those lads don't appear to have any cares at all.

I sigh. "What are you going to do about Gabe?"

"I don't know." She stops, brown eyes pleading. "He wouldn't sell you out, Essie. I know you think he's gone crazy, but he wouldn't do that."

No words come. I can only suck in a breath, shake my head.

"I'm just so sick of losing people." She sobs, then flashes her eyes at me. "Sorry, wrong audience. It's just…"

"Not fair," I finish for her. She clutches my arm. I clutch hers back. "Not even close to fair."

***

I force the lump of nausea down, squash my terror for Maya. I'm not up to this, but there's no choice. It's been almost twenty-four hours. Soon enough, Maya's absence will be noticed, and the circus will begin. I limp out of town, retracing our route. My fingers brush the handle of the carving knife in my pocket.

It's surprisingly easy to find Gabe's breach in the hedgerow. I switch off my torch and push through the brambles, ignoring the scratches they lay on my face. Flat against the hedge on the other side, I gain my bearings. There's a bitter smell in the air, like someone nearby has hosted an early bonfire party. I retrace our steps from last night, staying behind the treeline, now unlit by fairy lights. The place where Maya fell is burned into my mind, and I can't avoid looking at the spot. There's no sign she was even there. Tears threaten, but I blink them away and push on.

The expensive car is gone from the car park. Our spray paint is visible as I approach the building. Even in this darkness, it's clear I was right: Gabe would love the dripping blood effect on my letter *M*. My mouth twitches into an acidic sneer as I move towards the porch.

All the windows are dark this evening, but I duck underneath them all the same. I freeze for a moment, breath caught, remembering the dogs. Though I strain my ears, there's no scampering or growling. Maybe they're gone.

There was no time to come up with a proper plan to get in, so I just pray for inspiration. As I move to the front door, luck delivers, and I discover the source of the bonfire stink at the same time. One of the windows is smashed, the wooden sash scorched. I crouch low to the ground, then peer inside. It's the dining room, but not how I remember it from last night. Burnt out, the walls blackened, static drips of ceiling plaster hanging. The dark wood dining table is reduced to two remaining legs that stand crooked and defiant in the middle of a pile of ashes.

I steady myself against the ruined wall. What happened here after I escaped? Did Gabe come back and firebomb the place? Or maybe, an aching, hopeful voice in my head suggests, Maya set the fire and escaped through the window.

One more glance destroys that hope, though. The glass shards lie on the deep-pile carpet inside the dining room. It was broken from the outside. Why has the owner left it smashed in like this?

I work up the courage to stand, wrap my hand in my coat sleeve and push at the spikes of glass that cling to the lower frame. One of them falls inwards, landing with a clatter on top of its sisters on the floor. I hold my breath, but no one comes. Why are there no police?

After knocking a few more shards out, I squeeze though the gap into the dining room. The smell of burnt wood is overwhelming, and I cough silently into my hand. If I don't get out of this room, I'm going to pass out. I dart towards the door and open it a tiny bit. It leads into a dark, empty hallway. The smell is less powerful now but still hits the back of my throat. The flames seem to have halted in the dining room—there's no fire damage out here. Tiny fragments of glass have caught in the tread of my boots and they grate on the hardwood floor as I move.

The breath jams in my chest and I halt, reaching for the knife in my pocket. I can't hear anything at all; the house seems to be empty. And yet, it's a fight to make my feet move again down the dark wooden hall.

Heart hammering, knife in sweaty hand, I slink deeper into the house. An opulent, red-carpeted staircase looms out of the dark, marking the point of no return. If anyone is inside, I'm easy prey now, so far away from an exit. At the first door, I press my ear to the timber, so close I can smell the varnish.

Nothing but the thump of my own blood. Screwing my face up as tight as my aching throat, I reach out a shaky hand and open the door.

A dim light's on inside. I think I'm going to vomit. An icy electric shock bolts down all four limbs as I step inside.

Someone's there.

A wingback leather armchair faces away from me towards the carved marble fireplace, a pair of slippers visible underneath. He's in that chair, waiting for me to blunder into him. I can hear his breath. And here I am, like a parlour maid at the door.

I raise the blade and move deeper inside, circling the back of the chair silently. He'll see me soon and spring. I squeeze the knife…

The chair is empty.

No legs or feet protrude to meet the slippers. My breath whoops out of me, my legs weak from cold terror. I stumble further into the room.

A picture dominates the wall above the fireplace. A rich, minutely crafted oil painting of a striking couple standing behind a boy of about twelve. The boy has on a scholar's cap and gown, and his father's superior smirk. Looming behind them all, the sharp, down-turned face of an elderly man with that same, mean mouth. Maybe a grandfather.

With far less hair than in the magazine photo I found, Alex Langford might still be handsome if it wasn't for the glare in his blue eyes, the austere upward tilt of his chin. It's a while before I'm able to turn my back on that painting.

I sneak around the vast space, peering around corners and behind furniture.

Nothing.

I search the ground floor, growing less stealthy with each empty room.

No Langford, no dogs, no rifleman.

No Maya.

Back in the hallway, there's a door I didn't spot before, huddled in a dark wall under the staircase. The sort you might hide yourself, or someone else, behind.

I expect it to be locked, but it opens freely over a set of stone steps that descend into darkness.

A cellar.

A tomb.

Torch on, I step inside. If anyone's in the cellar, they already know I'm here, so there's no reason to hide. I descend the stairs on numb legs, whipping my torch around from left to right, down, then up. It's gritty underfoot, and the scrape of my boots echoes in the dank, mouldy air.

"Maya?"

Again, nothing.

This might be a trap. Someone could be on their way with a key to lock me down here, or worse.

I spin round, caught again in a horrible dilemma between saving Maya and saving myself. But the seconds stretch on and no one comes, so I choose Maya.

Deeper into the cellar, it smells of old coal and damp. My grinding footsteps are the only sound. On the far wall, my torchlight bounces off what looks like the inside of the coal hatch I fell on last night. A bulky chain entwines the handle of its doors. Below the hatch is a huge trough, built of brick about five-foot high. Presumably, it was used to store the coal in the days when that all seemed like a good idea. You could fit a couple of people in there. A hard nausea forms in the pit of my stomach as I force my legs towards it.

"Maya." I lean up and peep over the side, torchlight flaring.

It's empty. Only coal-grimed brick in there.

I collapse against the wall, gasping with relief and heartbreak all at once. Whether she's dead or alive, they've taken her somewhere. My face in my hands, I sob out loud, and all thoughts of safety evaporate from my exhausted mind. There's nothing to feel but the loss of Maya. I huddle on the floor, weeping, desperate, with no idea what to do next.

To stand and leave feels like giving up on her, but there's no sense in staying here to get caught. I've been tense on this cold, hard floor for so long my legs have seized up, and I scramble to a crouch. As my hand shoots out for balance, I touch something soft and pull it towards me. In the torchlight, I know it immediately. Maya's scarf. The green chiffon one she wore last night.

There's dry blood on it.

Breath caught in my throat, I lean over the lip of the trough. Maybe I missed her somehow. Eyes wide and searching, I sweep the torch around the concrete floor, along the walls.

Something catches my eye on the wall inside. Shapes in the coal dust clinging there.

E...S?

Traced by a finger?

Essie?

Wheels crunch on the driveway and headlights sweep over the wooden hatch, probe through the cracks and slide off to the right. The engine dies and a car door opens.

Thrusting Maya's scarf into my pocket, sure it's already too late, I bolt for the exit.

I'm halfway to the foot of the steps when footsteps rattle at the front door. There's no time to get out of the house before the driver comes in. I mount the cellar stairs two at a time, desperate to remember if I've left anything out of place up there. At the top, I pull the door closed, shutting myself in, then bolt back down and across the cellar, snapping the torch off. As I scramble and dive into the trough, I bash my shoulder on the far wall. The only way to stifle the yowl of pain is to hold my breath and bite my knuckle. I crouch inside the coal trough and grip the knife.

Tense male voices permeate from upstairs, but I can't make out the words. A phone rings and one of them answers it.

More indistinct words, then as the voice approaches the cellar door: "And *I* told *you*, it's not a problem anymore."

There's nothing but my heart thumping.

"I agree, Kerry. Least said, soonest mended."

The voice drifts higher. He must be going up that fancy staircase. "Right you are. Yeah, bye." Then the same voice calls down, "Lenny! Need some help?"

More footsteps up the stairs. This is as good a chance as I'm going to get. Ears ringing, I bolt across the cellar, up the steps, along the hallway and out the door. I run headlong across the drive and lawn and dart through Gabe's hedgerow portal. There's no slowing my pace until I'm a mile back along Worcester Road.

Chapter Fourteen

Seth leans against his office door and looks at me, eyes foggy, unreadable. The same plain-clothed policeman is back with questions for me. I can't remember his name.

"We can stop, if you like. Take a break?" He glances up at Seth, as if it's his decision.

"I'm fine." My voice sounds petulant, and I don't know why. It's not helping.

This was supposed to be simple. Call the police, file a missing person report. Set them on Gabe's trail without incriminating myself, and on the way to Langford's house to find Maya. Worry about the pictures Gabe took later. Maya's more important right now.

This is the third interview, and whether it's Seth or me, one of us is going to crack. I'm sure of it.

"So, the last time you saw Maya was…?"

"We went through this yesterday," I say. "Twice."

Stop with the attitude, Ess. Act nice, for God's sake.

The cop peers at his papers and then at me. "Estella, I'm —"

"Name's Essie. I've told you that at least three times as well."

Oh, much better… are you trying to get arrested?

Maybe I am. I take in a lung-stretching breath, trying to calm the churning in my stomach. It starts again when I see Seth's grim-set face. He's doing a fair job of hiding it, but he must hate me for the trouble I've brought him.

"For my benefit," the detective says slowly, grey eyes alert but not unkind. "You last saw Maya, when?"

"Monday." A shaky sigh escapes me. "Five days ago."

"That's the… 22nd of October, yeah?" He scratches on his notepad, but it's for effect because he only puts a line by something he's already written. "At a café."

"Yeah."

He flips a few pages back and reads from the notepad. "Where you work. Bri's… Braai?" He pronounces it 'Bray'.

"Yeah, same as yesterday." Christ, it's hot in here. My throat is sore. I take a gulp from my glass of water.

"What would you say was Maya's state of mind that day?"

You mean before they shot her? "Fine."

His head twitches to the side, nearest eyebrow raised. "No indication that she might be considering… going away?"

I shake my head.

"Because I went to see your boss yesterday after we spoke. He told me that there was an argument between you, Maya and someone else at the café that day."

What the hell, Bri?

He refers to his notepad again. "A male, approximately twenty, tall, slim with strawberry-blonde hair. Your boss didn't know him. Who was it, Essie?"

"A friend."

"A boyfriend?"

"No."

"Was Maya sleeping with him?"

I look up sharply. "No."

"Are you?"

"No!"

"What's his name?"

My heart thumps louder. "That was Gabe."

He looks at his notes, flips back. "The man you said was trying to force Maya into an act of vandalism at Alex

Langford's house."

"Yeah."

His eyebrows twitch up again. "Why would he do that?"

"You'd have to ask him."

"And why would Maya go along with such a thing?"

I've got nothing, just a shrug.

"Does Gabe have some kind of hold over Maya?"

"Not that I know of."

"What's Gabe's last name?"

"I don't know his last name."

"Could it be Aster?"

"It very well could be. Like I said I don't know."

"Do you know where he lives?"

"No."

"Or works?"

"Nope."

"A very mysterious friend." He smirks. "Can't even find him on CCTV or drone footage."

"Are you going to look for Maya, or not?"

Watch it, Ess.

He huffs. "We will do our very best to find her, Ms Glass. That's why I'm back. But you need to cooperate. And drop the attitude." His eyes fix on me. "Is there anything you can remember from that day, anything she said or did, that was out of the ordinary? Or that might give us some clue as to her whereabouts."

I turn my gaze to his. The image of those letters, etched into the coal, flashes. "I wish there was, Detective."

***

"Happy birthday, Ess." Lawrence brings the smell of the fires in from the streets.

Seth closes the vicarage door, cutting off the shouting from River Street, and what sounds like breaking glass. "Glad you made it through the madness."

Lawrence tries to smile as we enter the office, but his eyes are hollow and bloodshot in a grey face. I doubt he's slept in the last week. I haven't.

Since Maya's disappearance, it seems the whole town has gone crazy. The whole *country*. Like some invisible puppet strings are connecting the two, making them dance together. Except we know who the puppeteers are.

"Was it Gabe who wrote the letter?" Seth asks Lawrence.

The copy of the Worcester Echo is still lying on Seth's desk, and I read it again in disbelief.

I feel the public has a right to know that certain government ministers are conspiring with the Worcester-based firm ConservUnity to prevent the development of vital green technology.

I understand from reliable sources that it may soon be possible to produce unlimited, clean and free energy. However, in a bid to protect the profits of existing energy companies, CU are suppressing the research.

This will spell disaster for our planet. Not only will it prevent development of the CU product, it will stifle future research projects into climate change solutions. The reckless endangerment of us all must be stopped.

Anon

The next day, the same letter appeared in local newspapers across London and Birmingham. How Gabe persuaded them to print, I've no idea. Perhaps he knows someone in the press. Maya said he's got connections. And they don't monitor the local press so much.

"Unless it was an incredibly lucky guess, there are only a handful of people it could have been," I say as we enter Seth's office. "Seth didn't, I didn't... It's Gabe."

Seth...don't mention Jack... please don't mention Jack.

There's no way Jack wrote that letter, so Lawrence doesn't need to know about him. Whether he sees my pleading eyes or not, Seth keeps quiet.

"Stands to reason it's Gabe," says Lawrence. "Though we'll never know for sure. He's long gone. His flat is cleared, phone's out of service, the lot. Even Hallie can't get hold of him." His jaw twitches. "Good thing for him, because if I ever see him again, I'll rip his head off."

"Me too." I sniff. Covering for Gabe with that cop turned my stomach, and I'd love to pay him back one day... "But he hasn't sold me out on the prototype. Yet."

"He probably thinks he doesn't need to, now," says Lawrence. "The letter's done its job."

"I heard ConservUnity are suing the Echo for publishing," says Seth.

"Must have rung true, though," I say. "I mean, people protesting in the streets all over."

"Guess the backlash was inevitable." Lawrence picks up the newspaper, though he must have read the article hundreds of times.

He's right about the backlash. We have an army presence on the streets of every major city in England, a huge police presence everywhere else, and thousands of drones to plug the gaps.

"I had no idea we had that many cops in the world," I say, eyes on the newspaper. "They're trying to root out insurgent groups before they can take hold. If Gabe wanted to up the ante with that letter, he's done it."

The first time I read it, my heart was pounding. For a moment, I thought maybe I could come forward with the file, expose their game. Make them stop. And though my hate for Gabe still smouldered, I was glad for it. Then I remembered Maya's gone, and Jack trusted me with this thing. He'd be exposed too.

"I um... haven't had chance to get you a present, but..." Lawrence hands me a card without an envelope. It has a picture of a rainbow on it, so hope-filled it makes my eyes swell with tears.

"Thank you." My voice sounds thin and watery. "How did it go with the police?"

"They took me right off the train from Edinburgh. I didn't even know about Maya's disappearance. That's how I found out. In a police interrogation room." Lawrence pulls his t-shirt up, showing me the bruises across his chest and back.

Seth hisses through his teeth. I close my eyes.

Lawrence's t-shirt flops back down, leaving him somehow more exposed than before. "They think I killed her."

"From *Scotland*?" Seth huffs, shaking his head. "I think they know who killed her, Lawrence."

"We don't know she's dead," I snap.

Seth and Lawrence shrink back as I fire my gaze at one then the other.

Yes, we do, Ess. Or else, where is she?

It's a nasty, needling voice that's been in my ear for days. Since that detective came sniffing around last weekend, it's settled into my brain and hammered away with its nail-crusted mallet. My head is pounding from it.

"I see the cops are swarming the streets," says Lawrence. "Drones everywhere. Just a matter of time until the raids start."

Seth nods. "I was in Birmingham the other day and the army's out there, all tooled and tear-gassed up. I watched the TV footage from London, but it didn't really register until I saw it with my own eyes."

"It's all escalated so quickly." I look out of the window, as if expecting an insurrection to start on Seth's lawn.

"The riots were the excuse they needed," says Lawrence, following my eyes.

"If only Gabe were here to see it." There's a hard knot of bitterness in Seth's voice that echoes in my own chest.

For a moment, none of us can look each other in the eye.

"Christ. How did this happen?" I run a hand through my hair. I haven't brushed it in days, so my fingers don't get far before getting tangled. "Lawrence, what are you going to do?"

"There's nothing I can do. They've told me not to leave

town. So, the Edinburgh job's obviously not happening. Not that I want to go now. Not without Maya."

"Have you seen her parents?" Seth asks. "Did they come down from Liverpool?"

Before Lawrence can reply, a black pit opens beneath me, and I'm swallowed by it. Horrible and self-indulgent, breaking down in front of Lawrence, but I can't hold it in. Seth puts his arm around me as I shake and sob, pounding my fists on my knees like a spoiled princess in a faery tale. The waves of despair keep coming, while the others look on wordlessly and Seth's arm grows tense around me.

As my breathing slows, I say, "Seth, turn on the TV."

He tips his head at me. "Essie, come on. You don't need to see..."

I snatch the remote. "I *want* to see. They might mention Maya."

There's rolling footage of petrol bombs and looting in London. The occasional attempt at a coherent demonstration with banners demanding peaceful protest, investigations, indictments. The cameras skate past the signs and zoom in on the rioters. There's a long-range shot of water cannons exploding from slate-grey trucks, scattering bodies. They cut to footage of a crowd trying to dismantle the Scotland Yard sign, riot police throwing tear gas from the glass-enclosed foyer. Shots fire and the camera drops, the picture going black.

"Christ." Lawrence passes a shaky palm over his crewcut.

A brief report from Birmingham, with crowds climbing on the bronze Bull Ring bull, storming the Council House. Worcester Cathedral is taking a battering too.

The picture changes to a head shot of a bespectacled, ratty-looking man in a studio—it's Oliver Foster-Pugh, and the caption reminds me he's the Home Secretary. Seth sneers but turns up the volume.

"We are appealing for the ordinary, law-abiding people of this great country to stay calm, but stay off the streets. Let the authorities deal with the perpetrators of this senseless destruction and violence. We will bring them to justice and restore order to our communities."

Behind the camera, there's a clatter and a bang, and unintelligible shouting breaks out in the studio. The lights go out, leaving Foster-Pugh in silhouette against a Drowning Hands of Unity sign, which somehow survives the power cut. Foster-Pugh and his interviewer sit in silence, barely responding as the behind-the-scenes shouting is quelled.

"Mr Foster-Pugh." The interviewer is not about to have his shot at prime time sabotaged. "Can you confirm if there is any truth in the allegations regarding the Worcester-based company ConservUnity and a conspiracy to suppress solutions to climate change?"

Foster-Pugh sighs, and as if he possesses magical breath, the lights come back on, giving him centre stage. "I can tell you categorically, Matthew, that there is no truth in that scurrilous allegation whatsoever. ConservUnity are a reputable and honourable company at the forefront of the fight against climate change. The whole ethos of Unity is founded in the union of science and faith, both of which hold the value of integrity in highest regard.

"Climate change is the single biggest challenge our planet faces—one that CU is committed to solving on behalf of us all."

"And is the government conspiring with the company in any way?" asks Matthew.

Foster-Pugh looks straight into the lens again.

"I can promise you, with no hesitation whatsoever, that we are not."

"So, yes then," mutters Lawrence, with none of the cynical humour he'd have had only a week ago.

***

It's incredible, but I have to carry on as usual. Keep pretending I don't know what happened to Maya. Go to work. Go shopping. Go to bed. Repeat. Act normal. Even though normal isn't a thing anymore.

Brian's closing early since the riots kicked off. The curfew starts at seven, but he's sending everyone home by four. The Braai is out of town a little, so has missed the worst of it, but someone still graffitied '*Go back to Bongo Bongo land*' all over his shutter on Monday.

"No taxis will come into town," says Brian with a frown. "Want me to walk you home?"

I press my lips into a wry smile. "Nah. I'll be fine."

Brian looks relieved. I mean, he's more of target than me right now. I should be walking him home.

Still, my heart is jabbering as I step outside the Braai. Bank Lane is clear of sleeping bags, and I don't blame them. I hope they've found somewhere safe, away from the trouble.

Down River Street, gangs of dark-clad men gather and pace like panthers, eyeing passers-by.

The ubiquitous stink of bonfires is already in the air. From the suburbs, I assume. There are so many coppers in town, I can't see how anyone's burning anything here.

The shop next to *Kiss* has been smashed up, a haphazard swastika daubed on the sign above the door. Half-eaten chocolate bars lie scattered on the threshold, soggy pastry squashed into the pavement.

As I pause to peer through the splintered door, a figure bursts out of it, making me shriek. He's carrying a gaping holdall stuffed with cigarettes, which spill on the ground as he barrels into me. His brown eyes click to mine for a moment and widen. He pushes me in the chest, driving me backwards, and scampers away down Bank Lane. Half a minute later, there's a shout from the river. A shot booms out, followed by a cry and a splash.

Belatedly, I recognise the boy who ran into me. It was Leon, one of the younger lads who've been sleeping on Bank Lane. My God, did they shoot him?

When I pass close to the River Street gangs, their movement increases, as though my presence has animated them. My legs weaken, like these men are stealing my energy. Shadowed eyes follow me, and whispers grow.

I keep walking, swallowing the nausea.

As I approach Unity Street, there's a low whistle and a

clicking sound behind me. The kind of noises you make calling a dog to heal.

"Hey, bitch. Where you going?" It's almost a growl.

Is he talking to me? I do a jittery half-turn, my heart galloping.

Officer Harassment. And his dead-eyed assistant, Charlie. With guns. Not pointing at me, but they might as well be.

My legs are planted in the concrete as Harassment prowls towards me, Charlie at his tail. His eyes flick up and down my body, and I feel exposed. I clutch my bag, cursing myself for stowing the prototype in it.

"You shouldn't be walking around town on your own at a time like this. Anything could happen to you out here." He's close enough to touch me.

I pray he doesn't.

"Thanks for your concern." My breath catches in my throat. "But I'm fine."

His pudgy hand raises. Before he can make contact, I break my paralysis. Expecting him to make a grab, I whirl, flip my hair, and trot away.

At Seth's gate, I glance back. Harassment and Charlie still stand on the corner, muttering to each other.

Watching.

Chapter Fifteen

It's been almost three weeks since they took Maya. I've chewed my nails raw. My voice is hoarse from lack of sleep and too many cigarettes. I feel old.

They've mounted a search for her, but it's all a sham. Her parents appeared on the TV last week from Liverpool, exhausted and hollowed out, appealing for her return, unaware of the futility of their ordeal. I wanted to scream the truth at them through my TV screen.

We can't move on the prototype with police and drones everywhere, so we keep out of trouble and let the authorities do their thing. I still carry the file in my shoulder bag. I know it's a risk, but it's comforting to have it with me, so I can touch it and know it's there. And it makes me feel less guilty about the risk to Seth.

If I carry this file, they can't prove Seth knows anything.

They're watching the vicarage. I've seen cars parked in the lane at all hours. They've stopped short of arresting a Unity cleric for now, but how long will it be until we give them just cause to raid a member? I've offered to leave, but Seth won't hear of it.

Jack never replied to the messages I sent the night they took Maya. I guess CU are watching their employees in case of any more 'scurrilous allegations', so I haven't tried again. Do they know their prototype has gone? I guess not, or I'd be in jail. Or dead.

So, the days grind on, and I hide.

On Sunday, I can't face another day of lurking in the vestry while Seth does his services to the swelling congregation. Seems everyone's found religion since they quashed the riots. Gotta get those Good Citizen points up.

I message Lawrence: *We need to talk.*

He doesn't reply for maybe half an hour, then: *We can't, Essie. They'll be watching.*

My response: *Please.*

Another pause, then he sends me a jumble of letters, and: *11am. Don't get followed.*

It takes too long to recognise the letters as a postcode. I check the clock on the wall of the vestry. It's coming up to ten-thirty. Before I can lose my nerve, I burst out of the door into the church.

Seth has decorated the place in a cascade of poppies. It's Remembrance Day, and I don't know when he's had time to get it organised. My appearance has drawn curious stares, but I can't be concerned with that. Sophie and Mark are sitting in pews a few rows back. So, I guess when *Change Here* didn't work they turned to God.

Good luck with that one, guys. God's on a sabbatical, in case you hadn't noticed.

Seth's standing at the altar behind me. Among them all, his eyes weigh heaviest on my back as I stride down the nave.

There's no air to breathe until I reach the outside. I crouch down, my back against the sandstone wall of the church, and gasp in the warm, drizzly fog. Like a sauna, it eases my labouring chest.

While I'm on the ground, I programme the post code into my phone. The location looks like the old hospital site. It's about a mile and a half out of town to the south, as River Street becomes Balmford Road.

The streets are almost empty, and there are no police for once. The security response is dialling down now—there have been no more riots since last weekend and the population seems to have gone back to the semi-conscious state of complacency everyone enjoys so much. It's quiet enough for me to be sure I'm not being followed. As I pass, there's no resisting a glance up Potter Road to my old flat, though I can't see it from the main road. There's a wistful tug in my chest, as though I might go back there and turn time backwards, back to when Maya wasn't missing. Before Jack and his little brown envelope, Gabe and his crazy revenge plot.

I press on.

I'm a little early, but Lawrence skulks in the doorway of the crumbling ruin of the hospital.

He's a mess. A shocked squeal escapes me. Almost every part of his face is bruised and his nose is swollen. There's a bandage on his left arm.

His eyes dart about as I approach. When I'm close enough, he grabs my hand, pulls me through the swinging doors.

There's a sheared padlock in the porch area and then we're in an expansive, once-opulent lobby. A high-domed glass ceiling stretches above us. Some of the enormous panes of glass are missing, shattered on the floor. Nobody has bothered to sweep them up. Leaves and other debris collect in the crevices on the roof and on the panes of glass still intact. Here and there, that same debris has tumbled through the broken panels onto the dull, neglected floor of the lobby.

"Jesus, Lawrence," I say, eyeing his bandage.

"I know. I've had a few conversations with the police recently. I'm not sure they even care if I did anything to Maya anymore." His mouth pulls into a strained smile. "They keep asking about drones. I guess they know about the hacking. They've got my laptop, so… Delete the app off your phone."

"Already have. Run. They'll kill you if this carries on."

He shakes his head. "Maya."

My eyes fill with tears. Lawrence lifts his hand to my shoulder, and we cling to each other for a moment, trying to make that enough. Then he's glancing about again, as if expecting an ambush.

Why aren't you in jail, Lawrence? Why aren't I?

"I was born in this hospital." He shakes his head.

"Yeah." I look up at the shattered glass.

When they closed it a decade ago, they were supposed to replace it with a state-of-the-art medical centre in Worcester. That never happened. Then people forgot.

"Lawrence, what are we going to do?"

"About Maya, or about the prototype?"

"Both."

He chews his lip, kicks at a piece of glass on the floor. "Your ConservUnity mate's still off the grid?"

I nod, and he gives a loud, annoyed sigh.

"They'll be watching him, too, Lawrence."

A scratching sound echoes down from the ceiling. A squirrel scampers among the leaves up there. It picks its way up to one of the broken panes, sniffs at it, and skitters back out of sight.

On the mezzanine floor above us, there's a crunch of glass, a scrape of metal. Lawrence's head snaps up.

We freeze, eyes on the raised floor.

"Come on." He pulls me back though the door to the outside.

Lawrence strides among the rubble of the ruined car park, close to a mossy stone wall. The drizzle has stopped and the air is still and heavy.

"There was somebody in there," he says, his shoulders bunched and tense.

"I don't see how," I puff, trying to keep up with his pace.

"You weren't followed? You're sure?"

Were you followed, Lawrence?

"Yesss," I say. "If there was somebody there, they got here before me."

He stops, grabs my shoulders and stares into my face. "You have the prototype with you?"

"Yes." I bite the inside of my cheek.

"Give it to me," he barks.

I gape at him, clutching my bag tighter. "No. It's safer with me."

He narrows his eyes and looks me up and down. "Are you wired?"

"What the hell? Why would I be wired? You're not making sense."

His head flicks to the side, more to regain his senses than a denial, it seems. "I know. I'm sorry. I just… it's driving me crazy, all this."

His eyes fill with tears. I grab him in a sudden fierce hug, and though he hisses in pain at the impact, he clings to me just as tight. We pull back, and before I can react, he's ripped the bag from my shoulder.

"Lawrence!"

But he's delving in the bag, and whips out the crisp, white envelope. "This it?"

I lunge for it. "Give that back."

Avoiding my grab, he tears into it and pulls out an unremarkable black memory card. I dive forward, trying to wrest it from him, but he pushes me away, pocketing it inside his jacket.

"Give it back. Now." I slap his chest, only slightly guilty when he winces. "Have you completely lost your mind?"

He laughs. "Probably. But I think I've worked out what to do."

"What?" I'm still trying to snatch the prototype back while he blocks me with his arms.

"Best you don't know. It'll be safe, though. I promise." He looks around us. "You'd better go first. I'll hang around a bit."

"Screw you."

"It's for the best."

I glare at him, not moving.

"All right, I'll go." He sighs, stepping backward. "Don't make this into something. We can either help each other. Or we make it a whole lot worse for each other."

He leaves me gaping after him.

***

159

"Maybe he knows what he's doing," says Seth. "He said he'd worked it out."

"That's not the point. He had no right."

Seth sucks in his lower lip. I think he agrees with me, but Lawrence is his friend, after all.

"Well," he says, as I pour us a glass of wine each. "I, for one, am glad that damn thing's not all on you anymore."

I look at him with an absurd grin. "That damned thing might save your life one day."

"Yeah, and it might not, as w—"

A heavy knock on the door makes us both jump. Seth's eyes snap to mine, and I can tell he's thinking the same as me about that kind of knock.

"Go in the back," he says, moving to answer it.

My heart hammering, I scurry into the kitchen, and stumble to the left of the door frame as Seth opens the door.

"Good evening, Cleric Fielding," says a gruff voice, familiar, accustomed to aggression but now dripping with false charm. "We're looking for a young woman, Estella Glass. I understand she's been, erm... sleeping here recently? Would you happen to know her whereabouts?"

"Hi, Officer." Seth's voice lifts with attempted cheer. "Um, no I'm afraid I can't help. Essie did stay with me for a little while. In my *spare* room. But I think she might have gone up north somewhere. To see a cousin, I think. You know, her best friend disappearing like that—she's been in a bad way. Needed to get out of town for a bit..."

Jesus. Stop talking, Seth.

"Really?" asks the voice. It's Officer Harassment "That's weird. Because I thought I saw her walking this way up Unity Street around lunchtime today?"

Seth hesitates a beat too long. "Oh... maybe she's back, then. I–"

But he gets no further because there's a thud of the door. I peek out from my hiding place to see Officer Harassment push past Seth and into the living room. And there's Officer

Charlie behind him, restraining Seth against the wall with an arm across his chest.

Seth shoots a desperate look towards me and mouths '*Go*'. I don't want to leave him, but he might be better off if I run.

A second later, they've seen me, anyway.

It's a short chase across the kitchen before Officer Harassment grabs me by the hair, pulls me backwards, then slams me against the wall. The impact knocks the breath out of me. Before I can even scream, he's spun me round and handcuffed me at the front. He marches me through the house, past Charlie, Seth's anguished face, and into the darkness outside. A second police car is pulling on to the drive, making my heart stab in my chest. That one's for Seth, I know it.

Yeah, he's in trouble and it's all your fault. Christ, Ess. Is there anybody's life you don't screw up?

There's no time to prevent it. Officer Harassment pushes me into his car, not bothering to protect my head, which bangs on the roof. Charlie catches up, with his blank-eyed stare, and they climb in the front without speaking. Harassment fires the engine as I try to swallow the nausea.

Through the rear windscreen, the other two coppers march into Seth's hall. The car crawls inexorably away from the vicarage.

Chapter Sixteen

I'm in a cold, sterile interview room, sitting at a bare metal table on a hard, plastic chair. The walls are that sage colour which is supposed to soothe, but the coffee-and-sweat aroma of the last interrogation negates the effect. My head is killing me. To stem the pain, I press my palms against my brow, elbows braced on the table.

The door clunks, and I straighten in my seat as a bespectacled man in a brown suit enters, carrying a mug and a slim tablet. He places the mug in front of me. His complexion has the same pale, greenish shade as the walls.

"Wasn't sure if you drink tea or coffee, so I went with the generic crap from the machine which could be either."

Wow. Thanks.

"Can I get you anything else?" He peers at me, his eyes glassy and shot with capillaries. "Your head hurts?"

Gaze lowered to hide the tears, I nod.

He turns back, shouts through the door, "Ollie. Some paracetamol, please?"

The door closes, and I wince as the bang pierces my brain. He sits down opposite me while I keep my eyes on the mug of generic crap.

"I'm Detective Victoria," he says, and I glance up.

"Believe me, Estella, I understand. You don't spend twenty years in the police force with a name like mine and not develop a sense of humility."

"Essie." It's barely a murmur, though.

"Hmm?"

"My name's Essie. Not Estella. Hate that name."

"Okay, I get it. Essie." His accent is soft Merseyside, like Maya's. Is he involved in the search for her? Perhaps they've found her. My heart somersaults, though that can't be right, or I wouldn't be in this place.

"Here's my problem, Essie. I have all this information telling me you've been mixed up in some bad stuff." He shuffles in his seat and straightens the tablet.

The door bashes against the wall hard enough to make me jump and give a squeal. Ollie comes in. It turns out Ollie and Officer Harassment are one and the same. Cutesy name for such a psycho bully.

He glares at me as he tosses two pills on the table. One rolls off and I struggle to pick it up in my cuffed hands. This clearly pleases him. He smirks and leaves the room. There's nothing else, so I take a cautious sip of generic luke-warm drink to wash the pills down. It really is awful—like tea, coffee and stale water.

"Now, where was I?" says Detective Victoria. "Oh, yes… bad stuff."

"No."

His glasses flash in the lights from the bare bulb above. "I'm sorry?"

I inspect the mug. There's a monochrome Unity insignia on the side. "Where's Seth? Have you arrested him, too?"

"Essie, have you heard of an organisation called *Change Here*?"

My eyes stuck to the mug, I try to force my heartbeat to slow.

"Come on." He lowers his face, trying to scoop up my gaze. "*Change Here*. Banners all over town. Crashed the Day of Celebration, turned it into a riot. You didn't notice?"

I shake my head, but it's pointless.

"You'll be aware that any public expression of political opinion is a criminal offence under the Dissent and Congregation Act. Section four, Clauses twenty-two to twenty-six, to be precise."

The only way I can stop myself from shaking is to clench all my fingers and toes. My nails dig into my palms.

"Are you a member of *Change Here*, Essie?"
Can he hear my breathing quicken? I shake my head.
"Do you know a man called Gabe Aster?"
My eyes flicker up before I can restrain them.

Shit.

He smiles. "What's your relationship with Gabe, Essie?"
"I've never heard of him."

Smooth, Ess. They know you know him.

"Strange. Because you were seen with him on the 22nd of October in the café where you work. But you know that, don't you? Is he your lover?"
I shoot him a glare for an answer.
"Do you know where he is now?"
"I don't know *who* he is, so..."
He sighs and flips open the tablet case. "Maya Taheri is still missing."
"Yeah." My lip curls. "Anytime you want to do something about that would be good."
"Not really my department," he says flatly. "So, Maya's boyfriend is…" He makes a show of tapping on the tablet. "… Lawrence Clifton?"
"Yeah."
"How would you describe their relationship?"
"Heterosexual, I suppose."
"Did they argue a lot?" Past tense.
I clamp my mouth shut, confused. Who is this really about, Lawrence or Gabe?
"Could Lawrence have had something to do with Maya's disappearance?"
"What? No! He was in *Scotland,* for Christ's sake."
"Oh?" He rests an elbow on the table, stroking his chin. "Because when we accessed his email, we found train tickets. Edinburgh to Worcester. On the 24th of October. The day before Maya was reported missing."

I blink at him, eyes watering. "That's not true."

He leans back and smirks. "What about Seth Fielding?"

"What about him?"

"You've moved in with him?"

What the hell?

"I'm staying there for a while. Someone broke into my flat." I squint at him. "But you know that, don't you?"

"Are you sleeping with him?"

God, these people are obsessed with sex.

He waits with a raised eyebrow.

I say, "He's just a friend."

"Is that what he would say, if I asked him?"

"He might say mind your own business."

"That would be unwise of him." His gaze aims at me like a gun.

Is he going to ask about ConservUnity or the prototype? This is a fishing expedition.

Victoria consults his tablet again. "So, you took part in an attack on the house of Alex Langford on the night of the 26th of October."

He doesn't phrase it like a question. I shrink inside myself, shoulders slumped.

"Essie? You were there that night, weren't you? With Gabe?"

I shake my head.

"You weren't?"

I keep my face low and blank.

"Have you heard of Alex Langford?"

Oh, this pain in my skull. The paracetamol hasn't touched it. I put my palms back to my forehead to ease the throbbing. He reaches out and pulls them down.

"Essie, did Gabe explain to you why he was fixed on that house in particular?" His voice is quiet, almost kind. "I bet he didn't."

I frown, lift my eyes, wanting to see Victoria's expression, as if I could see the answer in his face.

"Did you throw the petrol bomb or did Gabe? Did he tell you to do it?"

"No." I bite in the rest. So Gabe *did* go back and firebomb the place that night.

Detective Victoria sighs and shakes his head. "Oh Essie. You've been played, love. Big time played." He takes off his glasses, chews one of the arms and sits back in his chair, scrutinising me. "You know Hallie Morris?"

Where's he going with this?

He nods. "You're aware of what happened to Hallie's brother Francis, aren't you? That he was killed?"

"Yeah."

"Were you also aware Francis was Gabe's best friend?" He peers at me. "No, I didn't think so. They went way back— well as far back as you kids can go, anyway."

"So…?"

"In the months following Francis' death, Gabe spent a lot of time trying to convince everyone that Alex Langford had him killed."

"Why would he say that?" I glare at Victoria. "From what I understand, you lot killed him. Are you saying Langford controls the police?"

He flushes, his eyebrows dropping so low they almost obscure his eyes. "It might interest you to learn that Langford tried to sue Francis' university magazine for defamation. Apparently in relation to an article published in October of last year. About his company. You can look it up."

"Why would I be interested in that?"

"It's possible you wouldn't. I just think you have a right to know what you're dealing with. And who to trust."

"I know who I'm dealing with, Detective. And who I can —"

There's a buzz from Victoria's pocket. He takes out his phone, reads something, purses his lips and rises from his chair.

"Excuse me, Essie. Urgent business. Be right back."

The door closes behind him and I'm alone. With a sigh, I let my shoulders slump and cradle my thumping head in cuffed hands. My mind sprints on so many interweaving tracks I can't make sense of any of them.

Gabe and Francis were friends... what if Langford did have Francis killed somehow? Even if Gabe only believed it... is that why he wanted to blow up CU, using *Change Here* as a cover? And settled for vandalising his house? Just an old vendetta, and Maya paid the price. My fingers twitch, as though around Gabe's throat.

One day, Gabe...

Victoria doesn't come back. They've taken my phone, so who knows what time it is. It's like I've been here for days. Thirst rages in my throat and belly, but no one comes. In desperation, I drink the foul stuff Victoria brought me. I pace around the little room. The second time past the door, I rattle the handle in a futile gesture of rebellion. The power starts clicking on and off, the cuts never long enough for the generators to kick in. The effect is like a slow, nightmarish strobe.

I sit back down in the chair and squeeze my eyes shut, thinking of Seth. Is the same thing happening to him somewhere? Or worse?

The door opens. It's a uniform—not Officer Ollie Harassment, though. This young officer brings me a sandwich and, thank God, a large glass of water.

"Wasn't sure if you were vegetarian, so I brought cheese," he mumbles.

He unlocks my handcuffs. His eyes are green and soft, but I wonder how long it will be before they harden.

"Thank you," I say, bleary with exhaustion. "Do you know when they're letting me go?"

"Sorry," he says with a brief smile of commiseration, and leaves.

I down the water in one, then plough through the stodgy sandwich. Time ticks on.

The bang of the door makes me start.

Harassment prowls in, grinning. "You get to stay the night." He slips behind me, and lifts a lock of my hair with a damp, slab-like hand. "Lucky me," he murmurs over my shoulder.

Sick to my stomach, I jerk my head away.

He sniggers, yanks me up on my feet and whispers, "Maybe I'll come and see you later."

Outside the interview room, we cut through a quiet, semi-dark office. The old-fashioned clock on the wall shows eleven-thirty. We cross a white-tiled corridor to a heavy, iron door labelled '*Custody Suite*'. With a shove, he pitches me through it.

Ten minutes later, I'm staring at a camera lens staring back at me from an upper corner of a blank, white cell. Behind me is another one of those heavy iron doors, this one labelled '*Custody Room 2*'.

At last my pulse slows down, but for how long? The hard, thin mattress lies directly on the floor, in the glare of the camera. There's nothing else in the room except a fusty male smell which I have no hope of escaping since there is no ventilation other than the door. And somehow, I doubt that they're going to prop that open to freshen the air.

Heavy footsteps approach in the corridor outside my room. I snap upright and turn, expecting the sweaty, odious features of Harassment to appear in the shuttered window, the clatter of the lock.

The footsteps move on. I let out my breath and switch the filthy pillow round to face the door.

The light is dim and I'm so exhausted my eyes won't stay open, but my mind won't rest. I lie uneasy, wondering why the interview stopped. What's happening to Seth? Is he in the same building, locked up like me? What have they done to him? Is this about Gabe, Langford's house, or are they trying to tie me in with Lawrence and Maya's disappearance somehow? Victoria didn't mention Jack or the prototype, which either means they don't know about it, or that they're holding back.

I can't think straight.

There's nothing you can do. Get some sleep, Ess.

I wish I could.

From down the corridor, a door bangs. A woman screams.

I'm rigid on the unyielding bed. My skin and eyes itch, my chest burns. There was night after night like this after my family died—my mind and body uncoupling. My brain disappearing down holes, replaying the police at the door, Darya's burnt and bloody clothes in a bag, the inquest, the press, my last fight with Willow. It's funny because in the time after she died, I couldn't remember what the fight had been about, just that we fought. Now I recall every word we yelled at each other.

It was the night before they went to Manchester, when I was working the migraine story to avoid going with them. Willow knew I was lying. She came into my room to say she was on to me and she was going to tell Mum and Dad. It escalated quickly—all the way to where I slapped her in the face. She pushed me back against my bedroom wall and stormed out. It was the last physical contact we ever had. It makes no sense to me now that I would forget something like that.

A tickle on my cheeks... there are tears coursing down them. It goes on for some time, this silent flow, without a sob or even a sigh. The tears work their soporific spell and my brain shuts up and shuts down.

***

The door opens with more clang than strictly necessary, jolting me awake into an instant of panic. Two men in dark suits march into the cell. They're calm and purposeful. I rise on frail legs still leaden with sleep, back up a couple of shaky steps, then switch course. The idea is to dodge in between

169

them somehow. There's no plan beyond that—it's sheer instinct.

I'm spared the dilemma—one of them lunges, seizes my wrist, spins me around and inelegantly backwards into him. He wrenches my head back. My free arm flails upwards. I try to push away, freeing my hand, slapping and scratching anything in reach. He grabs me by the throat and squeezes. I make a ragged gagging noise, and he closes his hand tighter on my windpipe. The noise stops.

"Ssh," he says in my ear.

I fall still and watch the hypoxic shapes bloom in my vision. It feels like my eyes are about to explode.

The other man springs into my field of view now with a hypodermic needle.

"Don't…" I try to say.

The man behind me yanks my head back again. He forces me down and I fall backwards to the floor, cradled in his lap like a child. There's time to register disgust at the intimacy, before my arm is pulled away from my body and the needle stabs into it.

Cold pressure where it sits for a moment and then it's gone and my whole body slackens against my will. In my head, I'm fighting. Why won't my muscles do anything?

My vision blurs as I look up at the man who injected me. He smirks and holds the needle up as though it's a Magnum '45 or something. He steps out of reach and peers down to watch my consciousness draining away.

The man cradling me moves away and my head bangs on the floor. As he comes into view, it's clear I've landed an impressive scratch down one of his cheeks. He swipes the blood away to stop it dripping on his shirt, then kicks out at me. The jab connects, probably with my ribs. It's hard to tell —my senses are shutting down.

"Bitch," is the last word I hear before it takes me completely.

Chapter Seventeen

There's a buzz in my ears, like a drone is stuck there. I try to flick it from my head, but I'm too weak.

Open your eyes, Ess.

I'm in the back of a moving car. The whine of its circuits must account for the buzz. My forehead is cold. I guess it's resting on the window.

While I congratulate myself for these deductions, my head pulses in response, and I moan.

"Morning, sweetheart," says a voice from the front.

Is it?

Grey light flops onto the dashboard, so it might be. Who are these people? Where are they taking me?

I lift my gaze a little to see two men in dark clothes in the front. Probably the ones who drugged me, but I can't be sure from this angle. Their shapes are familiar—one wiry and sharp at the wheel, the other with forearms bulging above immense hands like the ones that wrapped around my throat in the cell.

Who the hell are they? Police?

They've handcuffed me again, and the edges of the steel are digging into my wrists as they rest on my lap. The windows in the back are opaque. From the noise and blur of shapes, we're on a motorway but I have no clue which one. In a moment of inspiration, I try the door, but it's child-locked. I suppose it's just as well. To jump from a car going at least eighty on the motorway while wearing handcuffs would be suicide, anyway.

My head lolls back on the seat. God, I'm so tired—my vision is swimming. My throat and scalp are raw, and I'm guessing the grabby guy snapped one of my ribs before I passed out. It pinches with every breath.

Despite the pain and fear, I drift away into a troubled doze. When the car comes to a rude halt, I awake with a gasp, my head and ribs kicking back with no mercy.

The door opens and Grabby Guy peers in. The scratch I gave him is red and swollen, even in this dim light, and a smirk spreads over my face.

"Yeah, laugh away, sweetheart," he says, letting me see the gun tucked into his waistband. I'm not grinning anymore. Is it possible I'm still asleep, and this is just a horrific nightmare?

He jerks his chin. "Get out."

There's no dignified way to get out of a car in handcuffs with a broken rib and the last of an unknown tranquilizer fizzing in my system. My legs collapse under me and I end up in a heap on the concrete floor. Which gives Grabby Guy a perfect excuse to hustle me to my feet. His colleague strides ahead as he drags me across an empty, underground carpark.

They march me through a heavy door and we enter an industrial lift with doors at both ends. It's hot and airless, and reminds me of the lifts in the hospital where Darya was... No, that's not a helpful thought.

There's a strong smell of diesel in here, which is not like the hospital so I grab on to that.

The lift ascends to the top floor. As we step out, the diesel fumes give way to the aromas of new carpet, chipboard and paint. We're in an empty open-plan office space in the process of a refurb. The walls are clean and painted in a tasteful, muted grey-lilac. Rolls of cream carpet lie stacked nearby.

At the far end is a private office built from partitions that don't look particularly secure. I can't see where they're attached to the ceiling or floor, as if they've just landed here. Despite this, off-white vertical blinds hang closed, shielding the view inside. This is obviously our destination as Grabby shoves me forward into the space. Low beams of sunlight stab through the enormous windows, which look out onto an unfamiliar cityscape. Non-Grabby Guy moves ahead and taps on the door.

"Come," a woman's voice demands.

I go in, like walking through warm treacle.

Behind a desk and a cream leather chair stands a woman in maybe her late forties. I recognise her from somewhere. She's dressed in a tailored suit. Matching red-framed glasses perch on top of her French-pleated hair. Her eyes are alert, her skin black and smooth.

"Essie," she smiles warmly.

I try not to show her anything, but I'm mightily tempted by the chair in front of me.

"Please, sit." She gestures and takes her own seat. I flop down before my legs collapse, though what I really need is a pee.

Shifting her gaze behind me, the woman waves her monkeys out. "Thanks, guys—I'll take it from here. If you could wait by the lifts, that'd be terrific."

When they're gone, the woman regards me for a moment, then reaches into a desk drawer and comes out with a packet of biscuits. They're the gourmet chocolate cookie kind.

"Hungry?" She opens the packet.

I shake my head, and it pounds back.

"Hmm. God, I'm starving." She takes an enormous bite. "How about a cuppa?" she says through a mouthful of biscuit. Then, at the door, "Guys, could one of you just nip out and get us…?" To me: "Coffee or tea?"

"Er… tea."

"Sugar?"

"Just milk."

"Perfect." Back to Grabby and Non-Grabby: "Two white teas, please. No sugar. And whatever you're having. Thanks, guys."

She doesn't offer them any money. Through the gap in the door, Grabby and Non-Grabby are as confused as me, no doubt accustomed to aggression without the niceties. There's a brief discussion while they work out who should go and who should stay. In the end, Grabby goes.

The woman turns her attention back to me. She's caught me off-guard with the tea and biscuits, but I'm wary again. Those nutters work for her.

She looks at me and sighs. "We've got ourselves in a bit of a pickle, haven't we?"

Unsure what she is referring to, I say nothing.

"Essie. I'm sorry about the way you arrived just now." She wrestles another biscuit from the packet, inspects it. "Those two are… well, to be honest, they're vicious bastards. But they're good at keeping things on-plan, as it were. I–"

"Who the hell *are* you?" I snap. Who kidnaps you and *talks* like this?

She leans back in her chair and nibbles the biscuit, narrows her eyes. "You don't recognise me, do you?" The idea seems to amuse her, and she waves her hand in a delicate flick. "I'm Kerry Tyler."

The name chimes somewhere in my memory.

"The Homeland Environment minister?" She says this deliberately, as if talking to a stupid person. "MP for Worcester?"

Jeez. I am definitely still tranqued.

She gives me a sweet, patronising smile. "I really wanted to meet you. We have similar interests and, I believe, some common acquaintances."

There's no choice but to proceed as though this is happening for real, even if it is a tranq dream. "I really need a pee. Is there somewhere…?"

"Oh, of course. Sorry, you've had a long journey."

Have I?

"The loos aren't plumbed in yet, I'm afraid. New offices. So, you won't be able to flush but…" She slinks around me

174

to the door and says, "Ed. Our guest needs to visit the little girls' room, please."

Non-Grabby looks annoyed, possibly at the use of his real name, or at the thought of taking me to the loo. He does as he's told, though, removing my handcuffs with swift practiced movements and a sigh.

While he marches me past the lifts to the toilets, I peer out of the window trying to get an idea where I am. An unfamiliar skyline glows in the dim, pinkish light. It's a sizeable city—London? We both check the bathroom for escape routes, and then Ed waits outside the door.

When I've relieved myself, the mirror over the sink gives me a shock. A grey face stares back from feverish, huge-pupiled eyes. My hair and clothes are twisted and damp with sweat. I put my hand up to my throat and touch the bruises that bloom there.

They've plumbed the sinks, but as I splash cold water on my face Ed, clearly feeling I've had enough time, bursts in and marches me back to the office. Grabby has returned to his post by the lifts.

"You got me skimmed milk, yeah?" I say as we pass by and he shoots me a malevolent glare. He forms his fingers into a gun and mimes shooting at me. I try to glare back, but he must see I'm scared, and it only makes him sneer.

There's a lidded paper cup on the table. The scalding of my tongue and throat barely registers as the hot, weak tea goes down. Kerry reaches into another drawer and brings out a document wallet stuffed with papers, and a phone.

"Better? Good." She smiles tightly. "So, I wanted to talk to you about our mutual interests. As you might be aware, my portfolio includes oversight of domestic research relating to climate change. Yours, as I understand it, includes wilful disruption of the infrastructure supporting that research."

Oh, Christ.

I sip my tea, brow furrowed. "Where am I, exactly?"
She ignores my question. Her hand reclaims the reading

glasses from her hairdo, deposits them on her nose, then flips through her papers in a fluid dance. "I'm sorry about what happened to your family. Must have been difficult."

The gaze is milder this time, the mouth softer. She may just mean that a little, but my defences are up. I keep my silence, so she shrugs and turns the pages.

"Okay, then." She picks up her phone and swipes the screen. "These photos were taken a few weeks ago, on the 19th of October." She slides the phone towards me. I don't take my eyes off her.

"Go on," she says. "Have a look."

It's a picture of me and Jack at the river. We're sitting on the bench by the bridge. It's dark, but the photo is high resolution. My heart lurches as I remember the only time I've ever met Jack there.

The prototype.

No… Please let this end.

It's a close-up, I assume taken from the opposite bank. Jack's jaw is tense, his brow furrowed.

"There's a few. Have a scroll." She smirks.

With a shaky finger, I start to swipe the screen left. Jack's looking at me, I'm looking away. I'm looking at him, he's looking away. He's reaching into his pocket. There's a small envelope in my hands. The envelope has gone and I'm fiddling in my bag.

Kerry sashays towards me, plucks the phone from my fingers and rests against the desk, peering down at my face. I fix my gaze in front of me.

"Who's the man in the photos, Essie?"

There's no lie to tell, so I say nothing.

She leans closer. "Who were you with that night?"

I shake my head as my chest tightens.

"Okay. What's in the envelope?"

All I can do is shrug.

"Shall I tell you what I know?" she whispers. "I know who that man is. And I know that you know him."

176

Kerry returns to her side of the desk, letting me stew on that. Beads of sweat tickle my lip as she shuffles her papers, pulls one out and tosses it across to me. I watch it glide towards me until it's so close I can't avoid seeing what's written there.

"We recovered these from your message service files. They're messages between two accounts dating back to July of '33. The two handles: Vixie44 and FractalEyes."

My stomach cramps.

Her eyes flit over the paper, then back up to me. "The first account is yours. The second belongs to the man in the pictures."

Panic kindles inside me, and my heart is racing. Mine and Jack's conversations splash across the page. There's really no denying what they are. I look up from the desk. If she knows about me and Jack, she must know about the prototype. Is Jack in trouble now? This is moving too fast.

Kerry rocks back in her chair, obscuring her smirk with tented fingers. She snaps upright. "What's his name, Essie?"

"Apparently, you have his name—"

I try to swallow the lump in my throat. Her eyes won't leave mine.

"I do, but I want you to say it." She stares at me through the stretching silence.

God, I need a cigarette.

Sweat runs down my temples. "I don't know his name. We just chat."

"And meet to exchange envelopes. Are you in the habit of talking to strange men in secluded locations and not asking their names?"

I glare at her. "We never used our real names. You can't even prove it's the same person in the messages."

She doesn't bother to refute it. "What do you chat about?"

I nod at the papers on her desk. "Well, you know that too."

Her eyes fix on me, and I can't meet her gaze.

"What do you chat about?" she repeats, more slowly.

"Mainly what a bunch of clowns you are," I say. There's a smirk on my lips when I look up.

Snatching up a sheet of paper, she says, "In a conversation on the 27th of April of this year, you ask him for lithium. He replies, *'If you want drugs, I can get hold of anything.'*" She raises an eyebrow. "He's offering you recreational substances?"

I sneer. "Lithium has no recreational—"

She peers at me over her glasses. "Same evening, same conversation: He asks you what you're doing, you say, *'Channelling the destruction of the planet'*, he replies, *'Oooh sexy'.*" She licks her glossed lips.

"That's not—"

"If one of your friends told you a much older guy she'd never met was writing this stuff to her, offering her drugs, what would you do?"

Freak out. Like Maya did.

"What are you getting at, Kerry?"

"I'm trying to work out what a man well into his thirties might want from a... child."

"I'm *nineteen*."

"You were sixteen in the beginning, Essie." A theatrical frown. "That's not right."

I search the ceiling for cracks.

She dips into her file and comes out with more papers. "Okay. How about these messages? From TheOtherOne32?"

The temperature drops, my heart is pounding against my broken ribs.

"Not so friendly, are they?" she says.

I stay silent, but I'm thinking. If they have these, they must have the identity of the person who sent them.

Kerry picks up the two piles of papers, one in each hand. "It's interesting, though, if you cross-reference these sets of messages...." She gives a mischievous wink. "So... 11th of May at nine forty-seven is your first message from TheOtherOne32: *'You're going to die'*. And there were more

178

that night, weren't there? With details of what would happen to you? How you'd beg to die? *'I'll cut your throat and watch you bleed while you scream my name.'"*

The memory makes me wince. There's a whirl of nausea in my stomach. It *was* Toby, wasn't it? Because then he came back for me, trashed the flat, tried to attack me. For revenge.

It had to be Toby.

"Also 11th of May, at ten thirty-four," Kerry continues. "You to FractalEyes: *'Had one of those crazies message me tonight'*. FractalEyes to you: *'From the forums? Christ. I knew this would happen. What did he say?'* Blah blah blah, then FractalEyes*: 'Essie, you need to report this'*. And a little later*: 'Well, I need to see you, then. To make sure you're okay.'"*

She slaps the papers down on the desk. "Gotta hand it to him, that's quick work. We have pictures of that first night too."

My eyes snap up to meet hers, then she swipes her phone.

"15th of May. A couple of shots of you in the bar... a couple outside your front door..."

She slides the phone across the desk at me, and there's a picture of Jack and me, kissing. Or really me kissing Jack, but you can't see that from the photo.

"So, he got what he wanted."

I can feel myself flushing. "No! I mean, he—"

"What, you don't think this is a bit of a coincidence? You're telling me it never occurred to you that FractalEyes-the-scientist and TheOtherOne32-the-crazy might be one and the same?"

Did it occur to me? I did insist on meeting somewhere busy... No, this is wrong. She's messing with me. "You're full of shit, Kerry."

"More recently, on the 18th of October, FractalEyes is back." She reads in a flat, emotionless voice, "*'I won't hassle you anymore, promise. Sorry about that night. There's a reason I was weird, but I can't explain it right now. I just need to meet with you. Just once. It's not about us or that night. You have no reason to trust me but please say you will. It's really, really important or I wouldn't ask. Anywhere you*

179

want—you name the time and place.'" Her eyes drill into me. "What was so important?"

My mind is screaming *'Prototype'* so loud she can surely hear it. I keep silent, breath frozen.

"What did he mean by *'you have no reason to trust me'*? What did he do to you that first night?"

"Nothing." I stare at my knees.

"Not nothing," she says, pointing to her phone. "You did see him again, though. After ignoring his messages for months. So, it *was* important. That little envelope he gave you."

She wants me to doubt Jack, to give him up. I try to keep my face blank.

Kerry sighs, extracts some papers. "Okay. You say you don't know his real name. But he knows yours, here." She points at the print outs of our messages. "When you met him in the bar, what did he say his name was? You didn't call him FractalEyes all night."

I could make a name up for him, but what's the point? They've got everything already. Her next question's going to be about the prototype.

And I've just realised, she's right. He called me Essie in the conversation that night, days before we met for the first time. How did he have my real name before I gave it to him? Her eyes glitter—she has me cornered and confused.

"Homeland Environment," I say, by way of a side-step.

"Hmm." She purses her lips, her jaw twitching.

"Like, the environment—but just in England. Like the hurricane's gonna stop at customs. Honest to God, Kerry…" I shake my head. It's not even something I was consciously angry about until just now.

She narrows her eyes. Perhaps she wants to call Grabby back in to knock me about a bit more. With a closed-lipped smile, she cocks her head to display her forbearance. "So, I guess you started talking to this guy what, three months after all your family died? Were you still suffering from PTSD? I hear the support offered the families was a bit… slow in coming. But perhaps you were over it by then."

Over it?

My face fixes in a hard stare, my breath trapped in the base of my throat. If I could scratch that patronising smile off her face with my fingernails, I would.

"What was it like?" she goes on with a mawkish pout. "Waking up that first morning remembering they were all gone, and you were all alone? That you had no one in the world?"

Oh, you cold bitch.

"Not no one." I want it to sound defiant, but it's just a whisper. To hide my tears, I look down at the desk.

She keeps coming at me, though. "And now your best friend is missing. You don't have much luck, do you?"

That's the first time she's mentioned Maya to me.

Kerry points at the phone on the desk between us. "This man, Essie. People like him seek out people like you. Because you're vulnerable. Because you can be controlled."

I shake my head, try to tell her she's wrong. No one controls me. The tears are falling, though. A humiliating, involuntary sob bursts out, and I close my eyes against her smug smirk.

"Okay. Let's say you don't have a name for him, real or fictional. What *do* you know about him?"

I take a shaky breath and sniff. "He hates you lot."

She laughs. "What else?"

"Well… he likes Chinese food?"

She goes in the drawer again and comes out with a tablet device, which she taps into, then slides across the desk.

On the screen is Jack. He's sitting in what appears to be an interview room, a little less sparse than the one where Detective Victoria questioned me. Opposite sits a suited man who appears to be questioning him. The stamp on the camera roll reads 14/11/2034 18:47. Last year. The camera sits side on, between them and up high.

Kerry leans over and finger-zooms in on Jack's face. He

looks dreadful—the eye nearest the camera is purple and swollen. It's like he hasn't slept in days. His eyes are fixed on a point to the side of his interviewer's head.

The scattering of discarded coffee cups match their tired demeanours. It's a curious echo of my own situation. Kerry zooms the screen out so I can see both men, hits play, then leans back. The frozen figures start to move.

"Who messed up your face, Jack?" The interviewer speaks in a bland voice which sounds like this isn't the first time he's asked.

Jack gives a tiny flick of his head, a cynical bark of laughter. "Come on, Colin."

Colin, whoever he is, performs a weary nod. He plucks a sheet of paper from a pile in front of him and tosses it across the desk to Jack.

"You'll be aware of this, but for the recording, I'll explain. This is a complaint received by your former employer, from the parents of Lara Bennett, date of birth 12th August 2015. She was a student of yours?"

Jack gives one tiny nod, his eyes down.

"For the audio...?"

"Yesss."

"And you're aware of the nature of this complaint."

No response.

"Jack?"

Jack sighs. "Yes, I'm aware of the nature of the complaint."

"Would you like to explain, in your own words, the nature of the complaint?"

A pause—two beats, three.

"A misunderstanding."

"Misunderstanding?"

"Yeah."

"Come on."

Jack spreads his hands, palm up. "What do you want? Her parents complained, they were wrong. We all moved on."

"So, if I understand you correctly, you're asserting that the... *friendship* between you and Lara Bennett was not

182

inappropriate and did not contravene any Unity codes of conduct or safeguarding policies at the university."

"Yes. I am asserting that. There was nothing—"

"She's eighteen, Jack. *Eighteen.*"

"Nineteen."

"And you're what, thirty-one?" says Colin. "You seriously don't think this is inappropriate? With a student?"

"She's a grown up."

Colin picks up more papers, tosses them at Jack. "We have pictures here. Loads of them. You and Lara laughing on campus, you and Lara having a coffee on the library." And another one. "You and Lara in a bar."

Jack clutches his coffee like a lifeline. "So what? People go to bars."

Colin shakes his head. "When was the last time you saw Lara?"

"I've told you this already."

"Jack, if I was in your position, I'd make an effort to come across more helpful."

Jack sighs and says in a monotone, "About three weeks ago."

"The night of 23rd October, yeah?"

"If you say so."

"The night this picture was taken." Colin indicates the picture of Jack and Lara in the bar.

Jack gives a shrug. "Guess so." He's staring at the desk again.

"Lara's flatmate reported her missing on the evening of the 24th October. She's still missing. Got any theories about what might have happened to her?"

Kerry slides the tablet back towards herself and pauses, leaving Jack frozen in his misery. She peers at me.

"So, you see, you're not the first." Her face melts into a sympathetic smile. "Our mutual friend—shall we call him Jack?—likes to spend time with younger women, it seems. Much younger. Doesn't always work out well for them." In a quiet voice: "He didn't tell you about this, did he?"

Nope. But what is 'this'? Why is she showing me that stuff,

trying to make Jack out to be the bad guy? They've been watching me. She knows about the prototype, or suspects. And she wants me to give it up. That's what this is.

Isn't it?

"Essie." That smooth face warms again. "I'm just trying to show you that your loyalty is misplaced." She leans towards me. "If you reckon you and he have something special, you're mistaken. Jack's going down a treacherous road—I can't even begin to tell you." She tries to find my gaze. "I just don't want to see you pick the wrong side."

"Side?"

From the file, she takes out a slim, green envelope and pushes it delicately towards me. I shake my head.

"These documents will explain to you who Jack really is. Do yourself a favour. Read them."

"I don't need to read them."

She rises, comes around the desk, and places the envelope in my hands. "I think you should."

She calls Grabby and Non-Grabby back in. Snatching the envelope, Grabby shoves me towards the door.

"Essie," says Kerry, and Grabby spins me round to face her. "If you tell anyone, there'll be no proof you were ever here, got that? I'll deny all knowledge of those documents, and who do you think they'll believe?" She arranges her face into a sickly smile. "I'll be watching over you. Remember that. If you want to talk, you can talk to me."

I'm not sure if that's supposed to comfort or scare me.

When we're back in the baking carpark, Non-Grabby removes another syringe from his inside jacket pocket.

With no fight left, I close my eyes as Grabby fixes me in position. I let them stick the needle in my arm and drift away while they push me down into the back seat. The last thing I am aware of is the green envelope landing on my chest as one of them tosses it in after me.

Chapter Eighteen

All I want to do is lie here, eyes closed, until the shivering stops. There's a damp smell, faintly familiar, and a sickly burn in my throat, like it's awash with bile. My head throbs. I don't wish to know where I am. It won't be good.

Someone whimpers, and that forces me to lift my eyelids into a squint.

No one's here. That sound must have been me.

Sunlight glows from across the room, behind the unlined, cream curtains.

They took me back to my flat.

I'm in my old bed, and the air is musty and dead. Though uneasy about being here, I can't deny it feels good. Just to be free and not locked up. And alive.

Seth.

Still shuddering, I struggle to my feet and limp to the bathroom, clutching my head. I'm fully dressed, boots on, and that's a relief. In the mirror, the bruises on my neck are in full, indigo splendour. There's another on my upper arm, and when I lift my shirt, a big one on the side where they broke a rib. As I pull the shirt down, my stomach revolts. I just make it to the toilet before the bile bursts out of me in a stinging retch, and there's a stab like the rib has snapped again. It's a long time before I have the strength to stand up and wash my face.

In the living room, my trusty curtains are drawn, but in their purple light I can see enough.

The place is trashed all over again. There looks to be more purpose to the chaos, with drawers empty and strewn across the floor. My lamps lie smashed, their meshed works exposed, emitting a faint smell of gas. They've pulled our family portrait from the wall, slashed it from the frame at the top and down one side. The canvas has rolled up on itself, obscuring my mum's face. With a cry, I drop to my knees, trying to unfurl it, but it just curls back up. They must have searched for ages. The flat upstairs is still vacant, so they could have taken their time. No one would have cared.

Serene among the madness, on top of a green envelope on the sofa, lies my phone. Obviously, they've bugged it, but it doesn't matter. I snatch it up and press buttons with a shaky hand.

My heart thumps as Seth's phone rings and rings.

"Hello?" His voice is croaky and strained, like he has a cold.

"Seth." A sob bursts out of me.

"Essie. Christ. Are you okay? I've been calling the police station, but they said they'd released you. Went to your flat, but you weren't there. I was… I didn't know what to think."

"I'm okay." I wipe my nose on my sleeve. "Alive, anyway. What did they do to you?"

A sigh at the other end. "Nothing. Not really. Just a warning." He sounds tired, and tight, like he's lying.

"Did they hurt you?" A tide of rage rises from my stomach. "Did they…?"

"No. No, just questions... a lot of questions. They only searched the house. Nothing else." He releases another shaky breath to match my own. "What happened to you, Ess?"

"I'm fine. Just… gonna rest."

"Are you coming home to the vicarage?"

"Can't. Need to rest."

"But, we—"

"I'll call you in a bit. Don't go out." He's still trying to say something when I put the phone down. It would hurt too much, to have him ask me to come back again, when it's all I want to do.

At the window, I peep behind the curtains. Bright autumn sunshine probes the room and I hiss as it hits my aching eyes, but keep looking. There's no one on the street outside. Not even a car, which is strange. It's possible they're just a bit subtler than Toby.

The table still screams the word *BITCH*, my long-abandoned sketches strewn across it—the ones Toby, or whoever, didn't destroy. Maybe not Toby.

On the sofa, lies the envelope Tyler forced on me. Inside, the file about Jack.

I eye it as if it's going to spring at me and bite. I can't see any teeth there, but they're probably on the inside. On the outside, it's the plain sage colour of Detective Victoria's interrogation room.

After rifling through the kitchen drawers, I find a forgotten packet of cigarettes and a grubby blister pack of paracetamol. I pour myself a glass of flat cider from the fridge, slam down the painkillers, light up from the gas hob and ease down on the sofa. My rib kicks again as I inhale and try to think.

Maybe Detective Victoria would have ended up letting me go, but someone told him not to. Kerry Tyler was curious about me and Jack, but not about the prototype. Nothing about that.

Surely details of Jack's project must have come through her office. For approval or... something. Homeland Environment: that's her job. Was it her decision to pull the funding? Does she realise Jack stole the prototype? It's only a baby step then to connect the theft with the envelope we exchanged at the river. But then, why didn't she ask me about it? She had my flat searched, so she wants it.

And where is Jack? Have they done something to him, or has he run? Or is he too scared to contact me? Every question births more, and my head pounds with them.

That persuades me to read the file at last. The possibility of some answers.

I fumble for the green envelope and rip it open. Inside is a memory card with no label, blank and anonymous, and a single piece of notepaper. On the paper is scrawled: *His handle.*

When I shove it into my laptop, I'm prompted for a

password, and the note makes sense. I type *FractalEyes.* A screen appears, with an array of file icons.

With a shaky inhale, I click one open.

Sent by email to: j.riley@worcs.ac.uk
22nd October 2031
Dear Jack
Re: Unity Membership
I am delighted to inform you that following your successful completion of our application process, and receipt of your guarantors' statements, you are now a confirmed professional member of Unity.

As you are aware, our professional members are highly valued, because we understand your vital contribution to our union of the scientific and spiritual.

On receipt of your signed contract, I will contact you again with details of the many resources and support networks which are available.

I'd like to take this opportunity to welcome you to the Unity family. Your remarkable work in the fight against climate change will be an asset to the organisation and its endeavours.

Warmest wishes

Cleric Millie Rosser
Chair of Welcomers

***

Sent by email to: fractaljack@volition.co.uk
12th August 2031
Dear Jack
Re: Application for Teaching Post at Worcestershire University.

Further to our telephone conversation earlier today, I am pleased to inform you that your application for the post of Pastoral Lecturer has been successful. We will now continue to process your Unity membership application to enable you to take up your post and full responsibilities in due course.

I enclose the Unity Code of Conduct, Duty of Care Policies, and other documents which I'm sure you will find useful in your application process, as well as a vital framework for your values-based duties at the university.

I wish you luck in your application to Unity, and look forward to welcoming you to the organisation.

Yours sincerely

Ben Millicent
Head of Pastoral Recruitment

***

CONFIDENTIAL
WORCESTERSHIRE UNIVERSITY COMPLAINT FORM

Ref: 2034/1364

Date of complaint: 12th June 2034

Received by: Isobel Carter, Unity Membership number 30454—12

Complainant(s): Helena Bennett, Jonathan Bennett re Lara Bennett dob 12/08/2015

Complainee(s) (if applicable): Mr Jack Riley, Pastoral Lecturer in Chemistry, Worcestershire University. Unity Membership number 56344—1

Nature of complaint: Misconduct and inappropriate behaviour towards a student (Lara Bennett)

Initial Details:

Parents are alleging inappropriate behaviour displayed towards Lara throughout the 2033/34 academic year. This includes spending excessive amounts of time with Lara, being inappropriately 'friendly' towards her and socialising to an unusual degree.

Lara's parents also claim Mr Riley is exercising undue influence on Lara to change her career path in order that they might spend more time together. Lara recently informed her parents she wishes to transfer from studying medicine to an

189

alternative course—that of environmental chemistry, a course led by Mr Riley.

Mr and Mrs Bennett report significant behaviour change in Lara in the time since she began studying at the university in October 2033, when she met Mr Riley. Usually a calm and shy person, Lara has become progressively angry and volatile. This has caused significant friction at home, where Lara has been living while studying here at Worcestershire. Lara's parents believe this is due to the pressure resulting from her relationship with Mr Riley.

Actions Taken:

Case referred to the university safeguarding officer for priority 1 investigation 12th June 2034.

Initial safeguarding review to be arranged in 1 week (19th June 2034).

***

These documents seem authentic enough, but they would. I'm sure a cabinet minister's resources could stretch to forging a university complaint form. But if it's real, then… what?

He's much older, yes. I've wondered why he bothers with me. But he's never wanted anything—until he dropped the prototype, I mean. Never anything personal. I grabbed and kissed him, not the other way around. He didn't seem to enjoy it that much, and the only undue influence that night was the tequila.

But what would it look like from the outside? I wonder what happened to Lara, if they ever found her, what she would tell me about Jack if I could ask her. And if I was like Lara—if I still had parents—what would they think of Jack?

The next file is a series of photos. They're likely the ones described in the interview Tyler showed me. Jack is in all of them, always close to the same young, beautiful girl with long, almost black hair—Lara, I assume. In every one, her eyes sparkle as she beams at him. They're in a library, in a park, then in a bar, then at what looks like a summer ball. She's wearing a strapless cherry-red dress, and a matching orchid pinned in her hair, and talking earnestly to Jack. He looks good—sophisticated, and his bow tie is the same shade as her dress. I close the file.

Next up is a transcript, and after a page, I realise it's the full interview with the tenacious Colin, a clip of which Kerry played for me.

There are reams of it, mostly the same questions going around and around. What was Jack's relationship with Lara? Did he know where she was now? Had they ever slept together? Was he in love with her? Could she have run away? Had he done anything to hurt her? And had he killed her?

It's exhausting just reading them, let alone being forced to answer them. Jack's responses are polite initially, becoming exasperated. I skip to the last few pages.

CB: Okay. It's clear you don't want to co-operate with the Unity investigation any more than you did with the police.

JR: I'm *trying* to co-operate. I don't know what happened to Lara, is what I'm trying to tell you. If I did, don't you think I would have told the police?

CB: Nevertheless, we have the outstanding matter of the Bennetts' complaint, which—

JR: Which is completely unfounded.

CB: Which, you maintain, is unfounded. However, Unity, with me as their representative, are obliged to handle this with the utmost seriousness.

JR: For God's sake.

CB: I'm sure you'll agree that… it would be best if, for the time being, you were not such a high-profile member of the university faculty. Or of this organisation.

JR: You're suspending me?

CB: Not exactly. We're moving you… sideways.

JR: What?

CB: Your research is very important to Unity. To everyone. We understand how close you are to prototype now, and it would be a terrible shame if the project halted because of a… misunderstanding. I don't have to tell you a lot is riding on this project. So, while we must ensure that we discharge our obligations—regarding both the safeguarding of our students, and to the police investigation—we are also aware of the value of our most talented members and the work they do.

JR: What does that mean, exactly?

CB: It means project Cleanliness is moving.

JR: We don't call it that here. It's moving?

CB: Yes. Out of the university.

JR: Where to?

CB: ConservUnity.

JR: The Judgement Day people? Oh, no. I can't work for them, they're nut jobs. This project is public property, Colin. You can't do that.

CB: Alex Langford is a respected businessman. And a shrewd one. He's no nut job. And he's already invested significantly in the project. It's as much Langford's as it is yours.

JR: Oh, great. From what I've heard we'll be building the ark before the year's out.

CB: Think that's a different part of the bible... But, anyway, forget what you heard. You don't want to pay any attention to rumours and malicious gossip. CU is on the level. Your opinion of them is irrelevant. The project's moving to CU, and that's that. You can either move with it, or... not.

JR: And if I say not?

CB: Well, it's your decision. The project will be the poorer without you, but I can't force you to take part. Only...

JR: Only...?

CB: You'll remember that you signed an Intellectual Property Rights agreement at project initiation. That document clearly states that Unity holds the IPR for project Cleanliness.

JR: Oh, yeah. I remember.

CB: Then you'll recall the agreement also states that should you decide to leave the project, any attempt to build a similar product outside of Cleanliness would be considered intellectual property theft and would be prosecuted to the full extent of the law.

JR: I am aware of that too.

CB: As it stands, the full extent of that law includes a custodial sentence of up to fifteen years. Especially for a product so vital to the survival of the species, as it were. If someone were seen to be taking actions to profit personally from such a product, the courts would take a very dim view of that indeed.

JR: That would be bad, wouldn't it?

CB: It would be difficult for us to proceed without you. It might mean the end of the carbon capture solution we are so close to cracking.

JR: (Laughs) *We…*

CB: And of course, we would also have to consider what happens in relation to the Lara Bennett matter. *If* you were no longer a Unity affiliate.

JR: What do you mean by that?

CB: I mean we want to help you.

JR: Then why doesn't it feel like it?

***

The last document is a ConservUnity non-disclosure agreement tying Jack in more legal knots, but I don't even get past the first page.

They *blackmailed* him into working for them. Why would Tyler want me to see this? And why would she leave all this stuff in my hands? Unless it's all lies.

Was Gabe right about Langford having Hallie's brother killed? Was he involved in Lara Bennett's disappearance? No wonder Jack was in such a state when he gave me the prototype.

But there's a little chirping voice in the back of my mind. The tiny but incessant drilling keeps saying this: if he did nothing wrong, then why would he allow himself to be blackmailed? I mean, can you even blackmail someone with something they haven't done?

How sure are you, Essie? How sure he doesn't know what happened to Lara?

Yeah, he was gentlemanly enough when we met those times, even when I tried to suck his face off. But he would be, if he was under suspicion for something bad that happened to another girl.

Tyler's file has no information on the police investigation into Lara's disappearance. Whether that's a deliberate omission or because she doesn't have the documents, I can't be sure. Either way, I'm in the dark about how seriously Jack is caught in this. What I am certain of is he must be desperate if he agreed to move to CU. If they're as bad as he makes out in the transcript.

And your stalker, Essie?

No. No, no, no. Jack wouldn't do that. He understands how alone I am, how scared I was even though I pretended I wasn't. It was Toby. Toby came to the flat to hassle me. And broke in again.

Did he?

It wasn't Jack.

People like him seek out people like you…

But if it *was* Jack behind those vile messages, why didn't Tyler include that evidence in the file? That would have been the clincher, wouldn't it?

Nausea overtakes me again and I clutch my stomach, head stabbing, until it passes. What the hell was that stuff they gave me?

Tired of thinking, I message Jack: *We need to talk.* After it's sent, I remember Jack had a personal email address on the uni letter. Doesn't matter. They've probably hacked that, anyway.

There's no doubt somebody other than Jack is reading that right now, but I have no choice. I pause for a moment, staring at my phone as if expecting an instant response from him.

It's a long time before I can send the next three messages, the same words for different reasons. *Please call me* to Hallie, Maya and Gabe's phones. I want to call Lawrence, see if the prototype is safe, but that would be crazy.

For a few minutes, I can't bring myself to tie up the phone just in case. But I ring Seth back in the end. Because it's starting to dawn on me he's all I have.

Chapter Nineteen

Three weeks later, everyone is talking about Christmas. Maya is still missing—I can't think about tinsel and fairy lights. Even her parents are losing heart. They keep making the trip down from Liverpool, doing interviews with the police, the press, praying for a thread of hope. I haven't seen them or replied to their messages. How can I look them in the eye, knowing what I do?

The only part of her I have is the blood on the green chiffon scarf from Langford's cellar. They can't have seen it when they raided Seth's. I keep it in my bag—can't help it. To leave it behind would seem like another betrayal. The blood is flaking off. Soon even that will be gone, along with the fading scent of her vanilla perfume. Or perhaps it's just my memory of her smell.

I should have handed it in to the police, but there's no way to do that without admitting we were at that house. And what would be the point? There's zero chance they'd investigate Langford for Maya's disappearance. I bet they're covering up for him. They'd just throw me in jail for trespass, or criminal damage, or whatever. So, I keep it with me.

Lawrence is still under suspicion, real or fabricated. They haven't charged him with anything, or I would have heard. I haven't seen him since that day at the derelict hospital. All I got were two words in a message—*it's safe*—a couple of weeks ago, then radio silence. I think Hallie has skipped town—whether to join Gabe or escape him I don't know, or care, anymore.

I'm living in the old flat, after a brief return to the vicarage. It was getting weird with Seth—somehow tense. He said he didn't want me to leave, but it didn't ring true.

Dealing with all those messed up people all day, he didn't need another one lounging on his sofa when he got home. And anyway, short of locking me in the vestry, which would have opened a whole new can of weirdness, there's nothing he could do to keep me there. He settled for helping me get the lock fixed and a bolt fitted to the inside of the door.

I'm at the Braai every morning at seven to open up, like the old days. Back on permanent earlies, I finish around three, depending on how much prep Bri wants me to do for the dinner service. On the way home, I stop off to buy cider and some junk food for tea. Then I go home, bolt myself in, close the curtains and huddle in front of the telly until bedtime. When the power's out, I do some sketching by the light of my one remaining gas lamp, try not to think. Most of the time I find I'm drawing Maya, believing she's still alive —maybe scared and hiding.

Those letters, *E...S,* in the coal.

She *was* alive.

Tonight, I'm sketching Seth, just shading his chin when a message drops from Jack.

I'm so sorry. For everything.

Grabbing the laptop, I type with furious fingers.

Where have you been? I've been losing my mind.
His reply: *I know, sorry. Can we meet?*

I'm scared. Of who he is, what he might have done—and what I might do to him.

I type: *Need to think.*
Jack: *Understood. Sorry just—is it safe?*

Good question, Jack. My fingers pause over the keyboard. What can I tell him?

Me: *Yes.*

That's my best guess anyway.

Jack: *Thank you. It's asking too much, all of this.*

I shake my head, in disagreement or disbelief. But the conversation ends there because there's no right response for him.

He's left me feeling agitated, so I open the radio app. A jaunty Wham! song is playing—the website tells me it was number one fifty years ago today, as the DJ talks incongruously about a plane hijacking in the same week. I return to sketching Seth's chin.

Goodnight Essie, Jack says.

Though I daren't post anything, the forums have pulled me back in.

There's still an awful lot of anger about the CU conspiracy theory on PolitiWorld. I itch to tell them it's all true, but how long would it take for them to bust my door back down? Maybe going online wasn't such a good idea. Too much temptation.

***

A few days later, I'm walking home from the Braai. A fine mist with needles of drizzle is hitting my face when my phone rings. I glance at it and read Lawrence's name with a jolt.

"Lawrence?"

"Essie," Lawrence blurts. "I don't have much time, but… they found her."

My heart wakes up kicking. "Maya?"

"Yes." His voice cracks.

"She's alive?"

A pause. I stop walking, close my eyes, the phone clamped to my ear by a rigid hand.

Please… please….

Then, in a shaky whisper: "Oh, God, sorry. I mean they found her... her body."

I give a choking cry, only now realising how much hope I have been clutching. My legs fold, and I thud onto the damp pavement. My free hand covers my mouth as I gag in shock, and for a minute I think I'm about to vomit all over the stones. "No, Lawrence," I moan. "No... no... no..."

"Please." He's crying too. "Don't."

I can't stop. The world around me shuts down. Even my vision is fading, closing in from the outside, disappearing into a blackness I almost welcome.

Not Maya... no... please.

"Essie, listen to me." Lawrence's voice is sharp enough to snap an arm. I grow quiet, but I haven't the strength to get to my feet, just sit there in the middle of River Street, listening, rain soaking through my jeans. People are stepping around me, glancing down. No one stops.

"Lawrence, where did they find her? What—?"

"They're coming for me." Lawrence whispers.

"The police? Lawrence, you have to run."

"Yes. I just needed to tell you where... shit. Oh shit, Essie, they're here already."

"Lawrence!" I scream. "What's happening?"

There's a bang and a splintering sound, then a clatter so loud it almost pierces my ear drum. Like he dropped the phone. Or threw it.

"Lawrence?"

They're yelling for him to get down on the floor. There's the sound of blows landing in the distance, and Lawrence cries out in pain.

"LAWRENCE!" I struggle to my feet and start running, though God knows where. Lawrence is six or seven miles away, in Worcester.

There are more thumps, more screams and shouting. The phone goes dead. Gasping, I try to call him back but there's just a single, mournful out-of-service tone. I turn in circles on the pavement as if to read the answer in the River Street shop fronts. They're going to pin Maya's murder on Lawrence. We knew they would try, but it's really happening.

A sickening shock hits me. What if they know he has the prototype? The paving stones warp and stretch beneath me.

This time I know where I'm running to.

I don't know what he's done, if I can trust him, but he needs to know. My lungs are burning when I reach my front door.

Jack, I type into the laptop. *It's gone. I'm sorry.*

There's an immediate reply*: Are you referring to what I think you are?*

Me: *I think I am. I'm sorry. I can't explain on here. Can we meet?*

Jack: *We'd better. 8 tonight? Same place?*

Me: *Okay. I'm sorry.*

This time it's Jack who doesn't reply, but I'm not waiting for it.

As if it can bring Maya back, or make it not have happened at all, I climb under my duvet and scream over and over into my pillow. By the time I fall into a broken doze, there are more tears than feathers inside it.

***

On the way to the river, I overhear more than one conversation about Maya, and try to close my ears to it. It's impossible—everyone's talking about her. Against my will, I learn that they found her in a muddy ditch on a lane, the other side of town to Langford's house. There was no effort to conceal her body. They had no need for that, with a scapegoat lined up already. Her clothes were torn, and she had been beaten, and several people say shot. I drop my head and close my eyes, tears squeezing out of their corners. But closing them doesn't stop that image of her lying on Langford's lawn. My stomach convulses, forcing a hand to my mouth.

I pull my coat tighter around me. It's cold tonight and that should offer some relief, but it just makes my bones ache. In no time I'm on Worcester Road, outside the Braai. Through the window, Brian is sitting among his patrons, laughing at one of their jokes. It's just a window between us, but I've never been further away from the world that Brian inhabits, with its tasty food and warm lighting. I turn away from the glow and press on to the river.

Jack's sitting on Lila Etheridge's bench again, beside her plaque, staring at the water. Even seated he looks stooped, older. As I sit next to him, he offers me a cigarette, lights mine with a disposable lighter, and then sparks up his own.

"Didn't know you smoked." I blow a smoke ring to distract myself.

"I don't," he says, taking a profound drag. "Gave up five years ago."

"Well done, you."

"No one followed you?"

I shake my head, hoping I'm right. We smoke in silence for a minute. Angry with him for lying to me, I wait for him to make the first move. Still, I've let him down, too. We don't seem to be any good for each other these days.

"You lost the prototype?" His voice is tight.

"I'm sorry. Lawrence… took it from me. I tried to stop him. He said he had a plan, but I don't know what."

"Who's Lawrence?"

"Maya's boyfriend."

Jack sighs. "So, you told him about it?" He throws his cigarette into the river.

I give him an irritated side-eye. "We went to Gabe for help, like you asked," I say, bitterness rising in me. "Went to him, and all he did was blackmail us into…"

"Into what?" Jack frowns.

"Never mind." I crush my cigarette under my heel, take a breath in and blow it out, trying to slow my heart. "I asked Gabe, and he wouldn't help me. So I was going to ask Lawrence, but I changed my mind. But he found the prototype anyway in my bag, and he took it. Now they've arrested him."

All of this comes out in a splurge, like being sick on the floor.

"Christ, Essie."

"They don't know he's got the file," I say, hoping that's the truth. "And Lawrence doesn't know about you. He says it's safe, but I don't know where it is now." My hand rests on his shoulder. "I'm sorry." My voice shatters into a sob.

He puts his arm around me and pulls me closer. "It's not your fault, Essie. I should never have got you involved."

I shake my head against his chest.

There was nothing else you could do, because they've got you where they want you, haven't they, Jack?

Why can't I say this out loud? The words die on my numb lips. Perhaps saying it would make it real. Or I don't want to hear the answers.

He pulls away a little. "What did they arrest him for? Lawrence."

That poleaxes me. While I expel hysterical, hiccupping sobs, gasping for breath, he clutches my forearm.

When I can talk, I tell him about Maya. Which leads back to how she died—the whole mess with Gabe and his vendetta, the night at Langford's house. I don't want to tell him any of this, but the words burst free without permission.

Slowly, I gain control enough to hold back the whole experience with the police, Kerry Tyler, the stuff about Lara. And Seth's help. Seth's taken enough risks for me already, and Jack doesn't need to know about him right now. I can't lose another friend. That would kill me.

Jack's eyes are wide and glassy. "Jesus Christ," he says. "Are you sure?"

"I was *there*. I saw her go down." My voice catches, and I swallow down the bile. "If I hadn't almost broken my neck in a rock fall, I'd be dead too."

He stares at me, his jaw clenched, then looks ahead. We sit in silence, gazing at the cold river. The moon is glistening on the surface of the water, the way it was the night Gabe hung his first banner. If I hadn't come down here that night and seen it, would any of this ever have happened?

"Maybe Lawrence is being straight," I say. "And the prototype *is* safe."

"Maybe. But he'd better have put it somewhere really clever, because they'll have searched his place by now." He chews a fingernail, then picks at it with his other hand. "Do you think he'll talk?"

"I don't think so. Like I said, he doesn't know who you are. They're after him for Maya, not the prototype."

"Doesn't mean he won't offer it up though. As a sweetener."

"Lawrence wouldn't do that. He wants that thing made more than you do."

"But does he want it more than staying alive?"

He offers me another cigarette, has one himself and we sit and smoke them down to the filters without speaking once. He glances up and down the river path, takes my hand in his cold ones.

He pushes a little card into my palm and squeezes my fingers. "We can't use messages anymore. They're watching our accounts."

"I know."

"My personal number is on that card, use that one. Not the work one—that's monitored. Anything happens, anything at all, you ring me, okay? Doesn't matter what time it is. If Lawrence contacts you, if you find out where the prototype is, if they come after you… anything. Okay?" He takes another phone out of his pocket and hands it to me. "Use this phone. They'll be listening to yours."

"Yeah. Jack—"

"I have to go. We've been here too long already."

He stands up stiffly, glances around again, then down at me, his brow furrowed. "I'm so sorry about your friend, Essie."

True to form, he turns and leaves.

203

Chapter Twenty

The smells of mud and oily water drift up from the docks. They're a couple of miles away across a craggy park and cityscape wrapped in smog, but there's no mistaking that river scent. Seth and I trudge up the slow sweep of the hill from the pub, towards the church at the summit.

I walk on cold, numb legs, and it feels like the fog has seeped inside my head. Once there, it started screaming Maya's name.

We're bent against the whipping wind and rain. There's a powerful gust, and Seth grabs my hand to stop me getting blown into the road. We scurry on, and the church crawls into view, just over the brow. It's a dark stone gothic affair. The plain-type black and white sign at the gate says *Parish of Liverpool. Unity St George's*.

A glum, angular graveyard sits to the left as we approach the archway at the entrance. A few people are arriving just ahead of us, but no one lingers outside in the storm. As they file into the church, they reveal Brian, who loiters, smoking. His eyes are bloodshot and dark-circled, and the aroma of cigarettes on him makes me want one badly.

"Essie." Brian squeezes my shoulder. "Seth."

As we enter together, soft piano music is playing over the speakers either side of the altar. Brian murmurs something, then goes to join Mark and Sophie, huddled together on a pew a few rows from the front. It's almost a relief there's no space near them. My eyes fix on the back of their heads dipping sombrely, as if in prayer.

I've never spoken to any of them about the police. Or asked Brian what he told them. If I can't trust Brian, that's the last piece of scaffolding gone, and what happens then?

But the weight of the things we haven't said drags between us, too heavy to ignore, even for Maya's funeral.

They've removed half of the wooden pews and spread colourful prayer mats on the floor. The remaining seating is scattered at random intervals. There are people already praying. Others sit murmuring to each other.

The cleric, wearing white, bustles around a table in front of the altar. She turns and hands cups of something to Maya's mum and dad, and joins them on a nearby mat. Her mouth moves, but only the occasional sibilant carries. Maya's mum bows her head for a moment, then lifts it and smiles at the cleric. I want to go to them, but what can I say?

"Come on." Seth tugs gently at my hand.

A hard, bitter knot forms in my stomach as we find a pew. At each place is a single, beautiful photo of Maya. It's one of the studio shots she had done for her portfolio. She made me go with her that day in case the photographer was dodgy. She needn't have worried: I think he was more scared of us. In the picture, she's flashing her sexy, lopsided smile at the camera, like she's just said something sassy but not unkind.

My eyes blur with tears.

The church is decorated for Christmas, with holly and winter wreaths, and a tall spruce scattered with synthetic candles, which they have left unlit for the occasion.

Behind us, people crowd inside, many dressed in white with headscarves. The church is full, but there's nobody else from Balmford. No Lawrence.

They wouldn't grant permission for him to attend, even accompanied by prison officers. He must be frantic about not being here. I wrote to him to say I'll be thinking about him, but I doubt if he got the letter.

The cleric stands and helps Maya's dad up with a gentle arm. He shuffles over to join a crowd of men gathering at the altar. All of them wear white robes and look careworn and broken. They arrange themselves into rows, Maya's dad in the front. Behind us, the heavy wooden door opens to reveal a small white-clad group outside.

Someone at the front sounds a sweet, clear note for a

couple of beats and they all join in. It's the purest sound I've ever heard from the mouths of these haggard and chipped men. My tears spill as their voices soar. Seth grabs my hand, and he's crying too.

The group on the porch come forward. They're carrying someone.

Maya.

She's hidden, wrapped in a heavy white shroud, but the folds of the sheet trace the narrow curve of her shoulders. It's Maya lying on that wicker stretcher. It's the shape of her neck, her arms.

The fabric is pock-marked by raindrops, surrounded by red and yellow flowers. Though she passes within a foot of me down the nave, I can't reach her. My fingers probe inside my bag and stroke the green scarf.

As Maya and her attendants approach the front of the church, the choir crescendos and fades. The cleric takes her position at the lectern and the pallbearers lower Maya reverently to the floor before the altar. Draped in the shroud, she still looks naked and unprotected lying up there on her own. The choir and pallbearers bow to her and file away, taking positions on prayer mats and pews. Maya's dad eases himself down next to her mum.

There's silence, then rain pelting against the stained glass and the wrenching sobs of Maya's mum.

When the cleric speaks, it's in Arabic and I don't know what she's saying, but it doesn't matter. There are murmurs of response from the congregation. Seth joins in too, squeezing my hand briefly, and I feel like I'm intruding in a club where I don't belong.

Some of those on prayer mats bend to touch their foreheads to the floor, joining the cleric in the melodious chanting. I close my eyes, carried away on the waves of sound, my head spinning, my stomach churning.

The cleric uses English now, with soft inflection. She talks about Maya as a friend; the endurance of love, of God's love, of loved ones who will never lose her, and who will one day walk together with her again.

I try to find comfort in this, like I've tried before. But the hole I have in me is one person bigger. The tears are still falling but they're slower, more bitter, and I don't want relief from them. Seth reaches for my hand again, but I pull away. When I swallow, the hard, acrid lump in my chest is lodged there. Maya's mum is crying, and that's her place. I have no right, so I bite it in, rub the tears away.

The cleric introduces Maya's sister Leila, who speaks in a shaky but strong voice about Maya's sense of humour; her talent, her temper, her vanity, her kindness. At the end, she remains standing at the microphone.

A young man rises from a prayer mat at the front and sits at the huge church organ I hadn't noticed before. The first few notes he plays rip a hole in my heart even before Leila starts to sing *Ave Maria*. She sings in Arabic, and I don't know if the words are the same. They can't be, but the melody is unmistakable. Her voice is exquisite, pure and resolute.

We had *Ave Maria* at my family's funeral. It was partly a nod to Mum's intermittent Catholicism but also because I could never resist it. My heart still shatters when I hear it— although most of the rest of that day is a merciful blur now. I wonder if this one will be too. How can that be? Why wouldn't it be burned into my memory by the pain?

We all stand as Maya's body is carried away down the nave again. Her parents gather themselves and walk with exhausted dignity after her, other close family following with the cleric at the rear. Her mum is smiling at people as she leaves. She recognises me as she passes, reaches out and cups my tear-crusted cheek in her hand, then moves on. They follow Maya out into the storm.

My legs hold me up long enough to see them go, then I collapse onto the pew. Some of the tension left the room with Maya, and a melancholy relief takes its place. People murmur to each other in the congregation. Leila stands at the lectern, looking stranded up there now she has finished singing. I try to rise on shaky legs, meaning to approach her, but she turns and hugs the young organ player. I wonder if he's Maya's brother as Leila makes her way towards the door, stopping to talk to people.

"Essie." She bends to give me a hug. "Thank you for coming."

Her voice is soft and mildly scouse. So much like Maya's it hurts to hear it.

"No problem," I say, feeling stupid. "This is Seth. He… loved Maya too."

"I'm sorry for your loss." Seth's voice sounds calm and comfortable.

"Thank you." Leila flattens her lips and moves away.

Outside, the storm has died down to a swirly drizzle. The light is dull and oddly restful. I leave Seth chatting to the cleric and look for Maya's mum.

She's next to a stone buttress, talking to an elderly Asian man with a walking stick. I approach uncertainly, not wanting to break in, but she sees me and waves.

"Essie," she says. "How are you, sweetheart?"

She has the same slight Liverpudlian chime to her voice. The elderly man gazes at me.

"I'm… okay, thank you." You can't say you feel good at a funeral. "It was a lovely service."

"Thank you." Her eyes crinkle into a smile. How she can manage that, I don't know. "We have a talented family."

She reaches out her hand and Leila joins her, cuddling up to her wordlessly for a moment then stepping away.

My already-broken heart fractures again at the unconscious gesture. "I… I'm sorry Mrs Taheri, we have to go."

"It's okay. We're grateful you came so far for Maya today. She loved you, Essie."

I ache to tell her what happened to her daughter, to beg her forgiveness for my part in it. None of this is possible, and when I try to speak only a croak comes out.

Maya's mum puts her hand on my arm, and a mortifying, anguished sob bursts from me. She holds me in a warm, rose-scented hug, but it's all wrong. She should not be the comforter. Not today. I'm so ashamed fresh tears leak onto her shoulder, and she holds me tighter.

"Come on, Essie." Seth's voice is behind me, his hands guiding me away. I fall from her to him, hiding my face.

Over the top of my hair, he says, "I'm so deeply sorry for your loss, Mrs Taheri. Maya was a remarkable young woman. We all loved her very much."

That's how you behave Essie, you complete moron.

Seth leads me away, still sobbing, down the hill and back to the pub.

I fall into an empty sleep on the train home, my head rocking gently against the window. As we pull into New Street Station, I awake to find Seth's hand curled over mine.

***

Later, at home, I sit motionless, hollow, expecting to feel something—grief, relief, anger, loneliness.

There's only this unreal vibration in my head. Like I'm not here on the sofa in my own flat, but locked inside a circling drone. As if I might disappear into the drizzle outside and no one, not even me, would notice. I'm still in my funeral clothes: plain black dress with modest neck and hemline. Maya's green scarf is in my hands. I think it's to goad myself into grieving, but I feel nothing, except trapped.

My eyes seek the laptop, still showing the last page I read before leaving for Liverpool. In my daze, I forgot to shut it down. An article from the Birmingham University student paper, dated 9th October 2034.

Is the Government Suppressing Green Solutions?
Investigation by Francis Morris

We know we don't have much time left before the climate overcomes us. So why is this government pulling the funding for vital climate change research at a local university? Could it be to protect the enormous profits of the traditional power companies? *The Birmingham Question* is on the case, and will bring you answers…

When I press the back button, an almost identical article, with the same date stamp, comes up.

Is the Government Suppressing Green Solutions?
Investigation by Lara Bennett
We know we don't have much time left before the climate overcomes us. So why is this government pulling the funding for vital climate change research at this very university? Could it be to protect the enormous profits of the traditional power companies? *The Cryer* is on the case…

These twin articles. One by Lara, one by Hallie's brother. Were they friends, collaborators? This must be the story Hallie mentioned at our first *Change Here* meeting. The one that got her brother Francis killed, she said. Did the same thing happen to Lara? Detective Victoria said that Gabe blamed Langford for Francis' death. Was this article the reason? If Gabe's right, that would put Langford in the frame for Lara's disappearance too. Or her murder. And make Jack a convenient scapegoat, with their friendship all over campus.

And now Maya, too.

Bile rising in my throat, I type *Lara Bennett Worcester University missing 2034*. A local newspaper article is the first result, dated 28th October last year.

Local Student Still Missing.
Worcester student Lara Bennett, 19, has been missing for 4 days. She was last seen on the evening of 23rd October in a student bar accompanied by a male in his early thirties. Police are appealing for anyone who saw Lara that night, or might know the identity of the man she was with, to come forward and speak to them in confidence…

Oh, my God, Jack…

210

Were they trying to pin it on him? I should have trusted him. Told him I knew about Lara. Now it's too late. The buzzing in my head notches up. I close the browser and my eyes. That only intensifies the clamour, so I open them, and to distract my ears I put some music on the laptop. I listen to an old Radiohead song again and again.

On the screen, instead of a young Thom Yorke in a car, Langford sneers back at me. I fill up my glass with gin, down half, fill up, down all of it, and cough.

As I stare at the scarf, the green glimmers, and there's something else too. I know it's not real, but I see it.

E... S...

She was alive down in Langford's cellar. How long did they leave her, when she could have been saved? What did they do to stop her crying out? Screaming for me.

Alex Langford is a respected businessman...

Me and him in a room with no windows? He'd be a dead businessman.

I need to breathe the river again.

My keys, a torch and a knife go into my pocket. The knife that gouged *BITCH* into my table. I stuff Maya's scarf in my bag and escape into the damp, foggy air.

River Street is a whirl of celebration. Snowflake-shaped illuminations hang from the streetlights and glowing silver bells drape over my head.

I forgot. Christmas is the day after tomorrow. Seth'll be frantic trying to get everything done at church now. He lost a day to come with me to the funeral, and I never even thanked him. Just muttered a terse goodbye and turned away towards the flat.

I buy cigarettes at the newly refurbished shop next to *Kiss*. Another bottle of gin.

Bank Lane is empty of sleeping bags. Their occupants

211

have been arrested, harassed or just moved on so many times they've given up and sought somewhere else to carve out their days. I think of Andy, and I wonder where he is. I hope he found shelter from the storm.

But he's dead, I know that. Like Maya. Mum… Dad… Willow… Darya.

All the people on that train.

All the other trains.

The sleeping bags. The cellars.

And the people who speak out.

The vibration in my head resolves itself into a thrum of fury.

Broken branches are strewn across the road, but the river hasn't flooded. I sit on Lila Etheridge's bench and smoke. There's no moon to light the water tonight—it looks like a wide black hole surging to swallow the Earth.

I wish it would. Me first.

They've buried Maya, and someone has to pay for her death. To the wheels turning, it doesn't matter who. It helps, I guess, if an insignificant someone can be found to bear the cost, so the wheels can go on grinding.

They're pretending Lawrence came back from Scotland and killed her. So, the only one of us who bears no responsibility for Maya's death is facing the consequences.

No more.

Jack's card is in my hand. His personal number is there. It would be easy to dial it and talk to him. About the funeral. About the prototype. Beg him to help Lawrence and shut ConservUnity down. Put Langford in jail.

Jack wouldn't risk it. If that prototype works, it's one life weighed against billions of others.

Not just one life.

The screw top burns my hand as I open it. The gin burns my throat as I drink until I gag.

No. More.

I walk without knowing where. Just out of town. Away

from lights and life.

There's no memory of passing the train station, or climbing through the slash in the hedgerow. Gabe's portal. But that must be what I did, to be standing here under the fairy-lit trees again.

With no reason to hide, I march down the driveway this time. My four shadows bob about me. A hot, wet breeze blows in my face.

I have everything I need. A bottle. A lighter.

With a yank, I tear at the hem of my dress, ripping a section from the front. One last swig, and then I shove the fabric into the neck of the half-filled bottle.

"Langford!" I stride down his driveway to the door. "Come out and face me, you murdering bastard!"

Nothing.

Just my panting and alcoholic sweat. I check the nearby window, but the house is in darkness.

It's a cheap, polycotton dress, so the fabric wick burns as soon as I put the lighter to it, making me cough on the fumes. My skin sears. I lift the bottle to launch it at the window, unsure how long I have before it explodes.

Something cool presses into my temple, pushing my head to the side.

Gun.

My heart lurches, cold nausea in my chest.

"Put it down. Gently." The man's accent is weird. Like Southern USA, so it's not Langford. Of course, it's not. He's not coming out here.

I could disobey. Put up a fight. Throw the flames at him. But then he'll shoot me before I get a chance at Langford.

He bends with me as I place the burning gin on the ground, the gun never leaving my temple.

"Let's just be smart. No one needs to get hurt." His breath is on my neck.

A car revs behind us. The bottle stands quiet at my feet, the wick burning low, heat and ethanol stinging my nose.

"Good girl." He circles my waist and pulls me backwards, away from the flames. "That's right."

As he turns me with him, he gives me a prod towards the waiting vehicle. My feet move without conscious decision.

He opens the rear passenger door and motions me inside with the gun. "Get in."

When I don't move, he says, "You came here to meet the boss, didn't you?"

Not *meet* him, exactly.

And this guy forgot to search my pockets. I edge nearer the car.

Chapter Twenty-One

Bible Belt leans inside the car, shoves me over behind the driver's seat and climbs in. He points the gun at me, out of reach. He needn't worry, it's not escape I have on my mind.

The driver twists around, and the crew-cut, sneering lip and bicep bulges are unmistakable. Grabby Guy. He of the rib-cracking foot jab. Kerry Tyler's abuse monkey.

Kerry?

It's gratifying to see my scratch has left him with a scar.

I throw him a hate-filled grimace, but there's a stab of dread right where he kicked me. He looks way too alert, and my limbs are heavy and stiff, slow with gin. I lean my head back on the seat. My fingers trace the outline of the little knife in my pocket. They jerk away guiltily and instead fiddle with the torn hem of my dress. Bible Belt points his gun, his dark eyes glaring from behind fronds of sandy hair.

Keep it together, Ess.

Quiet and low, I let them think I've submitted. There'll be a chance later, when my head has cleared.

Why am I thinking of Willow right now? Of the time she caught Maya, Beth and me smoking behind The Grey Squirrel. The pub had been closed and boarded up for years, and a lot of local kids hung out there. We were about fifteen, smoking and giggling, standing around in the dense heat in stupid miniskirts, waiting for Beth's fella to turn up. Thinking about it, I bet it was Charlie she was seeing then—the same Charlie who's flouncing about in a copper's uniform these days, giving people the deadeye.

Willow was walking past on her way to work when she spotted us through the chicken wire fence. She had that frowning expression. I remember her eyes perfectly framed by the wire diamonds of the fence, her nose dead centre to the diamond below. She had no idea how silly she looked as she yelled for me to 'Drop that fag, now'. I just laughed at her.

Typically, Willow didn't tell Mum and Dad straight away. She waited until she could press her advantage. When I found out she'd been sacked for not turning up at work, we traded secrets. That was how we usually achieved our uneasy peace. Would I have kept all those secrets if I'd known they'd all be dead nine months later?

My ears whine with tension and booze as we drive on dark lanes. It's a snaking route, and the turns in the road make my guts churn. Grabby makes a murmured phone call on his earpiece, but I can't distinguish any words. Bet he's calling Langford. Or Kerry. Maybe both.

Our destination is indecipherable until we ease onto the main road into Worcester. Instead of crossing over the river into town, we stay on the western bank, heading north. Past clusters of houses and shops, the land becomes flat and industrial. As the water bends away to the east, we take a single-track road to meet it. The lane ends in a huge iron gate, which opens on our approach. I stare out of the window as we enter, my heart pounding, the ringing in my ears staccato.

It's a red brick Victorian factory, with tall sash windows. We glide onto cobblestones. Grabby pulls up on the far side of the courtyard.

Bible Belt slips out and opens my door. "Okay, honey, you're up."

Is he putting that accent on?

The gun points at my face as I climb out and sway against the car door. He slams it closed and steers me around the building to where Grabby is waiting. The air is warm, the smell of rain with the river water constricting my chest,

216

bringing waves of nausea.

Behind the façade, a gritty tarmac drive runs between the factory and a series of low-rise concrete buildings to our right. As they march me down it, cold white security lighting triggers to mark our progress. The bulbs blur in triplicate and I blink to clear the fog. Beyond these is a large shed with no windows. A low hum emanates from its walls. Probably a generator.

My legs tangle as we round the corner of the main building. Bible Belt grabs the neck of my dress to keep me on my feet. We walk along the rear of the building, stopping twenty yards short of the far corner, at a door set deep into the brick. To the left is a brass plaque. In shadow, but just about readable with swirly Victorian lettering.

ConservUnity, est. 2025.

My mind, not my hand this time, reaches for the knife, and my breathing swells. Langford could be right here. I'm close.

Grabby swipes a card against an entry system, it clicks, and Bible Belt pushes me ahead of them.

It's dark and cold inside, but at the other end of the hallway, light seeps under a door, bouncing off the tiles. Grabby moves ahead and pushes into the room, flooding light into the hall. The door pulls to behind him, and Bible Belt halts me in the fresh, silent gloom. In my ears, there's nothing but this needling whine and my own breathing.

Murmurs drift from the room, then Grabby's silhouette appears and gestures us in.

My lungs cramp as I stumble toward him. Grabby stays planted in the doorway, so I have to brush past him and his sneering face to get inside. How I'd like to punch that face. He moves to make way for Bible Belt then leaves.

One less to worry about…

I don't need anyone to tell me who the man waiting inside is. Broad enough to make his enormous mahogany desk seem

217

to scale, he looks like a retired heavyweight boxer in a sharp suit. A hint of bristle covers his shaved head, but it still glints in the angled spotlights. The sneer is the one I remember from the fireplace painting, the smugness from the magazine shots with Foster-Pugh.

He's reading a document, or pretending to. Swiping off his glasses, he slots them into the pocket of his waistcoat and squints up as we approach. The ringing in my ears kicks up a gear and my throat closes around a tight knot of hatred.

Bible Belt still has hold of my arm, and he brings me up a few feet from the desk. Langford's cold eyes snap up to mine.

He gestures to the chair in front of me. "Sit."

When I don't move, Bible Belt pulls me down, so I fall into the leather seat. He steps back, but looms over my shoulder, his threat heavy like the knowledge of the knife resting against my thigh.

"Do you know who I am?" asks the man behind the desk.

I nod, and then for devilment, point at the brass name plaque in front of him: *Alex Langford OBE,* in the same Victorian typeface as the sign outside.

"Last time I saw you, you were vandalising my house," he growls. "The cost of putting that right was more than you'll make in a lifetime." He screws up his eyes at me, but they still burn with fury through the lashes.

"You murdered my best friend." Though my voice is low, I shake with rage of my own.

He gives a flick of the head, a smirk. "Not me."

My hands itch to wrap round his throat, but Bible Belt is too close. I long for him to leave us alone.

"You left her to die. In your *basement*."

His mouth drops open, eyes bulge. It's only a moment, then he recovers, but my resolve bristles with pure satisfaction.

"I never met your scummy—"

"Maya. Was her name." My voice catches fire. "And we just buried her today. And she had more class in her little toenail than you could have in your wettest dream. Alex

218

Langford…O.B.E."

He rises, expels a contemptuous snort. "Oh? She had class, did she? Well, she didn't look very classy bleeding on my lawn."

"You f—" The word turns into a scream. My bag falls from my shoulder as I spring out of the chair onto the desk.

The knife is in my palm. He flinches back as I leap, but not far enough. The skin of his cheek gives way as the blade tears into it. I scream again. He roars like a bear, tries to slap me away. I cling to the desk, yelling, clambering forward to take a second shot. This time I'll go for the throat.

But it's *my* throat that takes a hit. Bible Belt is on me, one arm hooking into my windpipe. The other hand wrestles for the knife. I try to hold on, but the pressure weakens my grip. He yanks me backwards, spins and shoves. My face hits dark wood, my nose pressed to the varnished floorboards.

As I scramble to my knees, Bible Belt comes up behind me and kicks me down, then crouches to press the gun into my cheek. My muscles slacken and I lie panting and sobbing, nose bleeding.

I failed her.

Again.

Two gleaming black brogues plant themselves just shy of my face as the gun lifts away.

"Enough." Langford is gasping too. He crouches in front of me, face bleeding onto his shirt. His hand reaches up beyond my field of view and returns with the knife, still gleaming with his blood.

"That's enough," he whispers. "A *knife*?" He wipes the blade on the sleeve of my dress and pockets it. "What did you think was going to happen?"

As Langford's face recedes, Bible Belt's foot crushes into the top of my spine. "Are you gonna be good now, little girl?"

Exhausted and nauseous, I watch the black spots dance in my vision with the tiniest nod. He releases the pressure, yanks me up, and throws me in the chair. I huddle there, rubbing the back of my neck, blinking at the tears.

Langford dumps the contents of my bag on the desk: My phone, the scarf, purse, lipstick, cigarettes, lighter.

Jack's business card.

I close my eyes for a long moment.

Langford is interested in the scarf. He picks it up, runs it through his disgusting fingers. I can't tell from his expression if he recognises it.

Next, he searches through my purse, which doesn't hold his attention for long. He hands my phone to Bible Belt, who starts fiddling with it, pressing buttons.

"Code?" he barks behind me.

I could hold out, but what's the point? There are other battles to fight. "Twenty-four, zero four, thirty-three."

Langford gives me a wonky smirk. "Twenty-Four Four. The date of the attack that killed your family? Macabre."

How does he know that? "I try."

"Got it," says Bible Belt, like he's some kind of special agent, and taps buttons behind me. I glance his way, then down at my feet, worry cramping my face. Now they have everything—if they didn't before.

When I raise my eyes again, Langford is examining Jack's card, and I go cold.

"Well, well, Jack." He sniggers. "At it again, you dirty dog."

"That's not—"

"Oh, come on. It's not like I didn't know. This is a cutting-edge business we're dealing in here." He flips the card over. "Risky… Competitive. You don't think I'd employ anyone without a thorough understanding of who they are, do you?"

"So, you've been watching Jack." There's a prickle of fear in my rib cage.

He gives me a slow handclap. "Yay. You figured it out."

"Reading his messages. Tapping his phone?"

"You know, some say your generation's a dead loss, but with sharp minds like yours, the world's going to be in good hands."

That cuts through the remaining gin haze. "Well, we couldn't do any worse, could we?"

Calm it, Ess. He's trying to wind you up.

"I've been watching your friendship with Jack develop for some time, now," he says with a suggestive smirk. "It's cute."

"Oh, piss off," I mutter.

"Would you say Jack worries about you, Essie? Would you agree with that?"

Bible Belt slithers into my peripheral vision. He's holding my phone up to me as he moves. Filming.

"What the...? Turn it off." I spring up to grab the phone off him. He pulls it back, then with his free hand, pushes me away. I fall backwards into the chair with a bump, my teeth clamping painfully down on my tongue. A yelp escapes me, and Langford laughs.

"Woah. Pace yourself, girl," he says as Bible Belt resumes his filming. "It's going to be a long night."

Langford fiddles with Maya's scarf again, and I want to punch him.

"You're not the first, you know," he says. "Starstruck teenager, I mean. Jack's got a bit of a taste for it. Never right, is it? A man of his age."

"There are worse things, Alex." I raise my eyebrows. "And you're wasting your time. I know about Lara Bennett."

Bible Belt goes around to Langford's side of the desk, focussing the phone camera on my face as I glower at him.

"Do you?" says Langford in a supercilious voice. "Since you know so much, perhaps you can update me on Jack's whereabouts. He hasn't bothered showing up for work for a week."

"I don't...What the hell is wrong with you?" The last bit is to Bible Belt.

Bible Belt chuckles. "Enough, do you think?"

"Little bit more," says Langford. "Get some of the interrogation."

That's not a word I want to hear. I swallow, look up.

Langford leans forward on his desk. "And who do you think *furnished* you with the information about Lara Bennett?"

Did Kerry get that dossier from him? With Grabby, popping up everywhere like a rent-a-henchman, Tyler and Langford are obviously connected. Is Tyler in on the conspiracy to suppress Jack's research? She does work for Foster-Pugh, who's in it up to his neck.

Langford sighs, almost like he's bored. "There's a lot of things I know about Jack. And quite a lot of things I know about you."

"Such as?"

"You're a low-life criminal."

"That's rich."

"As well as vandalising my home, you have stolen my property."

"No." Though I know it's pointless.

Bible Belt moves closer, still pointing my own damn phone at me. I shoot him a glance of pure venom. Hope it kills him.

"And I'd like it back," says Langford. "So, I need you—or Jack if he ever shows up—to tell me where it is."

The penny drops, and now I know why Bible Belt is filming.

Langford takes my phone and addresses the camera. "So, Jack. Time to come out of the woodwork. Or are you planning to leave your girlfriend to clean up your crap again?"

"Jack," I scream. "Don't come here. He's—"

Bible Belt darts behind me and puts his hand over my mouth. I persist though, get his finger between my teeth, and clamp down. Bible Belt yells, yanks his hand away and smacks me on the side of the face with the other one.

By his smug grin, Langford got that on the footage. He plucks Jack's business card off the desk and fiddles with my phone.

As it makes the *message sent* noise, he sneers up at me. "We'll see, now, won't we?"

***

222

I keep seeing Willow's face. Perhaps I'm trying to channel some of her attitude to throw at Langford.

They've moved me to an enormous workshop. Its concrete walls and floor encase several rows of workbenches. They recede into half-darkness across the width of the room to windows that stretch high, almost to the ceiling twenty feet above us. They're screened with giant vertical blinds. The work surfaces are littered with bits of circuit board and components—steel cylinders that look like cheese graters, metal pipes, plastic.

On some of the benches, robotic arms lie dormant. To me they seem tense and watchful, like they're awaiting Langford's nod before they jump down and march towards me. There's a faint smell of electricity in here, and it's cold. This whole building is freezing.

Bible Belt has handcuffed me, each hand tethered to an arm of a chair near the first bench. To stop me attacking again? Possibly. Mostly for Jack's benefit, though, I think. I have nothing to fight with and though my head still buzzes with fury, I'm powerless. For now.

After a muttered conversation, Bible Belt hands the key to Langford and marches out.

We wait in silence. For an hour? Perhaps less, but the minutes swell before they pass.

Jack will come, despite my pleas. Where from, I don't know. Because thinking about it, I haven't heard from him in over a week either.

Langford dabs a hanky against his bloody cheek then plays with my knife, scraping it along the metal workbench he's leaning against, making a nerve-jangling screeching sound. In response, my left eye has developed a maddening twitch. Not my biggest problem, but its persistence makes me feel sluggish, weary.

I'm trying to look away—as far from him as I can. His bulk is still needling the edge of my awareness, and I know he's staring at me across the dim space.

"Taking his time, isn't he?" says Langford, making me jump. "Maybe he's not as bothered about you as we thought."

I pretend not to hear. Langford whistles tunelessly and I clench my teeth.

He pushes off the bench and stalks towards me, behind, in front again.

He holds the knife up, its pearly handle still soiled with his blood. "We could start without him."

My breathing grows shallow, like something's blocking my chest. I swallow bile and a dry, stale alcohol taste. When I close my aching eyes, Willow's face is there again, looking more mellow and sad than it ever did when she was alive. Her sharp eyebrows, so often lowered in a frown, are high in anguish.

"You think you're being a hero, is that it?" His voice grates the air. I open my eyes, and he's still pacing, his fist clamped on the knife. He stops in front of me and presses the knife under my chin. "Don't make me laugh."

My arms twitch against the cuffs. "I'm not taking hero advice from a greedy bastard bent on selling us out to save a few million in share dividends."

"It's *considerably* more than that." The knife pushes, cuts my skin, making me hiss. "And you stole my prototype."

"You stole it first."

He snorts. "You seem to find the idea of *commerce* difficult to understand."

"No, I get it. If you've got money, it's easy to *make* money." Warm blood tickles my neck. "Especially if you swoop in when all the work's done. And then screw the rest of us."

He presses harder with the knife. "That file is mine."

The blade burns.

"It was never yours, you murdering bastard. You'll—"

Langford slaps my cheek and my scream is as much hatred as pain. Droplets of blood fly across my vision.

Wiping the hand on his waistcoat, he looks like he's going to do it again. I flinch back. His phone beeps. A grin slithers across his face in the light from its screen.

Jack?

My heart hammers as I glare up at him. He fixes me with a stare, nostrils flaring, and pockets the knife.

The door from Langford's office bangs open. Jack staggers in, sprawling on the floor in front of me. Bible Belt follows, locking us all in the workshop, a look of gratification on his sharp face.

"Hello, Jack." Langford unbuttons his waistcoat and struts towards him, adjusting his shirt sleeves. "You're fired, by the way."

Jack struggles to a sitting position, but has no time to stand "Yeah? Well I resign." His voice is muffled by a bleeding lip, and his eyes are wide and watery as Langford towers over him like an abusive father. He peers past Langford's legs at me, eyes bulging as he takes in the handcuffs and blood.

"Get up," Langford says.

Jack scrambles to his feet, rising to his full height—at least six inches shorter than Langford. He backs away. "I think we should—"

"Shut up." Langford advances on him. "Where is it?"

"Where's what?" Jack asks as he flattens against the wall. His eyes flick back to me for a moment. "What have you done, Alex?"

"Jack, I'm *fine*." I'm not, but I have to do something. "Everybody just… relax."

Langford shoots me a sharp glare, but gestures to Bible Belt, who drags a swivel chair over next to me. Langford grabs Jack by the collar, spins and throws him. It's left to Bible Belt to prevent him clattering headfirst over the back of the chair. Jack struggles against the hold, punches Bible Belt in the gut, forcing him backwards, coughing. But he comes back, delivering a heavy smack to Jack's face, giving him a bloody nose to match his swelling lip.

"Stop." I look pleadingly at Jack.

His shoulders slump as Bible Belt shoves him into the chair and cuffs his hands behind him. Langford looms in front of us. Jack is breathing wetly through his nose. He eyes Langford with helpless loathing.

Langford drags another chair in front of Jack and sits on it backwards, his legs straggling the sides like an enormous, malevolent showgirl. "So, Jack?" he murmurs.

"You're wasting your breath. I've no idea where it is."

"But you did steal it."

Silence.

"Jack?" he says, harsher this time.

Jack nods, his eyes on the floor.

Langford gives a corresponding nod. "Yeah, you did. And why would you do that?" He's so close that if Jack lifts his head they'll touch noses. Langford's eyes rove Jack's face for a bizarrely intimate moment.

Jack shrugs. "Long story."

Langford pulls back and laughs. "I've got all night."

Jack looks up at him, lips clamped shut, eyebrows angled in a tortured expression, then his eyes slide away, towards the door.

"Door's locked," says Langford. "So… we got to the part where you stole the prototype from my company. Then you destroyed all the records. What's next?"

My shoulders cramp. My ribs seem to squeeze my heart into a knot so painful it makes a kick for freedom.

I'm next.

Chapter Twenty-Two

Not waiting for an answer, Langford rises and skips his chair towards me. It's a graceful move that reminds me of a cabaret again, but it's even less funny this time.

"You have the prototype now, don't you?" he says, cold eyes on me. "Don't lie."

"I don't—"

"She hasn't got it, Alex." Jack's voice splinters.

"The bitch can speak for herself." Langford's eyes are still on me.

I glower, but I'm grimly satisfied with the impression I've given him.

"You were about to tell me you don't know where the prototype is." He pushes his face close to mine, his breath puffing into my eyes. The back of his hand raises. "Go ahead and finish telling me that."

My heart is beating so hard and fast its rhythm echoes in my breath. I can't throw Lawrence under a bus. He's probably facing a life sentence. A sitting duck, stuck in prison where they can get to him whenever they like.

I fix Langford with a defiant smirk, raise an eyebrow and say, "I don't know where the prototype is."

He drives the back of his hand across my face, snapping it to the side. My chair rolls backwards with the impact.

"Stop!" Jack shouts.

"I'm okay," I say, but my face is burning.

Langford paces around the workshop picking up random detritus from the benches, throwing it back down. He's searching for something. Weapons… implements. Oh, Christ.

"Alex, please," says Jack, and in his voice is the edge of my own terror. "Let's talk about this."

"I'm finished talking to you," Langford says.

With a grunt, he abandons his search and wrests my knife from his pocket. A terrified squeak escapes me and Jack gasps out a curse. Langford reaches us in a quick moment and switches his eyes between us, his mouth twitching into a twisted smile. He leans towards me. The knife presses into my throat, stinging.

"No!" screams Jack.

Langford pulls back but keeps the blade high. Almost hypnotised, I watch my blood trickle down the handle, pooling in a hollow at the base of his thumb.

Langford's eyes burn into me. "Now, you talk to me, or there'll be more where that came from."

I close my eyes, sense Langford get closer, pause and pull away. When I open my eyes again, he's leering over Jack, whose head is so far back it's going to snap off.

"You've been way more trouble than you're worth. They told me you were the only one that could do this job. But everyone's expendable in the end."

Langford moves the blade to Jack's cheek, and swipes down. Jack screams, the left side of his face awash with blood.

He sneers back at me. "So, Essie. You tell me what you did with my file, or you're gonna be peeling bits of Jack off the floor."

There's no way out of this unless we surrender the prototype. Maybe they'll let us live if we go far away somewhere and stay there. That means Lawrence will go down with us, but he'll be alive if we can make a deal.

Maybe.

My mouth won't form the words, though. The tiny part of my brain still in control is refusing to budge.

"Okay, then." Placing the knife on the bench, Langford rifles through a drawer beneath. Eyes gleaming, he pulls out a hair dryer with a long handle, but no lead. I blink.

There's a click and a roar. The hair dryer shoots out a jet of blue fire.

Not a hair dryer. A blowtorch.

Langford's face stretches in a poisonous grin as he stalks towards Jack, the flame still spitting.

Jack whimpers. My breath is frozen. I try to swallow the nausea.

A phone rings behind us. I forgot Bible Belt lurking in the shadows back there. He holds out the phone. Judging by his relaxed posture, he's not in the least bit rattled by Langford's violence. "It's Kerry."

My eyes dart up to Langford's pinched face as he drops the blowtorch on the bench with a huff.

He snatches the phone. "Kerry, I'm a bit busy at the minute," he snaps, then listens. "No, I didn't see that. But we're nearly there, anyway." More listening. "You don't... Okay, hang on." He gestures to Bible Belt to unlock the door.

Murmuring on the phone, Langford leaves the room, then pops his head back in and beckons Bible Belt. He leaves too, locking us in.

Silence.

As we wait, I try to get a handle on what just happened, what will probably start happening again soon. My head is thumping with gin and horror, a burning in my chest to match the one at my bleeding throat.

"I'm sorry," says Jack. He sounds close to tears. "So sorry."

I shake my head. There's a camera mounted on the wall above the door, its gaze focused on us, red light blinking. Can they hear us if we talk?

Careful, Ess. Don't take any risks.

"What happened to Lara Bennett, Jack?" My voice is quiet, shaky.

He stares at the floor. In a whisper, he says, "This isn't a good time to talk about it."

I laugh bleakly. "When's good, then? Just asking 'cos we're going to be dead in about fifteen min—"

"I've no idea what happened to Lara, okay?" He's almost pleading. "That's the truth."

"Why me?" It hits me about two seconds afterwards that this is what I should have asked in the beginning

"What do you mean?"

"I mean why did you choose me that night?"

"What night?" His eyebrows rise.

I glance at him, irritated. The twisting motion burns the cut on my neck.

He snaps his head forward, as though to avoid my gaze. "You seemed... vulnerable. I was worried about you."

"Like you were worried about Lara?"

He clears his throat and swallows with a gulp in a naive display of uneasiness. I might have found it disarming once, but now it's just childish and grating.

"Because to me it's starting to look like you've been..." I can't think of a better word for it, "... grooming me."

His brow creases. "What the hell does that mean?"

"I'm young. I've got no one. My family are all dead. No one to intervene, if you should start... asking too much."

He flinches from the words he used himself. Good.

"You used me. You knew I'd do anything you asked, so you gave me that file and made me your mule."

"No," he snaps. "No. It wasn't like that. I honestly thought you could help. That you cared about this stuff."

"Don't. That's not fair. You know I do."

He shrugs.

A flare of anger scorches my insides. "Did you use Lara too? Like this? Some other way?"

"Lara was in trouble. She... had problems."

"Yeah, but did she have problems before she met *you*?"

Jack whips his head around. His cheek is still bleeding, and for a moment I wonder how we would appear to a casual observer—handcuffed to chairs in a locked room, soaked in blood, having this particular conversation.

He's looking at his feet now. He's more distressed than when Langford had the blowtorch. His pain gives me no joy. He's right—this is hardly the time. Still, now the box is open I can't close it.

"I read the article she wrote, Jack. About the withdrawal of your research grant. The suppression of climate change solutions. Did you ask her to publish it?"

"No!" His eyes are wide now, fixed on me. "I didn't realise she was going to do that, I swear."

"All the same, you bitched to her about it, didn't you? Got her on the case?"

He's shaking his head, tears in his eyes.

I glance up at the camera, aware this is reckless. I can't seem to stop, though. "And she got someone else involved, didn't she? Francis Morris. My friend's brother. He printed the same article in Birmingham. It got him killed."

Jack won't look at me, so I can't tell if this is news to him. I doubt it.

"Do you think the same thing happened to Lara?"

He nods once, slowly, his wet eyes fixed on the concrete floor. "Please…"

"Were you in love with her, Jack? I bet you were. There are *pictures* that say you were. Stop lying." I sob. "Just stop lying to me. You owe me that."

Jack stamps his feet in frustration. "For fuck's sake," he says. "She was pregnant, okay?" He glares at me. "I was trying to help her. I won't say any more than that. You already know too much. About someone you'll never meet and have no business knowing *anything* about. Are you satisfied?"

I glare at him, and he glares back, his teddy bear eyes burning with fury. We both breath raggedly into the silence.

"Was it your baby?" The question makes me nauseous. Though my tone is careful, his whole face clamps down, cold.

"No," he says. "And fuck you."

These last words slap against me, and drape between us like venomous bunting.

We ignore each other for a long time. I'm crying—and Jack is too, judging by his steady sniffing.

He's right.

Kerry Tyler wanted to get in my head, so she gave me enough bait to rattle me, just to see what I did next. What I did is what I always do—to go off half-cocked and make things worse. I swallow the knot rising in my chest.

All the same, Jack did use you, Essie.

And he can't wriggle out of that, no matter how indignant he plays it.

We sit like that, in freeze frame, for what surely must be hours. No one comes and neither of us speaks. Gradually, the tension between us subsides. Probably not because we forgive each other, more that we're both exhausted. I can hardly believe this is all happening on the same day we buried Maya. But the evidence is there each time I look down and see my torn funeral dress.

Every part of me is numb or aching. I glance at Jack to see how he's doing. At first, he looks like he's sleeping. His head is bowed, his red-brown hair hanging in his face, blood trickling onto his chest from the cut.

He turns with a little shaky smile. "I'm sorry. The Lara thing is just…."

The door opens. We both jolt upright.

Kerry's wearing jeans and a Christmas jumper. Her hair, though, is pulled into the usual sleek French pleat. Stilettoed boots clack on the concrete as she approaches us, riding a cloud of fresh, soapy perfume.

She switches her gaze from Jack to me, a flicker in her eyes. Her mouth and brow pull down in what might be shock at our condition. Neither of us responds with anything but a glare.

She tilts her head towards the door. "Lenny!"

In comes Grabby, followed by Langford. Bible Belt locks us all in again and lingers by the exit.

Kerry folds her arms. "Alex, can we remove the steel bracelets please?"

Langford nods to Bible Belt, who releases first Jack then me from the handcuffs.

The moment my left wrist is free, I've no idea what happens to my mind. The gin must still be swimming in there, because all the fear and pent up bitterness brims over. As Bible Belt steps behind us, I dive at Kerry, my hands reaching for her throat. If I'd thought it through, I would have realised I'd never get to her. But there's no thought at all, only rage.

"Bitch!" I scream, as Grabby seizes me from behind and drags me away. He throws me to the floor and towers over me, tense and ready to spring if I try again. Kerry stands impassive, only blinking at me a little.

"Not sure I deserved that," she says, voice even. "But my ex-husband would back you up, no doubt." She slips closer, and sideways to seal our eye contact around Grabby. "You should have come to me, Essie. We could have avoided this."

My lip curls. "Why would I come to you? Unless I felt like being fucked over again."

She pivots a little and turns a sly, lash-lined smirk on him. "Hello, Jack. I've heard such a lot about you. I'm pleased to meet you in the flesh."

Langford looms out of the shadows. His eyes are feverish and focused. "Okay. We're all here. Let's crack on."

Chapter Twenty-Three

Langford prowls towards us as I hunker on the floor, but Kerry holds out a hand to block his way.

Her eyes linger on me. "You still have no clue what you're up against, do you?"

Patronising cow. Only swear words come to mind, so I let it pass without comment, just a tic of my mouth.

"Let me help you." Kerry's voice is conspiratorial as she sits down next to me, so close our shoulders touch.

I lean away as she takes a slim device out of her pocket. She swipes and screens flash by—documents, pictures of Jack and me. I glimpse the picture of Jack and Lara at the ball. This is a copy of the file she gave me. The one which planted all the little seeds of doubt germinating tonight.

Bible Belt is holding another device up for Jack to see, and in its light, his face is flushed.

There's a picture of me leaving the Braai. *Swipe.* Me on River Street, passing the post office. *Swipe.* Me at my front door, taken from across the road. My shadow was taking pictures, and they have them.

Swipe.

There's an instant of searing heat in my nerve endings.

It's the inside of my flat. Belongings scattered, my defaced sketches, the *BITCH* etched into the table top, the torn family portrait.

"You broke into in my flat," I say.

Jack gasps. "What the… that's your *flat*?" He looks at Langford. "You did that?"

A chilly, feverish sensation steals over me, as if the world has spun off-kilter. Like the last six months of my life have been half-hidden the whole time.

234

"The death threats?" I only ask to bring myself back from the tornado that's hit me.

"Nope. That was, what's his name? Tony? Or else some random nut. Frankly, I don't care enough to find out. But it was useful." His mouth twists into a leer.

I swallow the nausea. "Why?"

Langford drifts over to the nearest workbench, where he dropped the blowtorch earlier. A cramp of fear knots my belly, but he only examines it, apparently fascinated by its form. "Leverage. You never know when you're going to need it." He triggers the burner for a moment, and Jack jolts in his chair. "It was a concern for me, I don't mind admitting, when Jack took up with another environmentalist. After what happened with Lara."

What?

"I had to keep him on the right track."

"Why didn't you just come and get me, if you thought I had the prototype? You could have taken it back."

"Good question." Langford raises his eyebrows at Kerry. "Hindsight is a wonderful thing, isn't it?"

She ignores him and swipes the device again. There's an image of me in waterproof gear, at night. I'm near a red brick wall, holding a spray can up, and scowling at the camera. Langford's house. One of the pictures Gabe snapped of us. How did she get hold of it? There are a few more of that night, but none of Maya. I'm not in the last photo, but it's of Langford's burnt-out dining room.

"Where did you get those?" I whisper, but I would be surprised to receive any kind of answer.

"Not a very flattering portfolio, is it?" says Kerry, pulling the tablet back to face her. "You could end up serving time if that lot got into the wrong hands."

I feel like I'm going to throw up. "You... None of this would stand up, anyway. It's all crap." But I'm trembling.

She shrugs, easing off the floor and brushing at the seat of her jeans. "And Jack... I mean, these vulnerable young

235

women… Lara…Essie…" she lets the sentence trail off for the drama. "Add to that your libellous letter to the papers, industrial espionage, intellectual property theft, intentional destruction of commercial records, tampering with evidence. It's not looking good for you either."

The letter? That was Jack? Not Gabe.

Jack's lip curls, but he stays silent as Kerry approaches him.

"Jack. Why get Essie involved at all, when she was already on our radar? Which you knew, because you put her there. Does she mean that little to you?"

I want to scream at her, but… why did he?

Kerry comes back to me, squats down, making the movement appear improbably elegant. "There's something else you should see."

No more.

I can't look away as she holds up the tablet again, showing me a shifting image of a place I know.

The vicarage.

The breath squeezes out of me. The drone circles the building, revealing the positions of all the armed officers, crouching ready to pounce.

"Seth's been a naughty boy, too." She shakes her head. "Aiding and abetting this criminal behaviour of yours. He's in as much trouble as you."

Sweat tickles down the side of my nose. On the screen, the drone is zooming in on the front door of the vicarage. I imagine Seth in there, rehearsing his Christmas mass, unaware of the storm about to break over him. I think of the church across the road.

A tear follows the track left by my sweat.

"I could make all this go away, Essie," she whispers, closing down the tablet. She rises effortlessly, beaming with satisfaction. "In exchange for one little gadget—your lives back. And Seth's in the clear."

I get to my knees, my feet, then up in her face.

"Essie," says Jack. "Careful."

Grabby strides over and clutches my arm, throwing me back onto the floor. My hip flares with pain as it hits the concrete. Dazed, I sit up, leaning against the steel frame of a workbench.

"Did you even have a plan to get this thing made when you stole it?" Kerry says to Jack. "You were never going to do it yourself—you haven't got the balls. Did you expect your girlfriend to take all your risks for you? You're a man-child."

His nostrils flare. "What's your cut, Tyler? You lot never do anything unless there's something in it for you. So, what's the deal? You make sure free energy never gets to market, and you get ten percent shares? Consultancy? Nice seat on a power company board?"

"Or were you gonna give it to your boss, Foster-Pugh?" I ask. "So his dad's *global energy empire* can get a big fat grant and make it? Would do wonders for profits, wouldn't it? *Free* energy."

She squints at me, and slinks close to Jack, almost brushing his knees. "I rather think you, of all people, would appreciate the value of a deal, Jack. You should be in jail right now, twice over. And when they find Lara's body—"

Jack springs up from the chair, but Grabby is there in a few strides. He forces Jack's arm up to his shoulder blades, then drives him headfirst into the wall and pins him there.

As angry as I am, there's no point in turning up the heat any more. Though it hurts me, I force my face into a small, conciliatory smile.

"Okay, Kerry." My eyes dart back to Jack. "I'm willing to talk about this. Just, let's… dial down the testosterone."

"I am in complete agreement with you on that. Lenny."

Grabby releases a panting Jack. They exchange a malevolent glance, and Jack flops down in his chair, his forehead bleeding.

"Can I…?" I point at another chair nearby.

Kerry nods and motions Langford, Grabby and Bible Belt to remove themselves. Langford purses his lips, but shambles away to a nearby workbench.

When we're seated for negotiations I say, "So, if we were to agree to surrender the prototype, *if*… This deal would kick in…?"

"When I have it in my hand," she says. "Not before."

"Okay… so there's a bit of an issue there," I say, thinking as fast as I can. "In that we would need to leave here. To physically recover the prototype."

"Hmm."

"Would that work for you?" I say.

Kerry holds out her hands, palms up. "Obviously not, Essie, no," she says.

"Then how are we supposed to get it to you?" asks Jack.

"You tell us where it is, we go and get it. Or we all go together—like a big old CU family outing."

"See, that's not possible," says Jack, warming up to the act. I hope he has a plan.

"Because…?" she says.

"Because, Kerry, we put some safeguards in place. As to the location of the prototype."

I see where he's going and think, *You genius*.

Kerry purses her lips. "I'm not in the mood to be screwed with."

"I'm not screwing with you, I swear," he says. "The prototype is safe, but none of us can access its whereabouts unless… certain conditions are met. In case of, well… scenarios like this."

Her eyes widen. He doesn't drop his gaze.

"You want me to let you go," she says. "So, you can go and find it and bring it back here?"

Jack shifts in his seat. "Yeah. Kerry, listen…"

Kerry gives a humourless chuckle. "I've no doubt that sounded like a plausible story in your head, Jack."

"You've got the pictures as insurance," I say—desperate, and too late.

"They're all yours, Alex," Kerry says in a monotone, rising from the chair.

As she passes Grabby, Kerry points down at the floor,

indicating, I guess, for him to stay.

Oh, great.

Bible Belt unlocks the door for her, and she glances back at us. I'm sure I catch a twitch of worry in her eyes as she turns to leave.

For a moment, we're all frozen. Then Bible Belt comes out with the handcuffs, snapping them on me while Grabby points his gun to inspire compliance. As Langford strides towards us, smirking, there's a muffled beeping sound. In my anxious state, I cry out, and my heart begins to pound. Langford pulls a phone from his pocket, presses a button, and the beeping stops.

He murmurs Bible Belt, who huffs and marches out, handing Grabby the bunch of keys. Langford turns back to Jack and me.

"Now. Where were we?" He holds up my knife.

My throat closes in on itself as Langford leans towards me.

"Alex," says Jack. "I'll tell you what happened to the prototype, okay? Everything I know. Put the knife down."

"You must think I was born yesterday." Langford pushes the blade under my chin and lifts, stretching my neck so far back I can't breathe. "You know what? Forget the file. I don't want it anymore."

"The knife, Alex," says Jack.

"You're going to build me another." Langford's eyes narrow on me, the knife a steady, cold pressure.

"What?" Jack's voice is raw.

"I don't care how long it takes. You'll build it. Or she'll get what's coming."

"Are—"

With a boom and a hellish squeal, the door connecting to Langford's office splinters. Its fragments blow into the workshop. A cannonball of fire follows in their wake. The nearest window shatters, rain pelting the workshop floor as I scream in unison with Jack. It hisses in the heat of the fire, steam and smoke mingling like a flooded barbeque.

"Fuck!" Langford's hand jolts, the blade slicing into my

chin. He and the knife move away, and I take in a rasping breath, coughing on the smoke invading the room. Jack is struggling at the cuffs. Futile as it is, I follow his lead.

Langford stumbles to the office door, an arm shielding his mouth from the dense black fronds of smoke reaching towards him.

The fire is spreading, grasping at the window frames, mounting the ceiling and consuming the tiles there. From the fierce roaring and heat, it's already all over the office. I think of Maya's scarf in there, and my heart cramps.

He's within a few yards of the door, and I can't believe he can stand the heat. I'm twenty feet away and the little hairs in my nose are singed. I pray for a second blast to blow his screwed-up head off his shoulders. I wouldn't even mind dying if I saw that happen first.

"You did this." Langford's mouth twists as he points at Jack.

Jack shakes his head and glances at me.

Breathing hard, Grabby rips the keys out of his pocket and sprints to a door behind us. He fumbles with the lock and then I feel a rush of sodden air at my back, blowing my hair in my face.

"Get *her* in Room One," Langford barks at Grabby over the clamour of the fire. A deep, bassy crack rings out and I picture the enormous desk fracturing in there. More poisonous fumes billow from the door. Jack doubles over, coughing.

"*You're* coming with me," Langford says to Jack.

"No," I say, but Grabby's releasing my handcuffs with a swift twist and tug.

He drags me to my feet, spins me round, and shoves me forward towards the door now open to the outside. Jack struggles and grunts, the handcuffs clinking against the metal post of the chair.

"No," Jack cries, his voice splintering. "Langford, bring her back. You'll get nothing from me…"

Grabby pushes me out of the door and the roar of the fire is replaced by the roar of heavy raindrops on the flat concrete roofs of the outbuildings. We're soaked instantly. I think about running, but Grabby has a gun. He pushes me with it and I slip on a slimy patch of tarmac and fall to my knees. This seems to annoy him more, and he yanks me up as a deep boom sounds in the workshop and Jack shrieks. I glance back to see fierce, flickering light spilling out. Another bomb, or something surrendering to the fire?

He drags me across to the first shed-type structure and slams me against it. My ear presses to the wall and the hum I noticed before tickles. Grabby is unlocking the door, pressing a knee up against me. I consider trying to grab the gun from behind, but before the thought is fully formed, he has it open.

Another furious shove, and I stumble clean across the room, smacking into the opposite wall. Lights explode in the darkness of my vision. I crumple to the floor with a sickening, shifting sensation in my head. By the time I straighten out, Grabby has gone, locking the door behind him.

From the direction of the workshop there's a shout of anger, a cry of pain that must be Jack, fire going wild. I bang on the door and shout again and again. I scream for Jack, for Langford to let me out, until I have no voice left and my fists are swollen and bleeding.

Sobbing, I collapse, back against the door.

The room I'm in looks like a cell. The floor is bare concrete and there's no furniture except a single, lumpy camp bed in the far corner, dressed only in dirty white sheets. The buzzing sound is louder in here, coming from behind the rear wall. The dimmest glow trickles from an ancient strip light overhead. As I sit trying to catch up with myself, it flickers a few times then returns to constant. A minute later, it flickers again.

On..off..on..off..on……..off..on..off..on……

I close my eyes.

Another explosion sounds a moment before the force hits my cell—a decp, ripping blast. There's an intense pressure in the air for a second, almost like a wave just below my hearing. The door clangs in its frame but doesn't blow open. It's followed by the sound of all the glass in the world smashing onto concrete. There's a clatter as shards of it smack against the shed I'm trapped in.

Had there been any windows in this room, they would have shattered too, and perhaps afforded me an escape—or shredded me from head to toe.

I try the door to see if the frame has weakened, but it holds fast. There's a new pattering noise, maybe plaster raining down. The light goes out, leaving me in utter blackness.

And silence.

Unable to breathe, I strain my ears for signs of life outside. Anything. That humming is back, emanating from the far wall. I'm pretty sure it houses a generator, because the resumption of the hum is followed by the maddening flicker of the light. I sigh, nostalgic for the darkness.

I could be the only one left alive, I realise with a jolt of horror. Images of Jack lying dismembered on what's left of the workshop floor flash behind my eyes.

Jack, and whoever bombed the place. Was it Gabe? Perhaps Hallie and the other *Change Here* members regrouped while I was broken with Maya's loss. I can't stop the vision coming at me in the flickering cell. All of them scattered by the blast, sliced up by flying debris.

Langford could be dead too, but it's too high a price to pay for that.

Chapter Twenty-Four

Exhaustion must have defeated me at some point, because the first clue he's there is the cold bite of a gun pressed into my cheek. When I open my eyes, the bulb is still flickering...

On.. off.. on.. off...

Langford mutters, "Get up," in my ear. The fumes of whisky and fire on him are nauseating. In the dull, intermittent light there's a pulsing hatred about him as he breathes down on me.

A moment of stillness stretches. I grapple with the fact he's alive, try to work out how to react. He's not patient: drags me to my feet and slams me against the wall then spins me round to face him. He forces my head back and the gun barrel into my mouth, making me cough reflexively. The dirty, metallic tang of it burns my tongue. I know I'm going to die. His lip twitches as he bares his clenched teeth. Something clicks, and I flinch in anticipation of the bullet.

Another beat goes by.

I'm not dead.

He's breathing hard, and my stomach clenches. The fire has blackened and crisped all of him—face and shirt, his bald head oily with sweat and dirt, hands dusty with soot. He tenses… exhales, swears, removes the gun.

I close my eyes, but that was a mistake. Pain sears my left eye as he slams me, not with a bullet, but with the barrel.

Warm blood trickles down my cheek. Everything tips sideways as the impact hits my brain, and I stagger. My legs seem to evaporate, and I begin to slide down the wall. He doesn't let me go down, supporting my whole weight by gripping my throat. I can't see anything out of the eye he hit.

"Well, aren't you a clever little bitch?" He pockets the gun with his other hand. "You and your boyfriend, and your scummy mates. Trying to destroy my business, steal my property." He shoves me harder against the wall, drawing a cry from me that makes his face cramp with satisfaction. "Were you trying to kill me? Doesn't matter. None of them survived the blast. Torn apart by their own bomb. I doubt they'll be able to identify any of them."

"You're lying." It's only a croak that escapes me.

Cold fear steals over me at the way he laughs. His grip loosens, giving me seconds to steady myself before his fist smacks into my mouth, knocking me into the wall. This time he steps back as I go down screaming and curl up on the floor at his feet. He kicks out, jabbing his foot into the rib Grabby broke, and I give a wheezing choke.

"Look at me."

There's no defying that command. The stabbing pain in my ribs makes me sob as I struggle to a sitting position and drag myself a few feet to the far wall. As I lean against it, the hum of the generator vibrates on my back. My good eye fixes on his face wavering in and out of darkness. My lip is bleeding so heavily there's little point in trying to stem the flow. We remain motionless for a moment, both gasping. A coughing fit overwhelms me and I taste more blood. Has he pierced my lung with that kick?

Langford appears to notice the flickering light and looks at the ceiling, frowning, then utters a curse. He removes a flashlight from his back pocket, then stalks across the room and stabs a finger at the light switch.

Off.

Torchlight burns my working retina as Langford approaches me. My limbs contract, as though trying to disappear into my body for protection. In a few steps, he's looming over me, his face hidden in darkness. With his free hand, he draws a phone out of his pocket. Its screen lights his features with a blue hue, and though the jaw is set, the fury in his eyes has cooled a little.

He lifts the torch again. "Tell me where the prototype is. I won't ask you again."

His voice is cooler, too. Cold.

"I told you. I don't know." I try to focus on his face even though he's not looking at me but back at his phone. "It's the truth."

The screen flickers as he taps something into it, a curt nod bobbing his head.

Between gasps, I say, "What have you done with Jack?"

His laugh barks out, and as if the sound operates an invisible switch, the buzz of the generator kicks up a notch. Dim orange lights, embedded behind iron cages high in the walls, judder on. Langford sneers at me in the new light and pockets the torch.

Still staring at me, he presses a button on his phone. From outside, there's another explosion. Further away, but bigger than the first two. A scream bursts from my lips as my chest contracts, my arms flailing over my head. When I look up, Langford only glares at me, the slightest narrowing of his eyes, not quite a blink.

Clanks on the roof.

Bricks? Are there bricks falling? I flinch down as if expecting them to break through the roof. Langford is leering over me, his face outlined in orange, flecks of it glinting in his eyes. The air is smoky now, with burning paper and plaster. Rubber. Some other chemical aroma. The whole place must be in flames. A muffled roar of fire, shattering glass.

There's no time to worry about out there. He grabs my arm, throws me into the centre of the room and climbs on top of me. Though I struggle, he straddles my chest, pinning my arms down with his knees. My rib stabs and I can hardly breathe.

He's going to kill me now.

Do I care?

My left eye is still blind and on fire, and my concussed

brain can't imagine any other way this could end. He stares at me with a weird expression—speculation, or detached scrutiny.

While he's distracted, I picture the gun in his pocket. If I can grab it, shoot this animal in the face...

But he snaps to and crushes his knees tighter into my sides, cracking my rib again, making me yelp.

"You were right about your friend. That gunshot wound was probably treatable." He smirks. "Reckon it was the tarpaulin that finished her off. Hard to breathe through those things." His smugness is suffocating as he leans in close to taste his victory. He's in my face, his hand clamped on my jaw. My cheek crushes into bone as his fingers hook. He dips his head. His teeth clamp onto my lower lip and bite down, sharp and stinging. What would have been a scream comes out of me as a muffled whine. Yet more blood washes onto my tongue.

He climbs off me. "Not feeling so clever now, are we?"

Something snaps in me, like a rotten rubber band. The wounds, the pain barely register as I twist and spring at him, screaming. "You murdering *bastard!*"

My fist smacks into his cheekbone with more strength than I knew I had left. He falls back with a cry. The impact stings my knuckles, but it's pure triumph. I'll do it forever if I can. Every nerve is alive with searing hatred as I lash out. The desire to rip his skin consumes me.

He dives out of range. We scramble to our feet at either end of the room, panting, glowering like mismatched boxers.

My head swims. These could be my last moments, and that forces me at him again. He's not quick enough. My nails connect, gouging a long gash from detestable right eye to chin. Parallel to the cut I made. I've given him tramlines. The thought brings a bitter grin to my face.

With a yell, he snatches my wrists and drives me back into the wall. In a moment that should be silent, there's the roar of fire outside, its bitter reek. I yank my arms, but his hold is intractable.

"Who'd miss a thieving little scumbag like you?" His eyes

glint orange as they burn into mine. "But first, I'll take my prototype back."

"I told you I don't have it. Are you deaf?"

"Cough it up, and you walk away with your miserable little life."

A bitter, hysterical laugh must have come from me. "I'm not a complete idiot, Langford. You can't let me live now. With all I've seen. What you've done."

Grasping both my wrists with one hand, he reaches inside his jacket for the gun. It presses hard into my forehead as he whispers, "You're right. You should have talked while you had the chance. You're done."

This is it, Ess.

I close my eyes, expecting only a shot to the head and burning oblivion. With a viscous jerk, but no real hope, I shoot out my knee.

It connects. A shriek escapes me as my rib stabs. Langford screams, and I open my eyes.

"You bitch!" Langford cradles his groin, turns away, and retches. The revolver hangs limply in his hand. Forgotten, only for seconds. I can't hesitate, but the world slows down as I advance on him.

He sees what I'm going for, and his grip on the gun tightens, but he can't straighten up to aim. Lifting a leg, I whip my boot into his face. Langford gives a gurgling scream and drops to his knees, releasing the gun.

An instant later, I'm holding it to *his* forehead, pressing it like I'm trying to break his skull. Maybe I am. His face is a half-mask of blood, flowing from a puncture the size and shape of my boot heel below his left eye. My lips twist as my vision blurs and dims. At least I've evened his face up for him.

I'm panting so hard the words have to fight their way out. "Who's done, Langford? Eh? Can't hear you." I shove his head back with the gun and whisper, "Not such a big man now, are we?"

He sneers. "You're not going to shoot me. You're not that stupid."

"Oh, I am." I push him again, ignoring the shuddering that has taken hold of my arms, my chest. "Really. Fucking. Stupid."

"Alex!" A woman's voice outside.

Langford's eyes shift from my face to the door as someone bangs on it.

"Alex, you in there?

Kerry.

She stalks inside, her stupid reindeer jumper sparkling red. "I saw the fire from across town. Has…What the hell is going on?"

"What you left us to." With the gun glued to Langford's face, I risk a glance her way.

She peers at me, then Langford, and gives a small tight nod. "Don't be daft, girl."

My mouth is dry and metallic as I give a strange, wheezy laugh. "Fuck off, *girl.*"

I tighten my trembling fingers on the gun as it slips on his forehead. He glares at me, silent, breathing steadily.

"Seriously." Kerry takes a step towards us. "You shoot him, you may as well blow your own head off next."

I wipe blood and snot from my chin with my free hand. "Be worth it."

"Or worse than death." She sidles closer. "Life in prison. Did you enjoy your night in that cell?" Closer. "Fancy another seven or eight thousand of those?"

A memory flashes of Officer Harassment leering over me, sweaty hands in my hair, and I flinch. My teeth clench, but my grasp is weakening. Almost against my will, the pressure from my hand to the gun eases.

Langford grins up at me.

Those hateful eyes watched Maya die. My fingers tighten on the trigger.

And *squeeze.*

Kerry lunges for the gun, knocking it out of my hand as it fires. The report roars in the tiny space. A firework stink ricochets after it. Langford screams a curse. Maybe he was expecting a bullet to hit him, like me before. Too bad, it missed. He's still there. On his knees, but alive.

When I turn, Kerry is kicking the gun behind her, towards the door. Someone is lurking there, and scoops it up. At Kerry's signal, he steps forward. Ed—he of the hypodermic needles. He doesn't have a needle now. It's a canister. There's a sharp tang of petrol as he opens it and starts tossing it about.

It splashes on concrete and patters on linen.

"Hey!" Langford gets up on unsteady feet and tries to grab for the jerrycan, but Ed dodges his lunge.

Eyes on my face, Kerry says, "Go home, Alex. Invent a reason you were never here."

Langford glares at her, but looks in too much pain to move. "This is my call."

She turns on him, teeth clenched. "Not anymore. There's more at stake than your *business*."

"I was taking care of it." His voice is low and tight.

"Yeah. I see how you were taking care of it." She glances back at me, looms closer to Langford. "You'd do well to remember who's really running this show, Alex. Go home."

His fists clench and as if he's going to start on her now. Perhaps saving it for another time, he backs against the wall.

Gently supporting me, Kerry escorts me out of this obscene prison cell and into the heat and damp of the outside. To our right, the ruin of the workshop looms, a dripping and smoking graveyard, backlit by dying flames. I don't want to look, but it's irresistible. Where are the fire engines? The alarms? Have they covered this up already?

The workshop is cloaked in profound darkness. There's incredible heat radiating from it, and a crisp odour of burnt paper. As we move to the front of the property down the tarmac drive, our feet grind on broken glass. It's not just shattered, it's *powdered,* like walking on compacted sand.

Behind us, there's a fierce *WOOOFFF* and fingers of light

reach under our feet as the shed ignites. Ed catches up, but I've no idea where Langford's gone.

There's no strength in my legs, and they collapse as we stagger across the cobblestones to a waiting car beyond. I slump into a half-huddle on the seat as Kerry sits in the front with Ed.

I'm bruised all over, sick, raw. Desperate to shut down, but my mind and the shivering won't let me go. My left eye is burning, warped and doubled shapes swimming in its field.

I can't stop the image of that creature's hands on Maya like they were on me. She would have broken sooner and much deeper—her life didn't toughen her like mine has.

How tough are you, Essie?

If Kerry had moved a little slower, the world would be rid of Langford. Tough enough.

After a short drive on a route I don't have the will to follow, we enter an underground car park. Kerry and Ed ease me out of the car. There's something parental about the way they help me up the stairs which is so long-absent I almost break down. But this fight's not over.

We exit the stairway through an iron door into an unadorned office facility. There's a reception desk and small waiting area, both unoccupied, in semi-darkness. She leads me towards an office off a corridor behind the reception. Ed takes up his station outside, giving me a sideways glance as we go by. The room is functionally furnished in beech effect but there's a shiny adjoining bathroom.

"You can clean up. No one will disturb you." Kerry gives me a tight smile and leaves.

They lock the door behind them.

It's not a kindness. They want me to remove the evidence of his attack. But who am I going to tell? I want his stench gone from me as much as they do.

I stay under the scalding water for a long time, trying to stop the shivering, to keep my mind empty and unfeeling. Desperate to ignore the bruising, the sting of my cuts, the bite mark on my lip. At some point, this is all going to come at me, but I can't deal with it now. Get through this next minute or two… just get through it and then we'll see. They'll probably kill me anyway, then it won't be a problem. I bury my face in the towel, as though a muffled sob doesn't count.

When I come out of the bathroom, wrapped in a gargantuan dressing gown, there are clean clothes waiting for me. It looks like one of Kerry's work dresses, wine red. It's tight across the chest, and a little too long. They haven't left me any shoes, so I pull my boots back on, with the blood soaked into the suede toes.

Is it my blood or his?

My eyes touch on the crumpled remains of my own outfit on the bathroom floor—my *funeral* outfit, torn and bloody.

To distract myself, I look in the mirror and can't hold back a hysterical chuckle. I look like an overgrown child, dressed up in her mum's work gear. Then I catch sight of the vivid bruise above my eye, the deep cut running in a jagged arc from just above my eyelid to my cheekbone. He must have come close to blinding me for good. There's a moment of danger when the thoughts begin to crowd in, but I shut them out by pinching my arm as hard as I can. It's the first thing I think of to do, but it seems to work.

Kerry is in the office when I return, bustling about with some papers.

She has a jumpy, discomforted air about her, an uncertain smile. "A little better?"

I don't have an answer to her question. She's cleaning up his mess.

Where is he now?

Need to keep it together. The pain when I pinch my arm shuts it all down again.

"Where's Jack? What have you done to Seth?" The screaming and the smoke have left my voice rasping, on the verge of collapse.

She must have noticed, because she pours me a glass of water from a jug on the desk. Some misfiring pride circuit in my brain makes me ignore it, though I'm parched, and my

251

head is thumping.

There's no way she's going to answer my questions—but, God, what if I already know? Even if Langford was lying and Jack didn't die in the explosion, they would surely have killed him anyway. And Seth... The thought drains whatever strength I've regained, and I fold into the chair beside me, my ears ringing.

"Essie–"

"You knew he was going to do this. When you left us there." My voice sounds flat and cold. Muffled by my swollen lip. I can't look at her, only blink the tears away. "Beat me to death. Was that your plan?"

"I...no. He was just supposed to scare you, to make you talk. I wouldn't..."

"What kind of a woman does that to another woman?" My voice shakes with rage and disbelief. The anger gives me the strength to meet her eyes, but she's looking down at her hands, plucking at a cuticle.

"What's the matter, Kerry? Lost your stomach for it?" My throat closes for a moment and I swallow. "The least you can do is look at me."

I swear there are tears welling under her heavily painted eyelashes. Could just be my imagination, though. Crocodile tears.

"Is Langford coming back?" My voice wavers and catches.

"Look—"

"Forget it. Nothing you people do shocks me anymore." I stand up, take a shaky breath. "You might as well kill me if you're going to, because at this point, I honestly don't give a shit."

Who knows if it's true as I stride across the room on steadier legs than I would have thought possible. I don't seem to care all that much. My hand grips the handle and pulls.

Of course, it's locked.

I nod, close my eyes, and lean my head on the door.

Trapped.

Chapter Twenty-Five

"Essie." Kerry's voice is steady.

I turn towards her.

"I didn't mean for that to happen to you," she says. "I'm sorry it did."

"You didn't know what a psycho he is? Come off it." Her show of contrition doesn't cool my fury one bit. "Oh, don't panic. I'm not going to the press, or anything."

We surely both notice I didn't say police.

"No one would believe you if you did," she says, with a ripple that might be genuine sadness in her eyes.

She's right, but I'm not naïve enough to think that means I get to walk away.

"Please. Sit down."

I don't have an enormous range of options, so I sit opposite her, and drain the glass of water. It eases the pulsing headache at least, and makes me a little more alert.

A long silence follows. Is she stalling? Waiting for my assassin? It doesn't matter. Jack's dead, Seth too, probably. Right now, I wouldn't care if I died, I just don't want *him* to be the one who does it.

I need to make something of the time I have left, so before I'm ready to hear it confirmed, I say, "Who blew up the workshop? He said they were all dead. Who's dead?"

But there's no reply, just a shake of the head, which to my exhausted mind means the worst. She seems to be reading one of the documents on her desk for an age. I shift in my seat. Despite my hopelessness, I'm maddened by her silence. To stop the images coming, I dig my nails into my palms. Images of Seth dead in a cell, Jack lying bleeding, of Langford standing over him while his life drains away.

Of him standing over Maya.

Kerry spins her chair round, opens a cupboard behind her, and comes out with a bottle of gin and two glasses. She pours a generous measure for us both, picks hers up and clinks it against mine.

Not keen to face my final living moments sober, I take as big a mouthful as my ruined lip will allow. It stings, but that's good.

From a drawer, she pulls a packet of cigarettes and a lighter, and holds them out to me. I shake my head. I can still smell the smoke from *him*, and it's like death.

The next swallow of gin eases the pain and helps me find my voice again. "You should have let me kill him."

She doesn't seem to have heard me. "It's such a bloody mess, Essie."

We both take a swig.

"I don't just mean this." She waves her glass around the office. "I mean the whole bloody circus. Politics. Makes a person hard over time, you know?"

I nod. I do know. My glass empties faster than is prudent.

"When you're new, everyone knows it. You're easy meat. You have to play along to get in the game." She stares at a spot on the wall beyond me. "You tell yourself once you're in, you're going to change it all from the inside. And you really believe it, too. At first." There's a misty, meditative glimmer in her expression which can't yet be the gin. "But they change you. One compromise at a time. They break you down, build you back up just like them. And suddenly you're playing *their* game." Her eyes rove my face, but I give her nothing.

"That's heart-breaking," I say, my bitterness flaring hot inside. "Game?" I point at my lacerated eye with a sharp, angry finger. "This is the game. What he did to me. That's the game you're all playing. That's okay with you, is it?" The tears loom again.

Her eyes flicker. "No, Essie. None of this is okay. But you're not that naïve." She tips her head to the side. "We're outsiders, you and me. If we don't find some way in, they'll make sure outside is where we stay."

I grimace at her. "We are not the same."

"I'm a black woman in politics, for Christ's sake. I've taken more than my fair share of crap. The harassment, the smears. One guy emailed this morning to inform me he plans to rape then lynch me. How far do you suppose I'd get if I didn't play a little dirty sometimes?"

I look at her coiffured hair, her expensive suit, her schooled posture, and a fire ball rockets around my stomach, into my throat. "That is a fantastic argument, Kerry. Use that one." My mouth twists, numb with bitterness.

"I never wanted any of this."

"Bullshit." It's unwise, this outburst. But they've burnt out my filter, and I can't hold it back. "You've got no problem at all with a spot of torture, a well-timed political killing or two."

"Wow. If they blew themselves up with their own bomb, how is that my fault?"

This draws a choked, outraged sob from me. "He murdered my friend Maya. She was a good person. She didn't do anything to deserve that. Or do you reckon that's just a proportional response to someone graffitiing your house?" I have to stop there because of the burning in my throat.

Mention of Maya sobers her, so I guess she's aware of what they did. Of course she is. They would have covered it up for him. Her and her boss. Langford's mate. They're all in this.

She doesn't change track. "You're happy to stay on the outside, then? Good for you and your moral absolutes. It's when you stick your head up, try for change—*meaningful* change, I mean. Not your juvenile whining for change. That's when things get nasty."

"I get it," I say, boiling with resentment. "We deserved what we got."

She snaps her eyes up. "I meant—"

"Oh, Kerry, relax. You've taught me my lesson. I'm not going to cause you any trouble. Neither of us has the prototype, so nobody wins. You live to sell the world another day."

"That's not me," she says, shaking her head.

"'Clever little bitch'. That's what he called me. Kicked the 'clever' right out of me, didn't he?"

She looks hunched and watery, like she's going to throw up, and I want to make her. I'm gasping, my head starting to swim. There's no time to go to pieces now, so I give my thigh a pinch under the desk. Hard enough to bruise. My breathing slows a little bit.

"So here I am." I gesture at my shattered body. "Back in my place: a broken-up victim for you to fuck with all over again. Well played, Kerry."

Her features cramp down on themselves as she looks at me. A few moments later, my cheeks sting with tears. I don't wipe them away. Let her see them, I'm finished pretending. I sob, my nose is streaming, but I don't hide. It's not just what they've done today. It's almost three years since the attack that ruined my life. Three years of their scheming and posturing. All the lies.

She watches me cry. Neither of us speaks for so long my tears dry up, leaving me parched and empty. I can't decipher what she's thinking, but there's no pity in her gaze, and she offers me no comfort.

"Where's the prototype, Essie?" she says. "Just tell me and we can all go home and forget all of this."

"Forget?" I expel a bitter laugh. "Yeah, okay. Except you already know Lawrence took it. I have no idea what happened to it after that. I don't even want to think about what you've done to him to get him to talk. He hasn't, or I'd be dead." I meet her gaze, square on. "You're right, though. I wouldn't tell you if I knew."

Her face is still and cold, but I won't drop my eyes.

"This technology we're all fighting over," she says, refilling my glass. "It wouldn't even get *made* unless someone thought they were going to rake in a shedload of money for it. Wouldn't have been dreamed of."

"Wouldn't have been *needed*," I say, but she ignores this,

or doesn't hear.

"And the whole time, the world's going to hell." The immaculate French pleat comes loose at one temple as she flicks her head. "It's just human nature—pointless to deny it. Sometimes I wonder what it says about us, though."

My mouth twitches. "I don't feel like it says anything about me."

"Like you're better than the rest of us." Her hands clench into fists. "In the short time we've been acquainted, you've proved yourself a vandal, a thief, and something remarkably close to a terrorist. So, don't come the virtuous heroine with me now, sweetheart. I see you."

Burning with hate, I swig my gin and glare. It doesn't faze her for even a beat.

"You people," she says, whipping her eyes up and down me, her lip curling. "You reckon yelling slogans and blowing stuff up is going to make a difference?"

It feels like I'm having this conversation over an immense distance, through air made of syrup. My eyes shift wistfully to the door, even though I'll never walk out of it.

"Or worse," she goes on. "You're sure it'll make no difference, but you do it anyway. Just so you can act smug while you watch the world go to shit."

She's clever. I always knew it. What I never realised until now was just how ruthless she is, how hard she'll work at convincing you she's right.

I've had my fill of those people of late and instead of subduing me it makes me fight harder. "What would make a difference? Selling us all out? Killing us? Will that save the world, Kerry? Better than something that could heal the shitty air?"

"Oh, grow up. No one's saving the world, here. We're done for... but the world will go on, whatever we do. Or don't."

"Jesus. You're a Judgement Day lunatic, too? Think you're one of the chosen ones, do you?"

With a snigger, she says, "No, not me. Good luck to the cockroaches, or whatever. But I *am* a realist. If humanity

257

stands any chance at all, it's not going to be down to some great epiphany where everybody starts sharing their toys. *Somebody's* going to have to make a mint out of it, or it won't happen." She shrugs one shoulder, sits back. "And it's my job to make it happen."

She fiddles with the desk calendar, as if measuring the time we have left. It's one of those sappy ones with motivational quotes on the back of each month. November's is facing me. I read it upside down.

"The oak fought the wind and was broken, the willow bent when it must and survived." Robert Jordan

What a load of shit.

Yeah, but Willow didn't bend for anybody, Ess.

"What are you and your mates going to do with the prototype anyway?" Kerry's haranguing yanks me back in the room. "Do you have the expertise, the capital, the means to produce this thing? Of course, you don't. You just want to stop *us* from making it. No moral high ground there, is there?"

Does that mean they're still alive?

I long to ask, but she wouldn't give me an answer, even if she knew.

"People can't afford energy, Kerry. Not people you know, granted, but there are millions of them. Wasting away while your mates get richer. If we could all have power for free, you don't reckon that's moral high ground?"

She rises from her chair, knuckles on the desk and fixes her eyes on me. "I need you to hand over that prototype. Or everything that happens after today is on you. I won't be able to stop it."

"I'm not buying your crap. This isn't on me. You're a liar. And a murderer."

"And you're going to end up dead with the rest of us," she

hisses.

"Good." I lean forward. "Bring it on, Kerry. I've got nothing to lose now. How about you?"

Kerry looks at my face, then her eyes drift downward. She recoils a little, blinking.

I'm digging my fingernails deep into my own arm, drawing blood. As if I haven't shed enough of that already.

"Why me, Kerry? I'm nobody." With the truth of that, the tears come back. "Why did you pick me to screw with?"

She purses her lips. "I didn't pick you. Jack did."

"What the hell are you talking about?"

"He never explained about Lara, did he?" She sighs. "Lara was a troublemaker, like you. An *environmentalist*."

"I know. And all about why she was killed. The articles in the student papers."

"That's not my area. I *do* know that Langford was given the go ahead to invest. All perfectly above board, mind."

"I bet it was."

"Jack was... reluctant, at first, about the new arrangements for the project. But he saw sense in the end."

Tired of the games, I rest my palm on my forehead. "I imagine the blackmail helped."

She ignores that. "I suppose when you came along— another young girl full of opinions—Langford was afraid of the same thing. So, he watched you. He needs Jack. Needed him. Jack was the only one who knew how to make this thing. He didn't want to lose his biggest asset. That *Change Here* group was the stupidest decision you ever made, Essie. Langford must have panicked when he found out about that. You only ever gave him more reasons to screw with you."

"What happened to Lara in the end? Did Langford kill her?"

She twitches her head again. More hair comes loose, sticking to her mouth, and she pulls it out. "I don't know anything about that."

We weigh each other up across the desk. I still have no idea what this woman is about. When I look down, I've scraped more skin off my arms. I didn't even feel it.

259

The decision happens like a turned page in her eyes. Likely she's hoping I'll lead her to the prototype. Or she's betting I'm unhinged enough to dispose of myself and save her the labour costs. And I wouldn't take that bet off her. She springs round her desk and crosses the room, removing a set of keys from a belt loop. The door clicks unlocked, and she cocks her head for me to follow, then slips over the threshold. Out through the reception area to another flight of stairs and down. There's no one here except the two of us. By the hazy, charcoal quality of the light, I guess it's just before sunrise.

Always darkest before the dawn.
Where did that come from, Ess? You sound like Kerry's corny calendar.

Then I'm concentrating on not giving in to the pain shooting up and down my body as we walk.

It's already hot and humid outside, despite the hour and the season. The clouds hang heavy and the air smells of fertile soil warming rapidly. That smell is the first pleasant thing I've experienced in some days, and it inspires in me a strong emotion I can't name right away. Nostalgia, perhaps? Sorrow?

Kerry seems to notice the smell too—she breathes in deeply and sighs. The green Range Rover that brought us here pulls up beside us.

"Somewhat redundantly..." Kerry says, "don't talk. To anyone. About anything. Don't make me regret letting you go because that's just going to work out badly for you. Understand?"

I nod, the gin making me feel like I'm in a dream. Or I'm still bleeding in that hateful cell, hallucinating my escape. Kerry hands me a business card.

"If the prototype should happen to...turn up, you call me, okay?" She narrows her eyes. "If I find out you knew where it was and didn't tell me, I will come after you. What you've done is a crime, so don't imagine I won't be able to get to you."

"What *I've* done?"

She glances up and down the empty street. "Ed will take you straight home. Do nothing for 24 hours, then you should go to the hospital. Anyone asks, you didn't see your attacker and you don't want to report it to the police. Stay low for a few weeks, do not attempt to contact any of your friends. I mean it. Then you can get on with your life." She pauses with a tight smile. "Minus the criminal activity. It's all pointless anyway."

I still don't understand why I'm getting out alive.

Kerry signals to Ed, who gets out of the car and comes around to our side.

"You know we'll be watching you. I mean *properly* watching you. Please be sensible, Essie."

For the second time since I met this woman, I'm not sure if she's offering a threat or a kindness.

The last thing she says to me is, "Take care of yourself."

Disingenuous given the circumstances, but I withhold comment.

With my release, a tsunami of shock hits me in the back of the car. My stale mouth fills with its tang, and I start shuddering, cold and drenched in sweat, heaving for breath. The tears won't stop. Ed glances at me a couple of times in the rear-view mirror. Satisfied there's no immediate medical danger, he ignores me. The blessed shutdown comes eventually.

I wake up aching, still shivering and crying in my own bed. A little later, I realise it's Christmas day.

The pills are in a kitchen drawer, the gin under the sink. It's a bottle my mum bought a few Decembers ago, probably our last Christmas. I've never been able to bring myself to drink it. It's so apt, it's inescapable as I break the seal.

The tablets spill out of their bottle into the palm of my hand. One big swallow is all it would take, and it all goes away...

You came all this way for this, Ess? After all the killing, the pain, the rage? You're giving up. Just like she bet you would...

No.

My phone is gone with everything else, so I have to walk there. It's still early. No one is on the streets this Christmas morning. Nobody sees me limping through the red heat haze, terrified of what I'll find.

He doesn't even wait for me to reach the vicarage door, but barrels down the path, catching me in a hug so tight I cry out.

"You're alive," he says through his tears, at the same time as I say, "You're not dead," through mine.

They didn't take him. Was that drone footage they showed me even real? Either way, it can wait.

"Is it safe?" I whisper in his ear.

He bobs his head against my cheek.

Nobody is tailing me, it seems. They probably reckon I won't dare go out yet, that I'm too damaged.

We go straight to the church. He helps me down the crumbly steps to the crypt, bends low behind the sarcophagus.

The lumpy, brown envelope is damp and mossy. At least Seth had the sense to fold the memory stick in bubble wrap.

He holds it up. "Let's hope it's a good copy. Encryption was a nightmare to untangle. What are you going to do with it?"

"Just keep it, I guess." My smile wobbles with the threat of tears. "Jack's dead. Nobody else I know can build it."

I close my eyes as Seth pulls me to him. "We'll think of something, Ess."

We.

Chapter Twenty-Six

24th April 2040

It came around quickly again. The seventh anniversary of the attack. Almost five years since I lost Maya. Even though Seth is here, I'll never get used to doing this day without her. I still awake with the same suffocating, sickened feeling.

It's scorching today. And swampy. The storm last night was supposed to freshen the air, but failed. Another one might be on the way. I still check the weather forecast, though why I can't say. They're losing credibility by the day now. I suppose it's more of a habit, a crutch against the chaos. The storms come at random intervals and no one seems to be able to explain them. Instead of checking weather apps, most people simply search the skies, and sniff the air.

I'm still working at the Braai, but I'm not sure for how much longer. Hardly anybody comes in to spend money anymore. The English Standard Service Income started at the beginning of the month. It's to compensate for the collapse in the service sector. They didn't want all the waitresses starving to death. It turns out as the end of the world approaches, the English don't rely on their tea and egg-and-cress sandwiches nearly as much as we thought.

I get a perverse kick out of the fact that the abbreviation for my new income is ESSI. That's how they say it, too. Like my name. For the first couple of weeks, I chuckled every time some politician said something like, "The ESSI is going make a huge difference to ordinary people's quality of life." The novelty has worn off now.

God knows how anyone's living on the pitiful sum you get. Perhaps because there's not much to spend it on anymore. Shops are empty half the time. Fuel supplies are low and sporadic. A lot of farmers have gone out of business. The countryside is a circus—wild sheep and cows running about crazy everywhere. I like it, and it's good news for the foxes. There's quite a few of those, too.

Most people my age are happy enough to knock about town doing nothing. You see them drifting along River Street like mist, listless and haunted, the same worried questions behind their eyes we all have.

Work is a must for me, and not only because I have more need than most. I don't care for too much time to ruminate. Busy is what keeps me going, though you can hardly call Bri's Braai busy. It's company at least.

The bluebells that used to line the lane have gone. There are only crisp and browning remnants. The best I can do is a sprig of forget-me-nots, huddled on the bank of a roadside brook against the glare of the sun. They're the same colour as bluebells, and to me a more pleasing shape, so I don't think Mum would mind too much. I pick one each for Mum, Dad, Willow and Darya, and then take another one for Maya. She's family too.

I'm not overly concerned as I check behind me. They still follow me half the time. And online, all the time. On the hottest days, if they're outside the house for a long shift, I usually take them some squash or water. They're only doing their job.

Amazing they still bother. I'm not that interesting. The risks I once took, the disregard I once had for my own life, horrify me now.

Today, there's no one following me. Perhaps they've decided to give me some space to mourn with dignity. I rather think it's a coincidence.

In a moment's pause on the road, I brush my sweaty hair out of my eyes and glance up. The turning to the crematorium is at the top of the steep incline ahead, set deep in eucalyptus trees. I take some generous gulps from my water bottle, bend forward in anticipation of the strain, and start up the hill.

I've been okay lately. There was a long time when I wasn't. With what they did—what *he* did. Now it seems he's everywhere. His surreptitious, sociopathic face all over the TV is a fact of life for me. Shocked me at first, when it wasn't as plain to everyone as the scar my knife left on his cheek. Those guarded, grey eyes that never share a smile with his mouth. How could anyone vote for that?

I came to terms with it, because what's the alternative? If I go public with what he did—while he's Prime Minister or anytime afterward—how does that end for me? And it's not just me in the equation.

I'll never be certain what really happened that night. Jack must be dead. They recovered no bodies, or even parts, from the explosion. His disappearance is easily dismissed as a troubled man running away from his problems.

Gabe and Hallie never showed up, dead or alive. The official story is that the two of them attacked the CU premises as revenge for the death of Hallie's brother and died in the blast. A slow tide of people started to believe this over time, but I'm not so certain.

Lawrence is in jail, serving a life sentence for Maya's murder. They won't let me visit him, so I have to make do with writing to him sometimes. Either my letters don't get through, or he simply doesn't reply.

So, I have come to whatever terms I can. Not all consequences are bad.

I lay the forget-me-nots on their plaque and flop on the wild grass. A few years ago, I'd have cut the greenery back to make it neat, but it doesn't seem right to do it anymore. If something green finds somewhere to flourish, I don't want to be the one to hack it down.

The marble plaque glitters. The embossed gold still spells out their names, just as jarring and unreal.

George Glass	(1985—2033)
Alice Glass	(1985—2033)
Willow Glass	(2010—2033)
Darya Glass	(2019—2033)

The ground is warm, already dry of last night's rain. I'm not wishing my name into the stone. The pain isn't as sharp or urgent, there's only a dense, tight ache in my chest.

The forget-me-nots look good, their petals tracing a satisfying shape against the marble. Like a child's drawing of a flower, wholesome and timeless against the grind of mortality all around me.

"Mum."

I've never spoken to any of them before. Not out loud; not properly formed words. Feels like a floodgate, but no more words come, just ideas. Imaginings of conversations, of the deeper understanding we could have had, of memories and empathy.

Or perhaps we wouldn't have. Maybe we'd have fought about it all. She might have said I was too young to start a family. And maybe I wouldn't have listened to her advice.

Why am I always saying 'maybe'?

While I trudge down the slope, the clouds congregate, brooding harbingers of The Storm Part II. It doesn't help with the heat at all, but forms a sweaty blanket for it to build under. I drain the last of my water at the bottom of the hill, and glance up at the sky. There may be time to get home before it breaks, but you can never be sure.

At the town end of Worcester Road, I pass the Braai and peer in the window. There's no one out front, so I guess Bri is in the kitchen, cooking food in case anyone stops by. I hesitate at the door, wondering if I should go in and see him. It would be nice to sit with him for a while. But I should get back. I press on, ignoring the hateful Unity sign. These days, instead of drowning hands, when I see the symbol, I imagine fingers gripping my throat.

Onto River Street, without even a glance down Bank Lane. No one hangs out there now, since they installed the spikes under the road surface. They're set to come up at random intervals to deter the rough sleepers, but they needn't have bothered. The community that used to flourish there has long since moved on, beaten down by too many losses, too much harassment. A sigh escapes me as I turn off the main road, towards home.

It's clear something is out of place before I near the gate. The atmosphere around the house seems distorted, spoiled. My first thought is something's wrong inside, and my stomach clenches. Then I see the source of my anxiety loitering on the *outside*, by the fence.

I stop dead on the pavement.

She appears so much older, the hair on her temples greying, her eyes sunken.

"Hello, Kerry."

Chapter Twenty-Seven

"Essie. You look well. Happy."

My eyes flick over her. "You don't."

Kerry peers down at herself, the faded t-shirt stretched over her chest and belly, both plumper than I remember. "Can't argue with that." She huffs out a laugh. "Can we talk?"

"What the hell could we have to talk about?" My voice sounds fierce, but I don't feel it. Her presence, so close to my home, today of all days, spins me off-kilter.

She checks behind her and reaches for the gate. "Can we go inside?" It's almost a plea.

"No." I block her way with my arm. "I don't want you in my house."

"Please." Her back stoops, creased eyes more miserable than I've ever seen them.

I grip the gate so tightly my knuckles turn white. "Why are you here? I did what you asked. Kept my mouth shut, caused you no trouble. What more can you want from me that you haven't already taken?"

"I—I don't want anyone to see us talking." She surveys the street again, hand still hovering on the gate next to my own. When a drone skitters overhead, her head bobs low. "For your sake, as much as mine."

She meets my eyes with a tired but steady gaze. Underneath the layer of anxiety, there's steel in her core.

I open the gate, leaving it ajar, and walk up the path. After a moment's pause, her clattering footsteps follow.

A baked, sugary aroma fills the house. Seth and Willow are in the kitchen, ostensibly baking cookies, but it seems more like a dough war. It's all over the floor, dusted in

Willow's dark cloud of hair, all down Seth's t-shirt. How did any of it survive to see the inside of the oven? Seth is making repeated, ineffectual attempts to stop Willow eating the mixture stuck to the worktop.

He grins as we pass the kitchen door, but it fades and his eyes flicker behind me as Kerry draws near. With a shake of my head, I hold a hand up for him to stay out of it. His jaw stiffens, but he doesn't intervene. Willow turns her big green eyes up at us, licking the dough from her fingers with an enormous grin.

Seth and Willow go back to their baking, but there's a tense edge to his voice as he resumes his instructions. I pass by the kitchen door, into the sitting room and Kerry follows.

"She's lovely." Kerry affects a soft purr. "Your daughter. How old is she?"

"She's two. You know that. Say what you came here to say and leave."

We sit on opposite sofas.

Willow and Seth have gone through to the dining room with the first batch of baked cookies. Through the glass door between us, Willow is already chomping on one, screwing up her face against the hot sugar. I suppress a stab of irritation at Seth for letting her eat one straight from the oven. He hasn't felt obliged to offer Kerry any, for which I give him silent thanks.

When I turn back to Kerry, she has tears in her eyes. My instant reaction—born of many nights in my own pain, rocking Willow to sleep—is to comfort her. I catch myself.

"I'm sorry." She blows her nose on a linen hankie. "I'm so sorry."

"Don't be." Though my insides are cold. "Seth was here from the start. Picked up the pieces you made out of me." At the sight of the scars on my arms, my shame flares. But for him, I'd be dead. We both would.

Seth's showing Willow the half-chewed cookie on his tongue. Crumbs fall from his lips onto the table and Willow is shaking with her belly laugh. The one she only ever does for him.

"Why are you here, Kerry?"

She laces her hands together, opens her mouth, closes it and sighs. "I don't know."

"If you came here, shaking us up like this without a reason —"

"I do have a reason," she says.

I fold my arms and wait.

"You probably heard, I resigned last month," she says, as if I should care. "Well, it wasn't just over the Foster-Pugh thing."

"No kidding."

Seth was raging about it. Oliver Foster-Pugh, still somehow Home Secretary, came up with a horrific new policy. Something about making Unity clergy root out people attending their services who may be in the country illegally. Kerry resigned in protest, but it didn't strike me as the kind of thing she'd get upset about. Not quit-her-job upset.

"Foster-Pugh is a nutter." Her hands are twisting, fingers bending back. "That Judgement Day stuff? All true. It was all him—he's been friends with Langford since they were kids."

"I know," I say, but she's not listening.

"They studied at Cambridge together. Foster-Pugh got into religious fundamentalism there—some nutty faction called *The Redemption Charter.* I mean, really." She holds her palms out. "There were loads of those groups flying round campuses in those days, apparently. I wouldn't know. Until Unity squeezed them all out. After that, I suppose he had to keep it under wraps. But *The Redemption Charter* is still a thing, and he's still a member. Langford too, I reckon, since his Plan A went tits up. And I've got the evidence to prove it." Her hands are rubbing her jeans now, up and down her thighs, as her eyes glint. "They've been preparing for *The End* for decades, not joking. Total sci-fi stuff. Secret bunkers, rockets into space, the lot. No surprise they're so excited now. Foster-Pugh was delighted when ConservUnity went up in flames, because he understands that was the best shot to stop the doomsday clock. He doesn't *want* to stop it."

"I can't believe that. Langford's his mate, and he lost his

business." But crazy as she sounds, it makes a weird kind of sense.

"Oh, Langford had it covered," she says, flapping a hand. "He was *massively* over-insured on that company. Nobody could tell, because no insurer would ever be able to properly assess the value of that tech. Langford made a killing on that explosion."

I wince as Jack's face flashes in my mind.

"Almost as if he *wanted* it to blow up." She turns wide eyes to me.

"He didn't seem like he wanted it blown up. He was livid." I shudder, look away.

"A clean slate, though," she says. "They said your mates blew themselves up attacking the workshop. Where's the DNA, then? They never found any on the site. And I know they're still looking for Gabe. The publicity clearly didn't do Langford's political ambitions any harm."

"Are you serious?"

"Completely," she says.

"He wouldn't blow *himself* up, would he?" Though the memory of his face in that shed flashes. His narrowed eyes when the last explosion sounded.

"Who knows? Three bombs went off. It's possible your mates set one, and he set the others."

"And you cleaned up the rest of his mess. Torched the place, got me to wash away the evidence." I shake my head, partly to reject her ramblings. Mostly because I can't believe how easily she's dragged me back into this nightmare.

She's not finished. "Foster-Pugh sold me out. I guess he knew how much stuff I'd got on him, so he did some of his own digging on me. And then I get *The Conversation* with him and Langford, in a discrete Westminster restaurant. I resigned the next day. They didn't give me any choice."

A vague curiosity stirs. How much does Foster-Pugh have on her? I push the thought away: this isn't my fight.

Kerry's still on the battlefield. "And you know this is all part of Langford's plan. Phase one: position himself as a global saviour in green tech. Phase two: a move into politics.

271

Become Prime Minister. Check." She draws a tick in the air.

"Kerry, stop."

"Phase three is the golden ticket. Set it up as PM. The control of the energy market with next generation carbon capture. Global power supply, free to produce. Sold at whatever price you want. Undercut the traditional power companies. Put them out of business in a month. All except one: Foster-Pugh Energy. Because they seem to have got their hands on the next gen carbon capture, and now they run the fucking world."

"I'm not interested."

She shrugs. "There are other ways it could go, but they all end in *cha-ching* for Alex Langford." Her eyes probe mine. "You're not the first of his victims, you know. I found out some stuff about him, too. Allegations of bullying, harassment, assault by former employees. All swept under the carpet. His daddy was the same way. Vicious bastard. I've seen the police reports. Used to beat him and his mum up. Explains a lot, don't you think?"

"Stop!" I hook my fingers in my hair. A memory flashes of that sharp, looming face in the background of Langford's family portrait. I shudder. "You sound mental, you know that?"

She purses her lips. "Yeah."

Seth and Willow have left the dining room. The front door bangs closed, and Willow's happy feet slap on the pavement outside, alongside Seth's lolloping ones. I suppose he's giving us some space, but I wish they hadn't gone.

My phone beeps. It's a text from Seth.

Call me if you need me. We're not going far x.

Kerry's haggard, lined eyes are watching me.

"You lot deserve each other," I say. "Is there a particular reason why I should care what happens to any of you?"

"None I can come up with. Except I wonder if you might be in the market for a little retribution?"

"Leave me out of your revenge trip, Kerry."

"It's more than that."

"Forget it. You're all toxic. And I don't want any part of your *game*."

"This has to make you angry, Essie. I know you. You can't walk away from this."

"You don't know me. You *watch* me." So tired now, I turn away. "You should go."

All this stuff—I thought I'd left it behind.

"There's something else." Her voice is wheedling.

There always is.

"Jack's alive."

I freeze with my back to her, close my eyes. "Leave me alone. I left you alone, didn't I?"

"It's the truth. He's alive, Essie. See?"

I turn slowly on trembling legs. She's holding her phone up to me with a picture of Jack. He looks leaner. Older and sunburnt, but it's him. A pink scar runs down his left cheek, where Langford sliced into it.

Heart hammering, I want to lunge and grab her phone, but I don't move. "Is this a trick?"

"No trick. Alive. He got out when the explosion wrecked the building. He's been hiding, but I found him."

"How?" My heart pounds in my throat. If Jack's alive...

"Well, he found me. Christmas time last year." She flaps her phone hand. "Doesn't matter, here's another thing. He's gonna rebuild the prototype. Since the original never turned up, he needs some backing from me."

All my nerve endings fire at once, sending white heat down my limbs, across my chest.

"You've been sitting on this for months. Why?" I understand in a flash. "Until you could use it to your advantage. You conniving—"

"Essie, it's not like that." She tips her head to the side. "Okay, perhaps it was like that in the beginning. But now—"

"Now you've had an epiphany and you want to save the world. Well you left that a bit late, Kerry. What's your angle?"

She's all wide-eyed earnest. Or faking it, I can't tell. "I need to make a living."

"Yep. There we go."

"Whatever you believe, does it really matter? You can be sure Langford and Foster-Pugh are working *their* angle. We can stop them, you and me. And Jack."

My head is spinning. Seth and Willow are back. Kerry hears them too and her face softens out of the hungry expression she's had for the last ten minutes. Seth's footsteps approach the door to the sitting room, pause and recede.

"Where's Jack?" I ask. "I want to talk to him."

Kerry pulls in a deep breath. "See, the thing about that—"

"You don't know. You're still playing games."

She removes her phone from a pocket. "No, I'm not. He sent me this picture to show you, so you'd believe he was alive. No location stamp, just the date. He'll tell us where he is when I can prove to him you've agreed to be involved."

Outside, an angry darkness descends. The shadows in the room grow.

"If that storm breaks, you can't stay here."

She nods. "I've got a driver waiting on River Street."

"Of course you have."

"So," she says, searching my face. "Are you in?"

Willow bursts in, followed by a harassed Seth.

"Mummy," she says, launching into my arms.

"Hi, baby girl." I nuzzle her curls, ignoring Kerry's huff.

Seth stares at Kerry, jaw muscles twitching. "Sorry, love. Willow wanted to see you."

"No, it's fine. Kerry's leaving, aren't you?"

Kerry screws up her lips and bites the inside of her mouth. Perhaps she can imagine her main chance slipping away. Outside it grows even darker, the pressure building in the air.

"Everything okay, Ess?" Seth looks at me, and back to Kerry, sitting tense, seemingly intimidated by his hostility.

"Everything's fine." I smile up at him. "Honestly."

He bends, kisses the top of my head and lifts Willow from my lap. She protests, but doesn't go full tantrum.

As he nears Kerry's sofa, she half-rises. "Hi. I'm K—"

"I know who you are. Don't fuck with us, Tyler." With Willow in his arms, he strides out.

I don't think I've ever loved him more.

Kerry says, "He doesn't like me much, does he?"

"Why would he?"

Her eyes shift to the wall above me, I guess to my sketch of Willow. The one Seth got framed last Christmas. "You named her Willow."

"Yeah."

"For your sister."

"Yeah." I'm not going to tell this woman that I want my Willow to be as strong and spiky and difficult as the namesake aunt she'll never meet. God knows, she's going to need to be all that.

She shrugs. "Are you in, or not? Because if you're not, I need to find someone else to build that thing. I'm certain Jack's not the only one who can do it."

The rain starts, enormous drops crashing into the windows, sounding like rubber bullets showering the building. A voracious wind gusts, making the house creak.

"Why do you want to build it, Kerry?"

"I would have thought that was obvious," she says, pointing to the craziness whipping outside. "We've got to do *something*, haven't we? We're almost out of options."

"What happened to 'someone's got to make a mint out of it'? Is it just the money? Or the payback?"

"Perhaps I've changed a bit," she says.

"Wish I could believe that." I stare out at the battering rain.

"Does it even matter? We can save everyone, the whole shebang. But that'll be the arseholes too, so you might as well get used to it. I suppose the question is, is it worth it? To give Willow a future worth having."

She's right, of course. I hate her for it, because at its heart, it's still classic Kerry tactics. Clever words and manipulation.

Seth and Willow are back in the dining room, laying the table for tea. I watch them, seriously considering Kerry's proposal for the first time.

In the room next door are all my reasons—to say yes. And to send her away. Seth's eyes reflect my anguish. I so badly want him to be in this with me, but I shake my head. After a long, frowning look he carries Willow back into the kitchen.

I take in a shuddery breath and let it out slowly while Kerry waits.

The Beginning

I've waited so long to get here. For Jack to reveal his location. For Hurricane Jezebel to pass over the island and turn her destructive rage on what's left of Florida. For José Marti airport to be patched up and reopened. Through a six-hour delay, and a ten-hour flight, with my dour chaperones. My latest shadows.

And now I'm here.

Kerry paid for my flight—grating, but necessary. Seth and I never had that kind of money, even before he left Unity.

I call them from baggage claim. Seth puts Willow on the phone, even though it's late there. Her sleep-muffled 'Mummy' makes my eyes sting with tears. I'm so far away from them.

Jack's waiting beyond the ropes, in a haze of heat and expectation. I wasn't sure how it would be, seeing him again. All through the flight, I couldn't settle to anything, the tension defeating any attempt at reading or sleep, my doomed effort to watch a film.

The scar on his cheek is worse in the flesh—vivid and protruding, like the one skirting my eye socket. Langford's legacies.

Our embrace is long.

"Friends of yours?" Jack jerks his head behind me, to my shadows.

"Yeah. They like to hang out with me. Sometimes I forget they're there."

It's not true. I never forget.

We walk along the crumbling, battered Malecón together, joining the Habaneros coming out from hiding.

Jezebel has left her mark here. Buildings lie flattened,

flood water dwells in any gullies and potholes it can find, resisting the pull of the sea. The people walk about, some stunned, some distraught. The clean-up has started, brigades of optimists sweeping and piling broken furniture at the side of the road.

We sit on the sea wall. The late afternoon sun throws pink rays on to the rocks below our dangling feet.

Jack offers me a cigarette, and I shake my head. He lights his own, and the wheel of the Zippo sounds like a blade.

I tell him about Willow and Seth, and home. Jack talks about his research in Havana, his slow progress in recreating the carbon capture tech here, the places he wants to show me, how much he loves Cuba. How it'll be under the Atlantic in a few years. He volunteers for the Wall Builders brigade, a troop reconstructing and reinforcing the sea defences. Here and there along the bay, he points out their work, the wall made wider and taller, to hold back the inevitable.

We discuss the hurricane, the havoc and death toll, the current trend of naming storms for biblical characters.

We go on like that until the real subject strangles the small talk.

"How did you get out?" I ask.

He stares at the rocks below. "I'm not sure. The second explosion came as Langford took my cuffs off. I just ran. Perhaps they tried to shoot. I can't really remember." He swallows, clouded eyes lifting to the ocean. "I just ran. What happened to you that night?"

The words quiver on my tongue for some moments, unwilling to fly. Finally, I point to my damaged eye, which still sees double sometimes. "Langford…"

The breath pushes out of him. "I'm sorry."

"Thank you." That's all. I can't see the point in obfuscation anymore.

We sit in silence while he smokes another cigarette and my courage grows.

"Jack. What happened to Lara?"

He sighs, opens his mouth, hesitates. "She was an environmentalist—"

"I know all that stuff. The project, the article she wrote. I mean, what happened to her?"

For some reason, he smiles. "Your forum posts always reminded me of the things she used to say."

When I don't respond, he says, "She came to me one day, because she was pregnant. She wouldn't tell me who. It didn't stop her campaigning. Made her more determined. That's when she wrote the article. A few weeks later, on her way home, she disappeared." He glances up at the sky. "It was him. There's no proof, of course. I just…"

I stare at him, a burning in my chest.

The tears in his eyes glow in the sun as he peers at a distant spot on the ocean. "They must have killed her, but her body was never found." He brushes at the crumbling stone beneath us. Bits of the wall fall away onto the foamy rocks below. "I tried to help her, but I probably made it worse for her. Definitely worse for me."

My throat closes into a choke I have to swallow. Hers was so nearly my story. "Why didn't you tell me this?"

He shakes his head, and turns towards me as his eyes grow grave and searching. "I only contacted Kerry because I thought she must have recovered the prototype. I couldn't get anywhere building it from scratch here and I was desperate. God knows, I regret it now. Even if it meant I got to see you again."

Eyes prickling, I nod.

He frowns at the horizon. "She strung me along for months before she admitted she didn't have it. Then came the bargaining, the threats. She could find me and have me killed. Have you killed. How can we trust her?"

My shadows are close by. Probably not in earshot, but I can't risk it.

"Don't know." I release a deep sigh. "But she's likely all we've got. There's two of us and one of her." I gaze at the strained and grieving faces all around us. Their weary eyes survey the receding floodwater, the beautiful, destroyed buildings glowing fractured red in the last of the light. "Maybe I just don't like the alterative."

279

A kerfuffle breaks out across the road. My surveillance monkeys whip their heads around, shoulders tensed. Two grubby-vested men are arguing over a piece of washed up furniture.

This is my chance.

Giving Jack a fervent hug, I find his pocket. "Don't look at it 'til we leave," I whisper.

His breath is hot on my neck. "Is that…?

I nod so he can feel it.

"How?"

"People always underestimate me." I pull away, glance at my shadows. Their eyes are back on us, but their postures are casual. "Poor, silly little Essie. Lost all her family. Her best friend. Got herself knocked up by a lapsed cleric. Careless."

Jack seems confused, his mouth working around half-formed words.

"We copied it, Jack. After Langford's house. The night they took Maya. I was going to turn myself in, but Seth wouldn't let me. We came up with the plan that night."

He gapes. "Why didn't you tell me?"

"I didn't trust you. With the Lara thing… I was confused. Scared of losing Seth. If anybody found out what we'd done."

His jaw stiffens. "You thought I'd killed her, didn't you?"

Did I? "None of that matters. We're here, now. And with that copy, we don't have to trust Kerry. We string her along. Build it without her. She won't realise 'til it's too late."

Jack stares at me for a long time, eyes slowly softening.

"Jack. Can you do that?"

He takes my hand and squints into the waning sun. "Yeah." His lips twitch in a smile. "I can do it."

THE END

Fantastic Books
Great Authors

darkstroke is
an imprint of
Crooked Cat Books

- Gripping Thrillers
- Cosy Mysteries
- Amazing Horrors
- Fascinating Historicals
- Exciting Fantasy
- Young Adult
- Non-Fiction

Discover us online
www.darkstroke.com

Find us on instagram:
www.instagram.com/darkstrokebooks

Printed in Great Britain
by Amazon